OLIVIA ELLIOTT

A Songbird for the Soldier

Book Four in The Pemberton Series

Contents

Don't miss out on Book 3.5 in *The Pemberton Series*! It's a free subscribers-only steamy novella called *The Bull of Bow Street Meets his Match,* and it can be downloaded when you sign up for my mailing list at oliviaelliottro mance.com. This book features Abigail Fernside's sister Harriet as the heroine.

One

The Hero Returns

I f Abigail didn't know any better, she would have said that the dowager Lady Winter was Captain Thomas Walpole's paramour. The petite older lady sat in the drawing room of Avery House—the Winter country residence—twisting a handkerchief in her lap and peering nervously out the front window.

"Do you think something has happened?" the dowager Lady Winter asked no one in particular.

Though the room was packed with people, not a one answered her question.

Her son, the very large and forbidding viscount Lord Richard Winter, glowered as he paced at the back of the room. The viscount's dazzlingly blonde and beautiful brother James sat teetering on the edge of an armchair as his stalwart friend Michael stood beside him with a hand on his shoulder. The two of them joined the dowager in directing their gazes out the window.

"Oh, my heart!" It was the dowager again, dabbing at her eyes with her handkerchief. "I cannot take too much more of this waiting."

The viscount's wife Lady Patience Winter stood near the window tapping her foot.

"Where are you, Thomas?" she said quietly.

Her question was picked up by her brooding husband at the back of the room.

"YES," he said. "WHERE THE BLOODY HELL ARE YOU?!"

His mother the dowager sent a frown in his direction, but he ignored her as he strode to the window where his wife stood and threw open the sash. Patience placed a comforting hand to her husband's wide back.

It was unmistakable—the sound of hooves trotting and wheels rolling over uneven ground. The company in the drawing room took in a collective breath, and everyone including Abigail came to their feet to see a carriage trundle into view from around a distant copse of trees. As it approached the house along the driveway, the dowager turned with a swirl of skirts and attempted to flee the drawing room.

"MOTHER!" bellowed Lord Winter. And then more calmly, "You will stay here."

"But . . . Thomas . . ." she said.

"You will stay here," repeated the viscount as he pressed past her and stepped swiftly from the room.

The company in the drawing room crowded around the window to watch as the carriage pulled up in front of the enormous house. Abigail could see the top of Lord Winter's dark head as he jogged down the steps to greet his friend who had—quite unbelievably—survived the final battle against

Bonaparte.

The Battle of Waterloo.

According to Lord Winter—a former major in His Majesty's army—it had been "a bloody mess". Abigail had choked on her soup when he had spat out those words over dinner. While all of England was celebrating the defeat of the French, the Winter residence had descended practically into mourning.

"Tens of thousands dead," said the viscount. "Not to mention those maimed for life. There will be a generation of British soldiers begging on the streets. It's nothing to celebrate."

He ripped a bread roll violently in half before continuing.

"If it wasn't for a bit of rain and the unlikely arrival of the Prussians, Wellington would have been on his back in the mud."

Abigail had glanced across the table to Patience who shook her pretty blonde head gently from side to side. Her husband was not done speaking.

"Not a word from bloody Thomas."

The bread roll continued to receive the brunt of Lord Winter's current mood.

"Richard! Language!" interrupted the dowager.

Richard gave his mother an icy glare.

"I will *bloody* wring his *bloody* neck the next time I see him." He enunciated each curse word for his mother's benefit.

"Really, Richard," said the dowager.

Patience placed a hand to her mouth to hide a smile, but Abigail couldn't laugh. It was all just a little too much. She could feel herself slowly shrinking, folding in on her own body and mind in an attempt to make herself smaller, less visible.

And that's how she felt now, standing in a crowd at the

window watching as Lord Winter stepped up to the carriage to greet the good captain. She could feel herself diminishing, becoming less and less important. It was the strangest sensation—almost as if she was watching a show at the theatre. The story was not hers. She was simply a member of the audience. Her life was of so little interest that she found the need to pay good money to watch someone else's more engaging life unfold in front of her.

On the driveway beneath the window, a footman opened the door to the carriage, and Abigail's heart gave a tiny flutter as Captain Thomas Walpole ducked his head out. He was wearing a deep blue jacket, and he had a pair of crutches in one hand, but he tossed them dramatically to the ground and accepted the footman's help in dismounting. As Lord Winter approached him, Captain Walpole balanced his weight on one leg and threw his arms as wide as his grin.

"I can't walk!" he declared jovially as if it were the best of news. "An iron ball went clean through my leg!"

Lord Winter took several long steps towards his friend and smothered him in an embrace.

"All right, all right," said Captain Walpole, eventually untangling himself. He glanced down at his crutches where they lay on the ground, then looked back up at the viscount.

"If we're going to do this, old boy, we'd best do it properly. I think you should carry me over the threshold."

"You bloody fool!" growled Lord Winter.

He was a large man, and though Captain Walpole was not slight by any means, the viscount managed to scoop his friend up into his arms.

"Ow!" said Captain Walpole. "Careful with the damsel, Richard. She's bruised and a little bit broken."

He followed this with a chuckle, and Patience burst out laughing beside Abigail at the window. At the sound of her laughter, Captain Walpole looked up to them and waved.

There was a crush to exit the drawing room as everyone rushed to greet Captain Walpole downstairs in the foyer. Abigail trailed behind. It wasn't her story after all. She was just a visitor.

She was still descending the blue-carpeted stairs when Lord Winter entered the house carrying his wounded soldier. He was followed closely by the footman carrying the two crutches.

Thomas—Captain Walpole, she reminded herself (it wouldn't do to be too familiar even in her thoughts)—was laughing as they entered the house. Lord Winter bowed his head down over his friend and planted a rough kiss on his forehead. At that very moment, Patience ran forward and threw her arms around the two of them. Abigail was not so much shocked as embarrassed to watch as her friend peppered the good captain's face with several loud kisses. Her husband didn't look put out at all by the display.

By the time Captain Walpole had been placed on his feet and handed one of his crutches, he was beaming like a man at his own wedding. Lord Winter's brother James and his friend Michael accompanied the dowager viscountess as they pressed themselves forward and into the captain's orbit. James reached out his hand, but Captain Walpole refused to take it.

"I'm afraid Richard and Patience have upped the ante," said Captain Walpole. "We're well beyond handshakes. It's kisses from hereon in."

He said it with a mischievous twinkle in his eye, and James let out a bark of laughter as he took the captain's face in both his hands and planted a hard kiss on the soldier's mouth. Abigail (still on the stairs—she had stopped her forward motion) looked to the dowager Lady Winter who was trying to stifle her laughter behind her handkerchief. Captain Walpole beckoned to Michael with his free hand.

"That one's going to be hard to top," he said. "But I'm sure you'll give it your best."

James playfully shoved Michael forward.

"Is this what happens when a man faces death?" asked Michael with a crooked smile. "Does he lose all sense of propriety and decorum?"

"He loses more than that," said Captain Walpole.

He spoke in a jovial tone, but his words caused the mood of the company to dip ever-so-slightly. Abigail felt the pause like a shimmer through her skin.

"Now give us a kiss!" said the captain, and with that, he lifted everyone up again on a celebratory tide.

They all applauded and laughed as Michael took the captain's head in his hand and placed a gentle kiss to his brow. Finally, Captain Walpole turned to the dowager Lady Winter.

"My love," he said. "You waited for me." He pressed a hand dramatically to his chest. "I half feared you would have married a Scottish earl by now and be frolicking in the highlands with several wee bairns clinging to your skirts."

The dowager Lady Winter swatted at his arm playfully.

"You mustn't tease an old lady, Captain," she said.

"Who's teasing?" said Captain Walpole, taking her hand in his free one. Balancing as best he could with the one crutch, he bowed slightly as he brought her hand to his lips.

The dowager's tinkling laughter spiralled its way up the staircase to Abigail's ears, and she was momentarily overwhelmed with the feeling that she was intruding upon a private family moment. She shouldn't be here. Not for this. She wanted to turn and run back up the stairs, but as the captain straightened himself, his face lifted to hers. When he clocked her presence, the smile dropped from his face for the briefest of moments, and Abigail's heart sank down into the floor. She had been right. She shouldn't be here.

But soon enough, his smile was back, and it seemed to be as genuine as ever.

"Miss Fernside. What a delightful surprise."

Everyone's eyes were on her now, and as she descended the remaining stairs, she could feel her face heating uncomfortably under their scrutiny. It took all her concentration to place one foot carefully in front of the other so as not to trip on the stairs and make even more of a scene. Arriving at the bottom of the stairs, she glanced up at the captain then quickly down.

"I'm . . . I'm . . . so glad to see you well," she said in her quiet voice.

"But I'm not well, Miss Fernside. I'm merely alive."

Abigail had been looking at her shoes, but when she heard him speak those words, she lifted her gaze to his. Up this close, she noticed what she had not from a distance: the dark sunken circles of his eyes, the raw red wound down the side of his neck half hidden by his longish brown hair, the way his free hand was shaking with the barest of trembling movements.

"Then I suppose alive will have to do," she said, forcing herself to lock eyes with him.

"That's the young lady I remember," said the captain softly. "Sharp as a tack."

Abigail couldn't help beaming up at him like a fool. He had

that effect on her. Not that she was special in any way—he had that effect on everybody. She could feel him hesitate before taking her hand in his.

Oh God, she really shouldn't be here.

She watched (and felt) him press the softest of kisses to her knuckles as his hair fell forward over his face, and she had to force herself to remain where she was, to not turn and flee up the stairs to her room. In all honesty, she had been beside herself with worry over him. She barely knew the man, had danced with him on only a handful of occasions nearly a year ago, and yet she felt a warm wash of relief to see him standing in front of her whole and alive. Her eyes began to sting as he released her hand, and she had to turn away from him to wipe (as casually as she could) at a tear that threatened to roll down her face.

"Who's for a drink?" asked Captain Walpole much too loudly, and the reception party murmured their cheerful agreement as they ushered him slowly up the staircase.

Abigail remained on the tiled floor of the foyer as she watched them all ascend the stairs. The captain shrugged off all offers for help, insisting on tackling the stairs on his own. He was thoroughly capable with both crutches now under his arms. Clearly, he didn't need anyone. Another tear made its way to the surface, and Abigail swiped at it angrily.

Why was the waif here? And why did it bother him so much?

Thomas knocked back his second brandy without taking his eyes from her delicate form as she sat quietly staring down at her feet. She was wearing white, and her wavy golden brown hair, though twisted up, was straining at its pins.

Alive will have to do.

She was right of course, and as he remembered it, she always was.

He had helped her with her dancing during the past Season in London. There were always a few young wallflowers who could do with an offer to dance, and she was one of them. He was happy to oblige these young ladies, to help lift their confidence and send them on their way to find a more suitable, more age-appropriate match.

How old could she possibly be?

Thomas shook his head. It didn't matter because it wasn't his business. He tried to shrug off the uncomfortable fact of his own advancing age. He liked to play the boyish rascal, but he was now firmly ensconced in his thirty-sixth year.

Thomas reached his empty glass towards Richard who raised an eyebrow.

"For luck," said Thomas. "I've been through a war."

Richard gave him a look as he lifted the decanter and refilled Thomas's glass.

"So," said Thomas, leaning back in his chair. "There must be some gossip I've missed. Do tell."

The company shifted a little uncomfortably. Thomas hated this aspect of coming home. Everyone was always so awkward around him, as if they thought that nothing ordinary was of any consequence any longer—not compared to what they imagined he must have been through. But what was the point of going through all that hell if not to protect the ordinary moments?

After a brief pause, the lovely and voluptuous Patience came to his rescue. Of course she did.

"The local vicar has only gone and married a former actress," supplied Patience with a saucy tilt of her head.

"No!" said Thomas. "My virgin ears."

That set off a chorus of laughter, and Michael happily intervened to supply some of the deliciously sordid details.

"You know what this means?" said Thomas. "We'll all have to attend church one of these Sundays."

James groaned, and Thomas couldn't help but smile at the beautiful man. He looked like a bloody angel—all golden curls and sun-kissed skin.

"No complaining," said Thomas. "The Good Lord would want us all to go as a family."

He lifted his chin in the waif's direction. She was no longer looking at her shoes but at James the angel.

"And what about you, Miss Fernside? Will you join us at church?"

She startled at the question directed her way.

"Oh, I . . . yes . . ." she said distractedly. And then, "I should be glad of the opportunity. I have much to atone for."

She pursed her pretty pink lips to keep from smiling and looked down at her shoes once more as the company fell into another round of laughter. Sitting there in her gauzy white dress, knees pressed together, head bowed slightly, she looked like the picture of angelic innocence. Her words had been delivered in a deadpan, as if she were absolutely serious, and Thomas was suddenly thrown off-balance by a wave of recognition.

This was what she had been like.

She lulled you with her meek and unassuming deportment only to knock you over with a rather clever jest or barb that seemed to surface as if from nowhere. She disconcerted him with these tiny little surprises. He remembered now how much he liked them—a little too much if he was being honest.

For a brief moment, he was dancing with her again just as he had done last Season, his hand holding her firmly at the waist. She had not been the best of dancers, and he was prepared to catch her if she stumbled. A part of him was hoping she might trip once more and fall against his chest so that he could have an excuse to wrap his arms around her and hold her close for just a moment. There was something about her that provoked a fierce protective instinct within him.

Thomas placed his hand over his left breast pocket and shifted uncomfortably in his seat. His leg was hurting him, his back was sore, and the wound on his neck was beginning to burn once more. He needed to apply the salve he had been given for his neck, he needed to lie down and stretch out . . . and he needed to put a little distance between himself and Miss Fernside. So he made his excuses. Certainly, no one begrudged him a rest after his journey, and Richard escorted him to the guest room that had been set aside for him.

As he swung himself down the blue-carpeted hall on his crutches, he could feel the large man deliberating beside him. He knew Richard like he knew his own rifle. The man was his best friend in this world and, he imagined, the next as well. Finally, they arrived outside his room.

"All right," said Thomas, looking up into his friend's concerned face. "Out with it. What is it you want to say to me?"

"You had several glasses of brandy." Richard rubbed at his short-cropped beard. "It's only two in the afternoon."

"Do I look foxed to you?" Thomas felt his irritation rise.

"How have you been sleeping?" asked Richard.

"Like a sweet innocent babe. I close my eyes, and it's all

sunshine and custard tarts and rolling in meadows."

Richard nodded thoughtfully which only served to heighten Thomas's annoyance.

"I could share the burden," said Richard as he opened the door to Thomas's room.

"Jesus, Richard. I'm a soldier, not a whiny little boy with a list of complaints. I told you it's all sunny fucking meadows and tarts."

"It's only that I noticed your hand." Richard looked down to Thomas's left hand where it trembled at his side.

"It's just the aftershock," said Thomas, pressing his hand to his leg to still the tremor. "It'll wear off soon."

Richard gave a low grunt. "I also noticed that you didn't correct mother."

Thomas stared at him.

"She called you *Captain*, and I have it on good authority that you are no longer a captain."

Thomas looked away from his friend and down the hall. He couldn't bring himself to maintain eye contact for this.

"I've been told you were given a battlefield promotion—two ranks up. You're a bloody lieutenant colonel. Were you even going to mention it?"

"No," said Thomas, still looking down the hallway.

"What happened?" Richard placed his hands to both Thomas's shoulders, and Thomas dragged his gaze back to his friend's face.

"You *know* what happened. They all died—soldiers, officers, horses. Shot down, sliced down, trampled, bludgeoned. The place was a graveyard well before it was over. I would never have been promoted if the situation hadn't been so desperate. Someone needed to hold the square against the French cavalry.

12

You know what some of those new recruits are like—jittery as all hell."

"And you held the square," said Richard.

It wasn't a question, and Thomas momentarily appreciated that fact, but he quickly brushed it aside.

"There was no one else to do it."

"You could have made lieutenant colonel years ago," said Richard. "You never put yourself forward. You could have traded in your captain's commission."

Thomas stared at his friend as the ire rose like bile in his throat.

"No one's life should be placed in my hands. I'm half drunk at two in the afternoon."

Richard gave him a hard look as he held his silence for what felt like a very long time.

"You may recall that *I've* placed my life in your hands more than once," he eventually said. "I would do it again."

And with that, he left Thomas staring after him as he strode down the hall.

Thomas shoved his way angrily into the bed chamber, stumbling and losing one of his crutches as he did so and landing with some force on his injured leg. Pain spiked through him like a hot skewer.

Bloody bollocking hell!

He managed to limp and lurch his way towards the bed. When he was finally laid flat on his back, he decided that he was never going to get up again. This was something he decided every single time he lay down. For several minutes, Thomas attempted to keep his eyes open, but fatigue crept over him like a heavy cat come to rest on his chest, and he finally surrendered to the sheer bloody weight of it and closed his eyes.

He saw smoke—a grey-blue haze. Shouts of men, weapons firing, the squelching sound of human flesh being rent. In the distance, barely made out beyond the haze, the line of French cavalry advancing. Hooves hitting the damp earth in unison. He could feel the earth shake with their advance. He had given the order to form the square—his men in red knelt and stood in formation, the bayonet ends of their muskets angled up and out. He had warned them that this would be a battle of the mind.

"Forget the soggy field, forget the men charging on horseback, forget the French, forget Bonaparte. In the next few minutes, the fight will be with yourself. Hold your fear tightly in hand. Don't let it loose. Don't fire your gun. Above all, don't break and run—it won't save you. Do nothing. It may feel as if you are waiting for death, waiting to be trampled underfoot, but you are simply waiting for the right moment."

The right moment was when the cavalry hit the thirty yard mark. If his men fired before then, they would waste their shot. No time to reload. The twenty yard mark was too close. Even an injured horse would keep galloping for a few heartbeats, and the square would be broken, allowing the remaining cavalry to enter and take them out from within.

Thomas had placed a hand to the shoulder of the young soldier trembling on his knee in front of him.

"TOGETHER!" he yelled over the din. "HOLD!"

The hoofbeats were a jumble of thuds as they ripped up the sodden ground on their advance.

"HOLD!"

As the cavalry passed the sixty yard mark, Thomas felt the young soldier in front of him try to stand. He gave the boy's shoulder a squeeze and pressed him down.

"HOLD!"

The horses were practically on them now, wild-eyed, slathering at their bits. Thomas lifted his musket.

"AIM!"

"FIRE!"

The ear-splitting retort of over a thousand muskets firing at once sent the world into a strange silence. Thomas watched with no particular satisfaction as the first horses stumbled and fell, blocking the remaining advance and allowing his men time to reload.

"AIM!" he yelled, but he couldn't even be sure that they heard him. He couldn't hear himself anymore.

"FIRE!"

It was a memory, but it was also a dream. As Thomas lowered his musket, he realised with a sense of odd foreboding that none of it was real. Yet his heart continued to race as he peered through the musket smoke. He had the strangest desire to turn, to look behind him.

What was he guarding? He couldn't remember.

As the smoke slowly lifted, he could make out the vague shape of a pale figure seated on a wooden chair in the middle of the muddy field. Thomas squinted, straining his eyes to see. It was a woman in a white dress. Her knees were pressed together, and she was peering down towards her lap. Slowly, she lifted her head and looked his way.

The waif, thought Thomas uncomfortably. *What's she doing here?*

Two

Never Part, No Never More!

Abigail could not decide on a dress to wear to dinner. She had several that were quite suitable for evening wear, but she did not want to draw too much attention to herself. If she could blend into the background, perhaps no one would notice how inappropriate it was for her to be there.

Yes, Patience had invited her. And yes, she often stayed for extended periods with the Winter family—but she had not realised Captain Walpole would be returning to recover at Avery House . . . and his presence made her presence inappropriate or, at the very least, not favourable. The captain should feel completely comfortable to recover among the bosom of his found family. She was practically a stranger, and he would have to make social niceties with her. Her presence would be a burden to his already tired person.

She looked down at the dresses she had thrown to the bed.

The pink gown was far too vibrant and brought out the flush in her cheeks, so that was a no. The silver was, well, silver. Also no.

Patience had encouraged her to purchase a bolt of iridescent green silk that shimmered like the leaves of a birch tree in summertime. The modiste had turned it into a rather slinky evening dress that made her feel as lovely as a tree nymph. So no.

Her maid Betsy was standing to the side. She was used to these sorts of extended deliberations and did not even bother to engage until Abigail's decision was made.

When Abigail finally descended the stairs for dinner, she was wearing a demure and understated midnight blue that made her face seem even paler than it already was. It was her least complimentary evening dress, and she was quite positive that it would attract no attention whatsoever.

Patience was waiting for her at the bottom of the stairs.

"Oh," she said. "I thought you would wear the green. You danced around the dressing room the first time you tried it on."

"I didn't think it would be an evening of dancing," said Abigail.

Patience scrunched up her face in disapproval. She herself was wearing an amethyst gown that would send any number of men into a tongue-tied trance. Abigail's friend was all curves and confidence, and though Abigail herself had taken a few lessons in self-assurance from her friend, she was finding that tonight, given the circumstances, she would much rather draw as little attention as possible.

"Have it your way," said Patience, "but you won't be able to do it forever."

"Do what?"

"Hide your light. It's not the sort of thing that can be doused with a homely dress."

"This dress isn't homely. It's quite refined."

"For a woman of fifty or so," said Patience with a quirk of her lips. "I'm sure the dowager will love it."

Abigail found it hard to pretend offence when she was laughing.

"Come along then," said Patience. "We're short of candles in the dining room, and we need you to brighten it up for us."

Abigail rolled her eyes as she allowed her friend to pull her along by the hand.

Dinner was an outwardly formal affair with the ladies in evening dress and the men in black. Captain Walpole looked exceptionally gaunt in black and white, but he was as quick to smile as ever. He lurched his way over to his chair which was pulled out for him by a footman. Of course, he refused to take his seat until the ladies had been seated first.

Apart from his initial greeting of her and Patience, Abigail noticed that the man did not lay eyes on her for a good part of the evening.

Well, mission accomplished.

The homely dress had done its homely job, and Abigail found herself relaxing somewhat. She tucked into her roast beef and glazed carrots with well-earned gusto as the conversation murmured about her. Michael—who was seated beside her—engaged her with questions about music and composition. They discussed Haydn, Mozart, and Beethoven, and Abigail found herself more at ease than ever. Just the once, she glanced from Michael and across the table to find Captain Walpole regarding her with a rather stricken look,

18

but he quickly directed his attention away to join the others in laughing at one of Patience's witticisms.

After dinner saw the men retire to the smoking room, and Abigail was quite happily left with Patience and the dowager to sit and sip sherry in the drawing room.

"I would insist we join them," said Patience, "but it turns out that I'm not at all fond of cheroots. The smell gets into my hair."

"I'm so happy to see that the good captain is his cheerful old self," said the dowager. "War has not taken that from him."

In actual fact, it seemed to Abigail that the good captain was hanging onto his old cheerful self by a very thin line.

Abigail looked to the older lady who had set down her sherry glass to lift up a sampler, a needle, and thread. She stabbed at her sampler and pulled the crimson thread taut before plunging the needle into the cloth once more.

"But his experiences *will* have taken a toll on him," said Patience. "We mustn't assume he is well."

Abigail wondered if Patience was speaking from personal experience with her own husband.

"Apart from his leg, he's as well as ever," said the dowager without looking up from her sewing. "Right as rain."

Patience tossed Abigail a look and shook her head.

"Would you be a dear?" asked the dowager, glancing over to Abigail. "Give us a song."

"It would be my pleasure, Lady Winter." Abigail stood and made her way over to the pianoforte.

"Nothing maudlin," called out the dowager, still attacking her sampler with her needle. "Don't make me cry."

"Of course not," said Abigail, seating herself at the pianoforte.

The feel of the bench beneath her, the sight of the familiar arrangement of white and black keys was like a balm for Abigail's nerves. It always had been, and she imagined it always would be. When she played, when she sang, it was as if nothing else in the world existed. She dissolved into the music and was lost on the lift and dip of each note, like a leaf carried along on the current of a stream. It was the most liberating feeling—the letting go of oneself.

Her fingers came down over the keys with a bright sense of impending mischief, and she picked up a lively and fairly inane tune with the title "Tho' you think by this to vex me". The dowager, she knew, would love such silly pap, and Patience would likely take Abigail's unspoken meaning. It was a duet for a man and a woman, but Abigail sang both parts herself, attempting to make her voice gruffer for the male portion. She glanced up just the once to find Patience practically shaking with the effort to politely hold in her howls of laughter.

When the song finally concluded on a series of "la la las" and a thrice repeated "Never never part, no never more!" the dowager was incandescent. Her sampler was thrust to the side, and she was applauding with appreciative enthusiasm. Patience very quickly came to her feet and approached Abigail at the pianoforte.

She leaned down and whispered, "You are a little devil," before pressing her lips together to stifle a laugh.

As the dowager's applause died out, the sound of clapping came to them from the entrance of the drawing room. When she turned in her seat, Abigail was fairly mortified to see Captain Walpole leaning against the doorframe, one crutch balanced against the wall so that he might use his hands to applaud.

How long had he been there?

"Next time, we'll sing it together," he chuckled before bursting into a round of "Never never part, no never more!"

He reached for his second crutch and swung himself into the room and up to the pianoforte. Abigail looked to Patience, but she had returned to her seat beside the dowager.

"Though I daresay you are quite adept at mimicking a man's voice," he added. "Very convincing, Miss Fernside."

His brown eyes were bright in their sunken sockets, and his longish hair fell forward into his face as he leaned over and picked up the book of songs sitting atop the pianoforte. Abigail could feel herself flush. Her sense of self had reemerged when she had stopped playing, and she was now only too well aware of how silly she must have appeared.

"It's one of my favourites," supplied the dowager from across the room.

Captain Walpole caught Abigail's eye as he said, "No doubt, my lady. No doubt. It's a rollicking good tune. Though I wonder if it is much of a tax on Miss Fernside's talents."

At the compliment, Abigail had to break eye contact. She looked down at the keys of the pianoforte since they were blocking the view to her feet. She could hear Captain Walpole tilt his second crutch against the instrument.

Taking his weight gingerly on his one good leg, he riffled through the book of songs in his hand and tutted.

"Quite a lot of nonsense here," he whispered, which made her smile. "I heard you play at the dowager Lady Winter's musicale last year. Not the pianoforte, but the harp, and it was decidedly more complex than this." He waved the book dismissively. "More meaningful as well. Would you do an old soldier a favour and play something that you yourself

21

find particularly moving?" He glanced across the room to the dowager. "If it's too maudlin, I promise to cheer her up."

Abigail wanted to grin but thought it might be too unlady-like, so she bit down on her lower lip instead as she looked up at him from under her lashes.

Thomas should not have stopped at the door to the drawing room. And when Miss Fernside had finished playing, he should not have engaged her over the ridiculous duet she had sung all on her lonesome. He certainly shouldn't have come all the way into the room. Nor should he have stood beside the pianoforte gazing down at the top of her head and a portion of her pale profile as she attempted to look past the keyboard to her shoes.

What was so bloody interesting about her feet? She was always looking at them.

The problem was that she had done it again—she had surprised him. Miss Fernside had chosen that particular song with a mind to make Patience laugh knowing full well that she could not do so politely with the dowager present. The waif was a wicked little thing—sharp as a blade, bright as a flame.

And now she was biting her lip in an obvious effort not to smile at him. She looked pleased with his request, and this in turn pleased him rather too much. She turned back to the pianoforte and plinked at a high note with one finger as she deliberated over her choice of song. Then she placed her fingers gently in position over the keys and began.

As the first several bars of gentle music rolled over him,

Thomas realised that even in his compliments, he had underestimated the waif's talent. The piece was completely unrecognisable to him yet devastating in its poignancy. He watched her face as she played, and to him it seemed as if she were somewhere else. Or perhaps someone else. Or perhaps no one at all. She had disappeared into the music, and God, it was mournful. It tugged at the end of a loose thread in his soul, and he half feared that he might unravel right there in the drawing room.

Bloody hell. He needed to sit down.

As if reading his mind, Patience appeared at his side. She had brought him a chair, and she offered him a hand as he lowered himself into it. The waif continued to play, eyes almost shut, completely from memory. Thomas had to close his own eyes to steady himself, to keep hold of that loose thread which threatened to undo him.

He had not cried when his good friends had fallen around him. He had not shed a tear when the young soldier kneeling in front of him in the square was later sliced open by a sabre, nor when he had been forced to end the lives of several lame horses writhing on the earth which was damp with the blood of the fallen. He had been sliced along his neck and shot in the leg, and he had not let out so much as a whimper. But now, sitting there in the drawing room, he felt the waif's music like the stroke of a gentle hand over his brow, and if he was not careful, he knew it would be enough to break down his grim resolve.

Miss Fernside's musical piece ended on what seemed to Thomas an odd note—as if there should be more to come. She opened her eyes and looked around the room in a way that suggested she was startled to find herself there. No one

23

spoke for what felt like a very long time, and the dowager sniffed through the silence, dabbing at her eyes with her handkerchief.

"I said nothing maudlin," she eventually protested. "But that was beautiful, my dear. Absolutely sublime."

Thomas took a tremulous breath.

"Well," he said (and the word sounded rather flippant to him given what he had just experienced). "Well. Miss Fernside. You appear to be swimming in a rather deep sea."

Fuck. What did he mean by that?

"That was . . ."

"You didn't like it," she said quietly.

"I more than liked it."

"You appear upset," she said.

Hell.

He needed to divert the conversation.

"Who might I ask is the composer? It sounded when you ended the piece as if there was more to come."

"I composed it," she said. "And you're quite observant. It *is* unfinished, so there is more to come."

"You composed it," he repeated like a fool, for he did not know what to say next.

Of course she bloody well composed it, you idiot.

Patience came to his rescue once more. Or perhaps she was coming to Miss Fernside's rescue.

"She's a marvel, my friend Abigail—a true marvel," she said from her seat across the room. "And now, I think she deserves to finish her glass of sherry."

The waif slid back the bench and came to her feet. Thomas reflexively stood, wincing as he accidentally took his weight on the wrong leg. Standing as he was, holding onto the back of the chair, he was partially blocking Miss Fernside's exit, but it was awkward for him to move without his crutches which were still resting against the pianoforte. He thought Miss Fernside would attempt to slide past him to join Patience and the dowager where they sat, but instead, she stopped right in front of him. All he could see was the top of her head as she looked down at her feet. Her golden brown hair rippled in waves against the restraint of her pins.

"Does it hurt?" she asked. "You shouldn't stand for me if it hurts."

"It's nothing I can't manage."

That caused her to look up at him, and her large hazel eyes seemed to give off a hint of incredulity.

"Will you join us for a glass of sherry?"

"Thank you, but not tonight," he said. "I should rest."

She glanced down at his left hand which was trembling at his side. He pressed it against his leg.

"Sleep well then," she said.

Several hours later, when all the house had been doused in darkness and silence, that was exactly what he was not doing as he sat in the drawing room with a glass of whisky in hand staring at the dark outline of the pianoforte. Moonlight shone through the windows, tinting the room in a faint silver-blue light.

Richard would not be pleased to see him drinking again, but Richard could go jump in a lake. Anyway, it wasn't two in the afternoon, and this was only his second glass, so . . .

Thomas decided to stop justifying his behaviour to himself. It really wasn't dignified. If he wanted a drink, he would bloody well have a drink. As he took another sip, he heard the soft shuffle of slippers over tile. Within moments, a small

25

pale figure entered the room and stepped gingerly across the carpet to a table in the far corner. She hadn't noticed him, and she might have left without once realising he was there. As he watched her lift something from the table, he took another swig of his whisky.

Despite the warm welcome of his friends, Thomas had felt all evening as if he were drowning in a sea of loneliness. The waif's presence with him now in that darkened room seemed to make everything just a little bit better. He didn't want her to leave, and he was not entirely sober, so he gave in to a selfish impulse and cleared his throat.

She let out a small squeak as she turned towards him with something in her hand.

"Oh, it's you," said Miss Fernside.

"What are you doing sneaking around the house at night like a burglar?" asked Thomas.

"Why, burgling of course."

Thomas smiled into the darkness.

Miss Fernside laughed nervously and raised the item in her hand.

"I had misplaced my spectacles," she said. "I couldn't sleep for wondering where I might have left them."

"I've never seen you wear them before."

"They're only for reading . . . and writing . . ."

"And composing," he added before taking another sip of his drink. He lifted the glass towards her. "Care for a whisky?"

"I . . . uh . . . all right. Yes. A whisky."

She stepped towards him and into the shaft of moonlight streaming in through one of the windows. Her hair was down, falling in little wavy rivulets over her shoulders. It was longer than he had imagined. She was wearing a pale blue dressing gown that tied at the waist, and he could see the hem of her white nightdress peeking out above her slippered feet.

"Come and sit then."

He gestured to a chair near him and then reached to the table beside him to refill his own glass. He hadn't another empty glass within reach, and the whisky had done a number on his more decorous impulses, so he simply handed her the glass from which he himself had just been drinking.

She didn't hesitate to take it from him, her fingers brushing his as he handed it over.

"To your health," said Miss Fernside before she took a rather large swig of the golden liquid. This resulted in a great deal of sputtering. He reached across to where she was seated and rubbed her on the back as he smiled.

"It's not sherry," he said. "You'll want to take smaller sips."

Miss Fernside coughed and cleared her throat.

"Serves me right. I was trying to look worldly."

At that, they both laughed.

"Why on earth would you want to look worldly?" asked Thomas.

Miss Fernside put up a finger as if to hold him off as she took a delicate little sip from the glass, this time without sputtering.

"Much better," she said. "It grows on you, doesn't it? Very warming."

"You haven't answered my question." Thomas leaned back in his chair and stretched his legs out in front of him.

She took a moment, as if thinking it over.

"I suppose I didn't want you to think I was as young and naive as I am."

"Hah!" laughed Thomas. He reached for the glass in her hand and took a sip himself, then handed it back to her. "You may be young, but I would not go so far as naive."

"Well, thank you."

She took another few sips, and she handed the glass back to him as if they had been drinking companions their entire lives.

As he examined the glass of whisky, she said, "It must have been a shock for you to find me here at Avery House. Patience had invited me to stay over the summer. I hadn't intended to intrude upon your homecoming."

He looked up at her, but she was gazing down at her feet once more.

"Shock isn't the word, Miss Fernside. I told you it was a delightful surprise, and it was."

The whisky must have been working its magic on her because she looked up and took the glass from his hand without any ceremony whatsoever.

"My turn," she said, taking a rather large sip.

Careful, thought Thomas.

He was feeling rather tipsy himself, and the waif did not have enough meat on her bones to absorb very much alcohol. He watched as she leaned back in her chair and stretched her dainty little legs out in front of her just as he had done. The sash of her dressing gown had come loose, and the garment fell open at her chest to reveal a great deal of pale skin above the scooped neckline of her nightdress.

"I enjoyed dancing with you last Season," she said, tilting her face towards him and against the back of the chair.

The movement caused her dressing gown to fall open even further. She was looking a little too relaxed.

"Give me that glass." Thomas reached over. "I think you've had enough."

She laughed as she held the glass of whisky up and out of his reach. Then quickly downed the rest of it, only to lift her face to his and give him a rather defiant smile. He had to resist an urge to lean over and kiss her.

"Have you ever danced with my sister?"

Thomas took the empty glass from her hand.

"Who is she?"

"Same name as me—Miss Fernside," she laughed. "Actually her name is Harriet. Etty for short."

"Can't say that I've met her."

"You would know if you had," said Miss Fernside. "She is perfect in every way. Auburn hair, green-blue eyes, as beautiful as a summer day and as clever as a fox. She's married now, but if you had seen her last Season, you would have been stumbling over yourself to ask her to dance. It would not have been a chore to entertain *her* for the evening."

Thomas wasn't so tipsy as to misunderstand Miss Fernside's sentiment here. She imagined herself to be a chore.

Well.

"Can your sister play the pianoforte?" asked Thomas.

"Sort of."

"Has she composed anything like the piece you played earlier?"

"No," said Miss Fernside somewhat warily.

He reached over and lifted a lock of her hair between his fingers.

"Does her hair strain at its pins as if it were struggling to break free?" he asked.

Miss Fernside was completely silent. She was watching him with wide eyes lit by the silvery light of the moon. The flutter of her pulse was visible at the base of her pale throat.

29

After a few moments, she sat up in the chair which caused her dressing gown to fall from one shoulder. They regarded each other for several long moments.

"I'd like another drink," she said finally.

Bloody hell.

"No, I shouldn't think that would be a good idea," said Thomas. "It's well past our bed time. I think it best that we retire. Come on."

He reached for his crutches and struggled to his feet. They made their way quietly up the stairs. On the top landing, Miss Fernside turned.

"Goodnight, Captain Walpole."

"Sweet dreams, Miss Fernside."

Thomas watched as she walked rather unsteadily down the hall to her room. He fought an impulse to follow her down the hall and put a hand to her shoulder. She would turn . . . and then? What he wanted was to sink his hands into the thick mass of her hair, pull her head back, and ravish her mouth quite soundly.

Instead, he fixed his feet to the floor until she had shut herself safely within the walls of her bed chamber.

Three

Only in this House

✦✦✦

"Up all night drinking whisky with a man nearly twice your age! I didn't think you had it in you, my dear." Abigail's mother had somehow found out about her little drinking session with Captain Walpole.

Both Abigail and her mother were sitting atop two rather large war horses in a muddy field. There was a light mist hanging over them, and in the distance, Abigail could see the scattered colourful shapes of bodies lying prone on the ground.

"Do you remember Mrs. Denver and her daughter Millicent?" asked her mother.

Abigail nodded slowly as she squinted her eyes into the distance. In her mind, she knew that she had only just seen Captain Walpole alive the night before, but now she worried that he was one of those bodies in the field. She squeezed at her horse's flanks, and he broke into a trot. Her mother somehow managed to keep pace with her which was strange because her mother had not ridden a horse in years.

"That girl Millicent was sixteen years old when she married Major Parker," continued her mother as they bounced along. "Sixteen! At twenty-one, you're practically an old maid in comparison. If you would only pay a little more attention to your appearance, Abigail. Your sister Harriet always manages to turn out well for an evening affair even if she does wear those terrible dingy dresses for her charity work at the prison. Every face in the room turns towards her when she enters. Posture isn't everything, but it's certainly half the battle. You'll not find Harriet bowing her head down to stare at her shoes when someone is talking to her. No one wants a mouse for a wife. Rodents aren't at all the fashion this Season."

Abigail was used to this sort of thing from her mother, but though she tried to let it all roll off her back, it didn't so much roll as grip at her shoulders like a vice. She clenched her jaw and tried to focus on guiding the horse. Her mother continued to talk as they approached the bodies strewn over the churned-up field.

"I expect Millicent's Major Parker looked a lot like that man over there," said her mother, pointing to a middle-aged corpse. "Except much more alive. He had a moustache as well and a tidy income. Millicent would want for nothing. Never mind the man was in his forties. Still quite handsome. Perhaps even more handsome than when he was younger. You'll not want a green husband, Abigail. They can be rather selfish—"

She leaned towards Abigail as they pulled their horses to a halt.

"—in the bed chamber."

"Mother!"

"I'm only telling the truth," replied her mother. "You'll want to put a little more effort into enticing the good captain. It sounds for some reason as if he's interested in you, my dear girl, and that sort of thing doesn't exactly happen to *you* every day."

Abigail could feel something snap inside her. She opened her mouth and yelled.

"OF COURSE HE'S NOT INTERESTED—WHO WOULD BE INTERESTED? HE'S JUST BEING NICE!"

Her mother didn't so much as flinch. She surveyed the scene in front of her.

"Abigail, I hate to say so, but this is hardly the place for a picnic. Although I suppose we could make do. Did you ask cook to pack us those lovely spice buns?"

"Pardon?"

"Spice buns, Abigail. Do I have to do everything myself?"

Abigail woke with her heart pounding and a frustrated scream waiting in her throat. She groaned and pressed a hand to her forehead. It felt like a giant was slowly squeezing at her temples. Trust her mother to elbow her way into Abigail's summer at Avery House. She slowly kicked herself free of the coverlet as Betsy bustled in and drew back the curtains to let in the morning light.

"Did you have sweet dreams?" asked Betsy quite innocently as she turned to Abigail from the window.

Sweet dreams.

With a sudden surge of complex emotion, the evening with Captain Walpole came rushing over her in a wave of jumbled images and broken conversation.

Oh dear God.

She had made quite a fool of herself. First at the pianoforte, singing that inane duet and then later when she had drunk rather too much from Captain Walpole's whisky glass. She was embarrassed about the duet, and though she knew she should be embarrassed about the whisky drinking, the appropriate embarrassment was crowded out by a rather warm and cosy feeling related to how casual and friendly it had been to share a glass with the captain in the middle of the night.

In the bright light of day, it did seem rather scandalous, but that was not how it had felt. He had seemed lonely and rather melancholy sitting in the dark. She couldn't very well have left him there on his own. And the whisky had allowed her to relax a little in his company. She had liked talking to him like that, with her legs stretched out and a warm buzz in her chest. She simply liked the feeling of his presence beside her in the dark. So what if he was just being nice? It felt rather lovely.

When Abigail arrived downstairs for breakfast, only James and Michael were at the table sipping tea and reading the paper. Neither Patience nor the dowager seemed terribly minded to ensure she was chaperoned around these two particular gentlemen, so she was quite used to taking tea or even breakfast as the only lady in the room. Patience would be out riding with Lord Winter at this time, and the dowager would still be abed.

"There's our little songbird," said Michael, folding his newspaper and placing it aside.

"Good morning," said Abigail.

She was always of two minds with the pair of them. Lord Winter's brother James was rather distressingly handsome, and Abigail found it quite difficult to engage with him. It wasn't so much that he made her nervous. It was simply that his appearance was rather distracting, and she had to spend a good deal of energy focussing on what he was saying or else she ended up losing the plot. James's dark-haired friend Michael, on the other hand, was attractive in a different way. He exuded a kind of amiability that set her immediately at ease.

"I'm thinking," said Michael, leaning forward and sliding a rack of toast towards her, "that we should take Thomas into the village for a pint this afternoon."

"Richard won't like that idea," said James over his newspaper. "He thinks Thomas is drinking too much as it is."

"All right," said Michael. "A steak-and-kidney pie, then. We could make a lunch of it."

"At the public house?" asked Abigail.

"That's right. The Stag and Hound." Michael leaned back looking quite pleased with himself. "Something nice and normal. Nothing fancy. Just a little outing to break up the day. It's not as if he can go riding or walking distances yet. He will be bored out of his mind."

"Yet?" said Abigail. "Is it expected his leg will heal properly?"

James lowered his paper to strike Abigail with the full force of his gloriously perfect face.

"His physician thinks so. It's possible he will make a complete recovery if he is diligent about the exercises that have been prescribed."

This was news to Abigail. She had imagined Captain Walpole would be on crutches for the rest of his life. Her heart lifted like a stupid little bird who had decided to take flight for no good reason.

"Will he be able to . . . to dance?" asked Abigail hesitantly.

"Will *who* be able to dance?"

It was Captain Walpole leaning on his crutches at the door to the morning room.

"Miss Fernside," said Michael cheerfully, "we must remember next time that when we speak of the Devil, he is likely to appear."

Abigail put her hand to her mouth to hide a smile as she turned to see Captain Walpole enter the room and manoeuvre himself into a chair beside her.

"Miss Fernside," he said.

She looked down at her plate before summoning a great deal of effort to lift her face and look him in the eye.

"How did you sleep?" he asked.

"I dreamed of my mother."

"So not well then," supplied Michael with a chuckle.

Abigail had to laugh.

"I take it you aren't insulted by the very rude man at the breakfast table," said Captain Walpole.

"Not at all. He's rather astute. I'm not sure one can be both astute *and* polite. In many cases, one precludes the other."

Captain Walpole gave her an odd assessing look before shifting his gaze to his empty cup and reaching a hand up to touch the side of his neck. The angle of the morning sun pouring in through the windows lit his brown hair so that Abigail could make out a few silver strands at his temple. Sliding her eyes across his profile, Abigail couldn't help but notice that his cheekbones cut a fine line. He was freshly shaven. When he removed his hand from his neck, she could see his wound—raised and raw. Had he been sliced with a sabre? Abigail wondered how much blood might pour from a wound such as his. If something like that ever happened to her, she was quite sure that she would immediately sink into a dead faint.

She lifted the tea pot and silently poured Captain Walpole a cup before seeing to her own. She could feel him watching her as she did so, and she tried her best to ignore the heat that was creeping up her neck.

"Thank you," he said.

"Not at all."

"What was it Mrs. Fernside was doing in your dream?"

"Mrs. Anderson," said Abigail.

"Excuse me?"

"My mother is no longer Mrs. Fernside. She remarried, so now she is Mrs. Anderson."

Abigail paused. *What could she tell him of her dream?*

"She was complaining that I hadn't brought spice buns for our picnic," said Abigail. "She was doing a lot of complaining really . . . mainly about me."

"Ah," said Captain Walpole. "Shall I have a word with her? Next time, you must invite me into your dream as well. I'll set Mrs. Anderson straight about where she can find those spice buns . . . among other things."

James and Michael had disappeared behind their newspapers, and Captain Walpole was regarding her in a way that made her feel quite embarrassed. She gave him a little twisted smile as a response before lowering her eyes to the table and fussing over a piece of toast. She had never pretended to pay so much attention to spreading a bit of jam, and she was only properly able to relax when Captain Walpole spread open his own portion of the newspaper.

As she took her first sips of tea, she surveyed the breakfast table. When else would she ever be sat alone with three bachelors chatting over toast?

Only in this house, she thought.

A few weeks ago, Abigail had been sitting with Patience in her dressing room. Patience had said she felt free here—free to do and say as she pleased.

"I could wear trousers and smoke a cigar if I liked, and no one would bat an eye. Well, except for Richard's mother, but she is surprisingly tolerant."

"Have you?" asked Abigail quite scandalised.

"Have I what?"

"Worn trousers and smoked a cigar?"

"Of course," said Patience mischievously. "And that's not the half of it."

Abigail had wondered what the other half of it might be. Now, as she sat at the breakfast table, she thought that perhaps it was staying up all night drinking whisky in your nightdress with a man who was no more than an acquaintance. The thought made her smile to herself. It made her want to do it again . . . in trousers . . . with a cigar in hand. It seemed to Abigail as if everyone else was capable of being themselves while it was always such a struggle for her to simply exist.

"We're going to The Stag and Hound for luncheon," said Michael to Captain Walpole. "Care to join us?"

"Who's going?" Captain Walpole spoke the words as he looked Abigail's way.

She certainly wouldn't be going unless Patience was. It was one thing to breakfast at Avery House with a group of bachelors. It was another thing entirely to be seen with them in public without a chaperone.

"The songbird here will come, won't you?" said Michael.

"I . . . yes . . . that is, if Patience will join us."

"And what about the cherub?" asked Captain Walpole,

tilting his chin towards James who was still hiding behind his paper.

"The cherub does as I say." Michael flicked at the back of James's paper with his finger. "He's coming."

Abigail very much hoped that Patience would not be otherwise occupied. She had never been to a public house before. She briefly acknowledged the fact that if this was what passed for excitement in her life, it was possibly a rather dull existence.

Nevermind, she thought. *Steak-and-kidney pie! In the village!*

The gentlemen disappeared after breakfast, and Abigail was left alone with the dowager Lady Winter since Patience was nowhere to be found. After a morning of reading to the dowager (she was very fond of Gothic romances) and playing music for the dowager and then sneaking off for a walk on her own so as not to have to entertain the dowager any longer, it was finally midday—hurrah! Michael had managed to track Patience down. Lord Winter was occupied with some urgent matters brought to him by his steward, so he would be remaining at home.

"As Patience's brother-in-law, I believe it falls to me to be her chaperone," said James. He turned his dazzling face to Patience before handing her up into the carriage. "So I hope you will be on your best behaviour."

"You will have a time of it, I'm sure," she laughed.

Patience took his hand. She was wearing a turquoise summer dress that accentuated all of her curves over which she had buttoned a rather low-cut spencer jacket in a glorious goldenrod. Abigail dropped her eyes to follow the slim lines of her own body down to the ground. She was wearing white again—well, technically, the dress was cream—and she had paired it with a faint blush-coloured jacket that buttoned up to the base of her neck. She knew she wasn't much to look at, but she thought the colour of the jacket suited her complexion, and that was certainly something.

Once Patience was seated in the carriage, James offered his hand to Abigail.

"And Patience will be *your* chaperone, Abigail . . . We're practically all sorted. There's just the matter of—"

"Who will be *your* chaperone, James?" asked Captain Walpole, swinging up behind Abigail.

"That always falls to me," said Michael. "If I didn't keep such a careful eye on him, he would have lost his innocence to the first bar maid who offered him a smile."

They all laughed, though Abigail thought that Michael and Captain Walpole laughed a good deal harder than the jest warranted.

She was quite enjoying herself already. Time at Avery House was nothing like being at home. With Harriet married and gone, it was just herself, her mother, and her mother's new husband Mr. Horace Anderson. Meals together consisted of her mother doing most of the talking in between bouts of silence punctuated by clinking cutlery. Mr. Anderson was a good man, and her mother only wanted the best for her, but it did sometimes feel as if she were waiting for the doors to open, to be let out into the wider world.

Musing upon it now as James helped her up into the carriage, Abigail wondered if it wasn't at least partially her own fault that those doors had remained shut for so long. She did have a habit of hiding herself. Spending time with her vivacious friend Patience certainly helped her feel more able to be herself in company. Patience was always so encouraging, and she certainly led by example—speaking her mind, laughing openly, and pursuing her passion as a portrait artist with determination and joy. Abigail's friend made her feel as if she too was funny and clever and even, on occasion, beautiful. Over the last two years, Abigail had come to like herself just a little bit more, but she still felt constrained by old doubts that continued to creep into her thoughts.

Captain Walpole was handed up into the carriage after the ladies, and Patience quickly shifted from her seat beside Abigail to the opposite seat in order to help him up and in without his crutches. He landed with a thump on the seat beside Abigail, knocking into the side of her as he sat clumsily down.

"Sorry," he said, dipping his head towards hers. "I'm rather ungainly these days. It's possible my career as a ballerina is over."

Abigail gave a little hiccup of a laugh.

"It's sad, I know," he said, patting her hand, "but you mustn't cry."

As James and Michael climbed in and sat themselves down on the bench beside Patience, Abigail noticed that Captain Walpole remained with the side of his arm and his leg pressed up against hers. There was room for her to shift over, but she could not bring herself to do so. The contact felt comforting, and Abigail luxuriated in the sensation as the carriage bumped its way into the village.

The Stag and Hound was just as Abigail had imagined it—rough-hewn tables and chairs, the scent of ale, a murmur of low voices punctuated with laughter. Small windows let in some light, but it was a cool room resting mostly in shadow. The owner—a small older man James referred to as Peterson—

came over to personally greet them. James recognised several of Lord Winter's tenants at one of the tables and excused himself to go and say hello while the rest of the party was seated.

"Back from the war, are you?" asked Peterson of Captain Walpole. "May I thank you for your exceptional service?"

"You can't know it was exceptional." Captain Walpole set his crutches against the table. "I clearly have trouble dodging musket shot."

That set Peterson chuckling.

"Modest and all," said the older man, rubbing a hand up and over his wispy blonde hair. "Drinks are on the house."

Michael slapped the table which made Abigail jump slightly in her seat.

"I knew it was a good idea to bring you along, Walpole."

"Is that all I am to you?" said Captain Walpole with a smile in his voice. "A free drinks ticket?"

As they placed their orders, Captain Walpole surprised them all by ordering a cup of coffee.

"What?" he said when they were all staring at him after Peterson had left the table. "If Patience is going to be so scandalous as to order a pint of ale, I have to do my best to create some balance in this world."

Abigail had done the expected thing of a lady and ordered the usual boring watered-down wine, though she was very much looking forward to her steak-and-kidney pie. When the drinks arrived, she watched as Captain Walpole wrapped his fingers around the handle of his coffee mug and was momentarily nearly unseated by a memory of the night before—*he had taken her hair between his fingers.*

How had she not remembered this until now? What had

he said? For the life of her, she couldn't recall, but she knew it was something nice. She had a vague feeling of having wanted to prolong the evening and an adjacent memory of her disappointment when he had ushered her up to bed.

Sweet Dreams.

Heat flooded her face.

"Are you all right, Miss Fernside?" asked Captain Walpole.

"Yes. Yes, I'm quite fine, thank you." She picked up her glass and knocked back half the wine in one go.

"Thirsty?" he added.

"Rather," she said.

Patience and Michael had their heads together chatting about something or other. Michael was a huge patron of the arts, and he always had much to discuss with her regarding her portrait painting, not to mention the gossip that swirled around the world of art and artists. As these two were lost together in their own little conversational world, Captain Walpole regarded Abigail with a gaze so direct, she felt quite as if she were standing naked in front of him.

"Don't," he said quietly just as she was about to look down at the table.

"Don't what?" she asked in almost a whisper.

"Don't look away."

Abigail was vaguely aware of Patience laughing at something Michael had said. She gazed into Captain Walpole's sad eyes as she fought every fibre in her body telling her to hide. Her pulse began to race, and she knew a moment that felt a lot like the night before when he had taken her hair in his hand. Her belly was warm, and a gentle ache began to swell between her legs as she regarded the man in front of her.

When James stepped up to the table and clapped Captain

Walpole on the back, the spell was broken, and Abigail found herself staring down into her wine glass with some relief.

"I found a friend of yours," said James brightly as he squeezed the captain's shoulder. "He's been very illuminating."

A young man stepped up to the table from just behind James. He had an arm in a sling under his jacket and a heavy bandage covering one eye. Captain Walpole immediately rose to his feet, or rather his good leg, when he registered the sight of the injured man.

"Lieutenant Colonel Walpole," said the young man. "You won't remember me, but—"

"Private Henson."

The young soldier's good eye shone brightly.

"You *do* remember me. Well . . . I just wanted to say how grateful I was . . . I am . . . for your guidance on the field. I should not have . . . I mean I would likely not be here . . . if you hadn't . . ." He broke off to look down at the captain's injured leg.

Captain Walpole or rather *Lieutenant Colonel Walpole* shoved out his hand to take the young man's.

"You did well," he said, which caused Private Henson to smile though his good eye was brimming with tears. "Your parents should be very proud."

"Thank you, Sir. Thank you."

"Have you a job to come home to?" asked the lieutenant colonel with genuine concern lacing his words.

"My father's farm."

"Ah, good."

The two soldiers regarded each other for a moment longer in a silence that carried the weight of all they had lost on that field. Eventually, Private Henson excused himself but not before clasping Lieutenant Colonel Walpole's hand in both of his.

As everyone resumed their seats at the table, there was not a word spoken. They watched the lieutenant colonel take a sip of his coffee as if nothing at all had just transpired. It was Michael who finally took the bull by the horns.

"Well," he said. *"Lieutenant Colonel Walpole,* you've been rather unforthcoming."

Patience cleared her throat beside him, and Michael threw her a look.

"Did you know?" he asked.

She tilted her head guiltily: "Yes, but he clearly didn't want to say, so . . ."

The lieutenant colonel had been staring into his coffee cup as they spoke, but he finally looked up.

"Can we just leave it?" he said with some irritation.

It was at that moment that their pies arrived, and Abigail realised with a pang of disappointment that she would not be able to enjoy eating hers. Her stomach was all knotted with confused sympathy and concern for the man seated across from her, the man who had two minutes ago asked her not to look away.

Fuck, thought Thomas. *Fuck.*

They were all watching him eat his bloody pie like it was some sort of show. He looked up and set down his fork.

"Tomorrow, I think we should play a round of cards," he said as he tried his best to shrug off the unwelcome feelings that were vying for his attention.

"About this promotion of yours," said Michael.

Thomas turned on him angrily.

"It's not really a promotion when there's no one else to fill the position because everyone's fucking dead, Michael!"

Hell. There were ladies at the table. What was wrong with him?

Patience slid back her chair and stood.

"Abigail, will you join me for a walk through the village?"

Thomas couldn't bear to look over at the waif. What must she think of him? He closed his eyes to steady himself as he heard her shift her chair to stand. When the ladies had left, James slipped around to seat himself beside Thomas.

"We know it was hard," said James.

"No," said Thomas icily. "You *think* it was hard. To *know* it was hard, you would have had to have been there."

He pressed his hand to his thigh beneath the table to keep the tremor at bay. He saw James and Michael exchange a look. That was all he needed—these two do-gooders talking to Richard, and then Richard sitting him down like a little boy for a little talk.

"If everyone would kindly fuck off for a moment," said Thomas, "I might be able to actually enjoy my pie."

"Fine," said James, lifting both his hands with palms turned out in surrender. "We're not trying to upset you."

If James wasn't so damn good-looking, Thomas might have actually punched him in the face. Instead, he continued to eat his pie as if nothing at all was the matter. He had to force it down since not only was he no longer hungry, but he was feeling slightly nauseous as well.

How could he have spoken like that in front of the waif? Good Lord.

He knew Patience would forgive him, but Miss Fernside

was too delicate to be left standing within firing range. He should make his excuses and leave Avery House before he managed to upset her any further.

In the end, Thomas hired a local driver to take him back to Avery House before the ladies returned from their walk. He would have to apologise to them, but he couldn't do it with James and Michael watching over him like two broody hens. He spent the remainder of the afternoon holed up in his room, lying on his bed and staring up at the canopy. James eventually came knocking.

"Can I come in?" He poked his golden head around the doorjamb.

"Will you leave if I say no?" asked Thomas with some petulance.

"No."

"Then be my guest."

James entered the room and closed the door behind him. He sat down on the bed beside Thomas and then swung his legs up to lie down beside his friend.

"What are we looking at?" asked James, peering up into the canopy.

"I think I should leave," said Thomas.

"Don't be an idiot. We love you, so you must stay."

"I don't think Miss Fernside loves me. What the hell was I thinking?"

"Michael tends to erode one's impulse control," said James. "He would try the patience of a saint. You mustn't punish yourself."

Thomas was still staring up at the canopy, but he could feel James take his hand.

"Come to dinner," said James. "I promise, all will be well."

He lifted Thomas's hand to his lips. "We love you. You always have a home here."

Thomas could feel a tear crowding into the outside corner of one eye. It beaded and rolled, sliding from his temple down into his ear.

When James finally left, Thomas resigned himself to the evening. He decided that it would be best if he could make his way down early to find Patience and the waif before the others congregated.

He found Miss Fernside first. She was wearing a shimmering dress of green silk that reminded him of the way light plays through the leaves of the trees in the forest. The fabric was cut in a different fashion from her usual dresses, and it wrapped itself around her figure in a way that made him drop his eyes from her face to her bosom and hips before he had to wrench them back up again. They were both standing at the bottom of the main staircase, he on his crutches, and the waif with her hand to the bannister.

"Miss Fernside," he said. "I must apologise for my terrible display this afternoon. It was unbecoming, crude, and—"

"—honest," she added.

He simply stared at her. Her lovely golden brown hair was swept up in a twist at the nape of her neck, but several wavy tendrils had already sprung free.

"I hardly think you need to apologise for telling the truth." Miss Fernside stepped towards him.

"I should not have cursed. I should have been more restrained."

"Your friends deserve to know how you feel," she said.

"But—" he started to protest.

"Might I be counted as a friend?" she asked.

48

"Yes . . . of course . . . Miss Fernside, I . . ."

"Then there's no need for an apology," she continued. "And Patience certainly doesn't need one. You should hear the oaths she utters when a painting is not going to plan—she sounds like a workman down at the docks."

Thomas could feel the grim line of his mouth breaking into a partial smile despite the misery that threatened to overwhelm him. Her words were like a sip of cool water in the middle of a desert. While they were enough to see him through the evening, he knew that a few drams of whiskey wouldn't go begging once everyone else was abed.

Four

Muffins

D inner was a relatively lively affair, all things considered. Patience told some rather funny stories about the crotchety genius Mr. Turner, and Thomas felt himself relaxing back into his usual role at Avery House.

"Mr. Turner will grab the paintbrush right out of your hand," said Patience, "and set about fixing your painting according to his own whims without so much as a how-do-you-do?"

Thomas watched Richard who in turn was watching his wife with a look of such abject devotion it made his heart hurt to witness it.

"I've seen Turner spit on his own paintings," said Michael.

"Really, Michael! We're eating," scolded the dowager.

"Out of disgust?" asked Thomas.

"No, for want of paint thinner," said Michael, which set the whole table laughing.

Miss Fernside's face lit with merriment. Thomas shifted his

gaze to the curve of her bosom, then up and along the sweep of her collarbone, over her shoulder and down, tracing the willowy line of her arm with his eyes. He had to subdue an urge that was gradually drawing strength. Not everything about him was injured. She glanced his way, but catching his eye, quickly dropped her face down to her plate and made a show of pushing a green bean around with her fork.

Thomas was used to having a beautiful woman hanging off his arm, and very occasionally, in the more discreet corners of society, a gentleman or two. He was always the focal point of any party, especially when it came to the ladies. A few drinks, a few games, a little flirting, and it was only ever a bit of fun— nothing serious. A widow here, an actress there. Of course, he would not dream of seducing an innocent. There was nothing fair about that. Young ladies in their first few Seasons were looking for marriage, and Thomas had never been so inclined. Marriage seemed like a rather big boot coming down in the middle of all the fun. He imagined that no matter how lovely the young lady, he would eventually resent her, not simply for shackling him to her ankle but for forcing him to hide those aspects of himself that she might find both intolerable and, let's be honest, also illegal.

Miss Fernside stabbed at her bean and took it between her teeth.

"What do you say, Thomas?" It was Richard.

"About what?"

"Michael wants to organise a card tournament tomorrow afternoon."

"Oh, yes, that would be good fun," said Thomas.

He glanced back towards Miss Fernside who was dabbing at her soft lips with a white napkin.

"Do you play, Miss Fernside?"

She looked rather startled to be called out at the table.

"Me? No, I'm afraid I don't."

"Then you'll have to learn," said Thomas. "How else are you to win tomorrow's tournament?"

She looked somewhat alarmed by this.

"Don't worry," he said. "I'm an excellent teacher."

The waif's off-limits, he reminded himself, but he wasn't really listening.

Abigail curled up on her side under the bed covers. The day had been a lot to take in, and she found it soothing to pull her knees into her chest. It made her feel smaller and less noticeable, not that there was anyone in the room to notice her, but still. She and Patience had spent a great deal of time talking as they walked about the village, and it had been an eye-opening conversation as far as Abigail was concerned.

"Not every injury is one of the body," said Patience. "A soldier returns with so many unseen wounds, it's a miracle he is still standing at all. Thomas will be quite devastated at his behaviour this afternoon, but we must do our best to put him at ease. He's hurting."

Abigail was not sure how she would be able to put him at ease. He had seemed quite angry, and it was just a little bit frightening if she thought about it too much. Captain . . . no, Lieutenant Colonel Walpole had always seemed so bright and jovial. He was the one who put others at ease, not the other way around.

"I'll do my best," said Abigail.

"It's possible he's having nightmares," said Patience. "Attacks of the nerves are quite common for returning soldiers as well. Have you noticed the tremor in his hand?"

Abigail nodded. She thought of the way he pressed it to his thigh.

When she and Patience had returned to the public house to find Lieutenant Colonel Walpole had already left, Abigail knew that she would have to be brave that evening in order to do her part. Bravery required that one did not shrink or hide, and so Abigail had donned her lovely green dress. It was not a dress in which one could disappear as Abigail was usually wont to do, and she knew it would force her forward to do what she must. He had been waiting for her at the bottom of the stairs with such a grave expression on his face, it made her want to cry.

"Miss Fernside."

The way he said her name with such inflected misery—it squeezed at her heart.

But in the end, she had done it. She had been bold in dismissing his apology, as bold as it was possible for her to be. She had even made him crack a smile.

Abigail turned over onto her back in the bed and forced herself to stretch out like a starfish. As she breathed quietly into the dark room, she heard a sound in the hallway—a rather large thump. Abigail scrambled from her bed and fumbled to light a candle. Then she tiptoed to the door and cracked it open. Her candle cast a slice of light across the hall. It was the lieutenant colonel. He was on the floor fumbling for his crutches in the dark.

"Lieutenant Colonel Walpole," she said softly.

"Don't call me that." He struggled unsuccessfully to stand.

"What should I call you?" she asked, opening up the door a little wider and stepping into the hall. She crouched down and placing her candle on the floor so that he might take her shoulder.

She had to wrap an arm around the man to steady him, and the contact of having her body slide up against his was decidedly intoxicating. He turned his head to look at her, and she was struck by how close his face was. She could smell whisky and something else . . . a scent that was entirely his own which made her want to lean into him and inhale. Of course, she did no such thing.

"Well," said Lieutenant Colonel Walpole as his hand slid behind her neck to take hold of her opposite shoulder, "women who embrace me as you're doing now usually call me Thomas."

Abigail did not like the thought of these other women who embraced him, and a brief, violent sensation rose in her breast as she struggled to stand with his weight. Thomas, however, was remarkably ungainly, and they both ended up on their bottoms on the floor, each with one arm around the other.

"You've been drinking," she said.

"Not too much."

"But enough to make standing a problem."

"Standing is always a problem when one is lame," he replied.

"Don't be obtuse!" said Abigail.

"Ah, there she is! My little dagger." He pulled her closer to him as he leaned back against the wall, and Abigail found herself melting into his side. She was suddenly aware of her state of undress—she was only wearing a thin summer nightrail. Not even a dressing gown.

They sat like that for several minutes, neither saying a word.

Abigail could feel the soft rise and fall of Thomas's breath as he held her in the candlelight. Eventually, she felt his head tilt down to rest over hers, and she instinctively nestled into his shoulder. She could see his hand trembling where it lay on his lap, and she very bravely reached over to take it in hers.

"It's all right," she said.

"I'm afraid nothing's all right," murmured Thomas against her head. "Nothing at all."

"It will get better," said Abigail.

She felt him kiss the top of her head, and her entire body responded with a flush of warmth. She lifted her face to look at him.

"I missed you," he said quietly, "after last Season. It was always such a joy to dance with you."

"I find that hard to believe," whispered Abigail. "You appeared to be avoiding me at the end."

"Waifs are off-limits."

"I'm a waif, am I?"

"Oh, yes. You are the waifiest waif in the whole wide world."

There was something about the way they were sat on the floor holding each other in the candlelit hallway that made Abigail feel as if she could say things she would never say in the light of day.

"I don't think you should be spending each evening drinking."

"Ah, the waif is also a nag. It gets even better."

"I'm not a nag! I'm concerned for you."

"Why?" asked Thomas.

He was drunk, Abigail reminded herself. He may not even remember this conversation the next morning.

"Why do you think?" she asked softly.

He took her chin in his hand, and his brown eyes were hard as he stared down into hers. Abigail's breathing became rather heavy under his gaze.

"You've taken a fancy to me," he said. "I know. I've probably encouraged it somewhat, and I apologise for that—old habits die hard I'm afraid. But here's what you don't understand. This won't end in wedding bells and happily-ever-afters. I'm not that sort of gentleman."

"How will it end?" she asked.

"Resentment on my part. Tears on yours. And you would be ruined for a proper marriage."

"A *proper* marriage," said Abigail. "What is that?"

"One in which you would be cherished above all others."

Despite his words, he tilted her chin to one side and pressed his face against her neck. She could feel him inhale. The gentle intimate contact made her skin fizz like a glass of champagne.

"You make it so hard when you smell so damn lovely," he said.

After a lingering moment, he lifted his head, released her chin, and leaned back against the wall.

The candle on the floor sputtered and went out, allowing the darkness to slide over them like a cloak.

"How would it start?" she whispered.

"Excuse me?" said Thomas into the dark.

"You said how it would end, but I'm wondering how it would begin."

Abigail held her breath as Thomas tightened his grip around her waist. She felt him take a breath that shuddered through him as he exhaled.

"A chance encounter," he said. "In a darkened hall. You would be wearing nothing but a very thin white nightdress through which I would be able to see your nipples by the light of the candle you were holding."

"Oh."

It was more a puff of air than a sound.

"We might end up sitting on the floor in the dark leaning against the wall in an embrace that neither one of us wished to relinquish despite its impropriety."

Abigail could feel his fingers at her waist stroking gently against the thin cotton of her nightdress. His body moved to take in another breath.

"Being lame as I am, you would oblige me by coming to straddle my lap, and my hand would slip under your nightdress and up along the back of one silky thigh as you bowed your head to kiss me."

Abigail could feel an aching sensation swell between her legs, and she held her breath as she tried not to squirm against him.

"What would the kiss be like?" she whispered.

"It would be soft as a sunset, sweet as honey. We could never have enough." His voice was a rasp, and he pulled her even closer against his side. "As we kissed, my fingers would stroke the back of your thigh before gliding up to tease you between your legs. I imagine you would be as wet as October . . . as wet as you are now listening to my words."

Abigail blushed into the darkness. He wasn't wrong. She tilted her head down to rest comfortably against his shoulder.

"And then?" she whispered.

Thomas was hoarse when he spoke.

"I would want to have your breasts out in the open. But you would probably be shy about it, so I wouldn't press you."

"Perhaps I would not be so shy," whispered Abigail.

"Oho! Are you telling this story, or am I?"

Abigail gave up a small laugh into the darkness.

"Miss Fernside," said Thomas, and she thought that for a brief moment, he sounded almost sober. "You are exquisite in every way. You must not think otherwise. It's only that it will end poorly . . . I couldn't do that to you."

"How very noble of you," said Abigail, slowly untangling herself from his embrace. His words hurt her despite his intention not to do so. "Let's try to get you on your feet, shall we?"

It was a struggle, but somehow they managed it down the hall in the dark to Thomas's bed chamber.

"On your way then," he said as he turned to her. "No more chance encounters in the dark."

Abigail didn't particularly like the implication in his tone, and she surprised herself by standing up just a little taller.

"That's entirely up to you . . . Thomas."

It was the first time she had used his Christian name out loud, and it felt . . . somehow right. He was Thomas. Not Captain Walpole or the lieutenant colonel. Just Thomas. Just a man. Certainly not her be all and end all, regardless of how wet she may still be between her legs.

"If you don't drink yourself into a stupor every night," she continued. "I won't be forced to come to your rescue."

Thomas shook his head with a soft smile.

"Sharp as a dagger," he said. "Bright as a flame."

They looked at each other for several seconds before he spoke again.

"Goodnight, Miss Fernside."

Then he turned and fumbled his way into the room.

Abigail did not find Thomas at breakfast the next morning which was quite fine with her.

She had thought for just a moment that . . . He had made her feel . . . special. But she wasn't special—not to him anyway. He had made that quite clear. If they had done what she had been inclined to do last night, she would have been ruined for a "proper marriage", and he would be resentful—of her!

Fine, she thought as she hacked rather angrily at her muffin with a knife. *Of course it's fine. I knew what he was like. It had only been a silly girlish hope . . . not even a hope really. A stupid wish. A dream. A fanciful tale I told myself.*

Abigail had seen Thomas with many sophisticated ladies at various functions she had attended around London the year before. He was more than popular. He might have danced the occasional pity dance with her, but he had always disappeared at some point in the evening, and there had usually been a beautiful woman making her excuses to leave at about the same time. Abigail knew this because she had spent an entire Season watching him, willing him to look her way. She had been quite besotted.

Naive, she corrected herself. *Unworldly and naive.*

"What did that muffin ever do to you?" asked Patience from her place at the breakfast table.

Abigail looked up. It was just the two of them this morning.

"It doesn't think I'm very special, so I'm punishing it."

"Well, in that case, hack away! Give it no quarter!"

"Thank you." Abigail gave a nod of her head. "Precisely my thoughts."

They both laughed as Abigail massacred the remainder of her muffin. As she was doing so, Lord Winter entered the breakfast room with James at his side. He stopped short, and

Abigail immediately ceased her laughter and put down her knife. The viscount looked from Abigail's mangled muffin to Patience who gave him a look.

"Abigail's muffin has been unkind to her," said Patience by way of explanation.

"Oh, really?" said Lord Winter in his low rumble.

Abigail was always a little intimidated by the viscount. He had a rather serious air about him, and he did sometimes raise his voice. She had watched him exchange loud words with Patience on occasion, and though Patience stood her ground, often challenging him at a similar volume, Abigail had to fight the urge to hide under a table.

Now, she could feel Lord Winter's gaze as it came to rest on her face. She looked down at her plate. There were muffin bits everywhere—she would eat them of course. She wouldn't want to be wasteful.

"Where's Thomas?" he asked.

He knows, thought Abigail. *Or at least, he suspects.*

She lifted the edge of the table cloth and glanced under the table. It seemed like a nice cosy space down there. She could bring a few cushions and a book. She might never have to come out.

"He hasn't come down yet," said James. "Shall I fetch him?"

"No," said Lord Winter to James though he was looking at Patience once more. "I'll go myself."

After breakfast, Patience chased Abigail out into the hall and took her arm.

"Let's go for a stroll," she said, directing her friend out of the house and into the garden.

Abigail inhaled the scent of roses and mock orange and let out a small sigh. Blue delphiniums speared their way up towards a blue sky, and white daisies bobbed their heads in the gentle breeze as if acknowledging the ladies as they passed by.

"The thing about muffins," said Patience, "is that no matter how delicious they may seem, they're also rather idiotic creatures with no sense of finesse, rarely even a sense of themselves."

Abigail stopped walking and looked at her friend.

"Muffins?" she said.

"Muffins." Patience nodded. The corners of her mouth were only slightly turned up. "Sometimes they need a little help."

Abigail thought back to the evening before with Thomas. The hurt was still raw in her breast.

"No," said Abigail in a way that made her friend's eyes open wide. "No. A muffin is not a child . . . and . . . and neither am I."

She pulled her spine up a little straighter and stood a little taller as she walked on past a swathe of huge crimson poppies whose papery petals flopped open to reveal dramatic black centres.

Looking at the poppies, Abigail realised that what she needed most was not Thomas at all, but simply a little more confidence. She needed to cultivate her own garden of joy and hope rather than expecting someone else to provide those things for her.

"Just to be clear," said Patience. "The muffin in question is Thomas, correct?"

Abigail stopped to pick a daisy.

"Not anymore." She sniffed at the flower in her hand.

"Do you know who has a good sense of muffins?" asked Patience, her eyes bright with humour. "My sister Grace."

"But she's only eleven years old."

"Nearly twelve."

"Oh, well then," said Abigail, "I stand corrected."

"I'm serious," said Patience. "She actually gave me some very good advice when I was wooing Richard."

Abigail had to laugh at that.

"You wooed Lord Winter?"

"He was rather coy," said Patience with a smile and a far-away look in her eye. "He needed a bit of a nudge."

Abigail looked down at the white daisy she was holding. She couldn't even imagine nudging a man like Lord Winter in the direction Patience was implying. Her friend was so bold and daring—nothing at all like herself.

"Patience," she said hesitantly, "I want to ask you . . . and this has nothing to do with Thomas—you must believe me on that count. It's just that my mother is so . . . and you know how it is with Harriet . . . I feel as if I don't know anything about . . . and it sort of eats away at you, the not knowing and the wondering. It's certainly not good for my confidence."

"Amorous congress," said Patience, taking the daisy from Abigail's hand and twirling its petals softly against her cheek. "I was wondering when you might ask."

Abigail couldn't help the somewhat embarrassed smile that broke out across her face. She gave Patience a playful shove.

"You could have made that a little easier then."

"I suppose I could have," Patience laughed. "Come along." She tugged Abigail back towards the house. "I have a folder full of diagrams."

"You what?"

"They are quite immodest. I drew them when my friend Serafina explained everything to me. She's a very good teacher—pays great attention to detail."

Abigail had to place a hand to her mouth to cover a grin. The morning was looking up.

Thomas woke late that morning with a sticky mouth and a throbbing head. He rolled over onto his back and winced. A disconcerting feeling lay over him like a damp sheet that he could not quite manage to kick free of his body, and he wondered if he had done something foolish the night before. Likely, he had simply told Richard where to shove his overblown sympathy and offers to talk.

Thomas swung his feet over the side of the bed and sat up. He squeezed his eyes shut and then opened them once more and waited for them to focus on the room. He was still dressed as he had been the day before—not a good sign. He looked down to his lap where he could see a rather violent erection straining to break free of his trousers. It had been a long time since he had been with a woman, and it would be some time before he would be with another, trapped as he was in this country house with not a single available woman in sight. James and Michael would be no help on that front either, devoted as they were to each other.

He rubbed his hands up over his face, and it was only when he removed them that he noticed the piece of folded paper on his bedside table. He reached over and picked it up.

The word '*URGENT!*' was scrawled in what he knew from experience to be his own drunken hand. He unfolded the paper.

It read, *You nearly compromised the waif! Stop drinking. Stop.*

Stop. STOP!

When Thomas closed his eyes, he heard Miss Fernside's whispered voice coming to him through the darkness: "Perhaps I would not be so shy."

Bleeding hell!

He looked down at the erection still pressing up against his trousers.

"You little fucker," he said.

At that very moment, the door to his bed chamber swung open without so much as a knock, and Richard stepped the full mass of his hulking body into the room.

"Jesus, Thomas. You look like the Devil's own arse."

"I feel like it." Thomas surreptitiously slid the piece of paper under his pillow.

"Is it helping?" asked Richard.

"Is what helping?"

"The chronic inebriation," said Richard. "As medicine goes, you've had some rather large doses. Surely, it should be working by now."

"Very funny." Thomas struggled to remove his cravat and failed miserably.

Richard stepped up to him and untangled the cravat from around Thomas's neck. Thomas tilted his face up to his friend and smiled.

"You love me," he said.

"Shut up, Thomas."

"What about my cufflinks?" Thomas reached his wrist towards Richard. "I'll need help with those as well."

Richard bowed his head dutifully to the task.

The man truly does love me, thought Thomas.

The fact was as extraordinary as it was wondrous, and

Thomas never tired of wallowing in it like a pig in mud. Once upon a time, they had been friends in the way that soldiers are often friends—guarded acquaintances in camp, brothers in battle, strangers at home. That had changed the night Major Richard Winter had happened upon him and a devilishly handsome Portuguese farmer in the woods beside their army encampment. To say that Richard found them in a compromising position would be to do the word 'compromising' a disservice. This had been no innocent stolen kiss in the dark. When Thomas had looked up and seen the huge bearded major standing silently in the moonlight, fear had risen like a thick sludge in his throat, and it had nearly choked him.

The legal punishment for his deviance was a hanging. Even if it were not taken so far, the social punishment would be not only a shunning, but the loss of the only employment he had ever known—the only source of meaning in his life. Richard had turned away swiftly, striding back to the camp on his huge legs, while Thomas had fallen over in a panic as he tried unsuccessfully to get his trousers back on.

The next morning, Thomas had gagged down his breakfast in silence among the crowd of officers, occasionally stealing glances Richard's way. Just the once did the major's eyes come to rest on his, and when they did, he gave a short sharp tilt of his head before getting up and walking off behind one of the tents. Thomas put down his metal cup and surreptitiously followed.

Behind the tent, the major turned on him with a ferocity beyond anything he could have anticipated. The man was red in the face.

"Do you have a fucking death wish, Walpole?!" he whispered

angrily. "It's a bloody army encampment!"

Thomas had quailed.

"It's not what you . . . It wasn't . . ."

"Do you think I'm an imbecile, Captain?"

"No."

"Do you think any of the other men here are imbeciles?"

"No, Sir," said Thomas.

"My advice," said the major, "is to keep it in your fucking trousers until we get home. It's not worth the risk."

Thomas didn't quite believe the words he was hearing. He would never have guessed that the major had a predilection for men.

"I'm not that way inclined," said the major as if reading his mind.

"Then . . . why?"

Major Winter stared at him for a good few moments before answering.

"I've experienced enough hate in my life to recognise affection for the blessing that it is," he said on a whisper. "Your secret is safe with me . . . but Captain, seriously, you must take more care!"

And that had been that. The huge major with the guarded heart had given Thomas a gift that day. He had seen Thomas, and he had accepted him without question.

In his bed chamber, Thomas looked up into the face of his friend. Richard removed the second cuff-link, and Thomas pulled his shirt up over his head.

"I'll have a bath sent up," said Richard.

When he turned to leave, Thomas called out after him.

"I'll stop. Drinking, that is."

Richard paused on his way out and turned.

"Why?" he asked.

"Because you want me to, and I like nothing more than to please you, you great lummox."

"Why?" The question was louder this time.

Thomas stared at him.

"Is it because of Miss Fernside?" asked Richard.

"How did y—?" started Thomas. Then, "Yes. I may have said some things."

"Did you *do* some things?" Richard's voice was much darker now.

"Of course not!"

Richard made a sound like a growl in his chest before turning to leave Thomas alone in his room.

"Of course not," said Thomas once more to himself.

Five

Lucky Stars

Bathed and dressed and fed and watered, Thomas was feeling marginally better. He wasn't entirely sure what to expect when he encountered Miss Fernside that day. He imagined he had embarrassed her, possibly even hurt her. Thomas had dealt with the occasional infatuation directed his way before, and it was all quite a lot of disappointment and tears and general horribleness.

When he found Miss Fernside in the games room, however, she did not look to have been affected by his behaviour in the slightest. If anything, she seemed rather disturbingly jubilant as she bounced in her seat.

"That's twenty-one," she said. "And a king beats your ten, so . . ."

"The buttons are yours," declared Michael, laughing. "See? It's not so hard, is it?"

Miss Fernside looked his way as Thomas entered the room,

and he was momentarily struck by the rosy glow of her usually pale complexion. She was wearing a summer dress of a pinkish plummy colour, and her smile stabbed him like a bayonet to the belly.

"Thomas," she said. She turned back to Michael. "He won't permit me to call him by his proper title." Then swivelling her head to Thomas once more. "We're just warming up with Vingt-et-un. Next, Michael is going to teach me Whist."

Thomas looked to Michael who gave him an infuriating grin.

"That's wonderful, Miss Fernside."

"I wonder how much I might win in the card room at Almack's," said Miss Fernside as she shuffled the cards. "I was always too afraid to poke my head in through that door."

"They don't gamble with buttons at Almack's," said Thomas.

"I should hope not," she said, dealing out a card to Michael and then one to herself.

"You might lose all your pin money in one fell swoop," said Thomas, though why he was trying to warn her off, he couldn't quite say. She was most certainly not his business.

"Pin money?" Abigail peeled up her card to take a look. "You think my mother gives me pin money?"

She dealt herself another card as Michael tossed Thomas a pitying glance.

There was something Thomas was missing, and it looked like neither Miss Fernside nor Michael were willing to enlighten him. This thought was interrupted by Patience's voice at the door.

"We're here!"

She stepped in with James at her side. Thomas always marvelled to see them together, their two golden-haired heads bobbing side-by-side, both beautiful mouths curved into rather infectious smiles, and always a glance between them as if they were in the possession of some hidden jest.

The jest would be Richard, thought Thomas. *Only these two would have the nerve to poke fun at him.*

"But that makes five," said Thomas. "If we're going to play Whist, who will be sitting out?"

"No one," said Michael. "The songbird and I will be playing as one. That way, I can teach her the game as we play."

Thomas was paired with Patience, and the team of Michael and Miss Fernside was paired with James. Though it turned out to be quite a lot of fun—and just what Thomas had needed to replace the glass of whisky he didn't have in his hand—he couldn't help but feel unreasonably bothered by the way Michael was sat with his arm over the back of Miss Fernside's chair. Occasionally, the man would cup his hand to her ear in order to whisper an instruction, and Thomas was reminded of how it had felt to press his face into the side of her satiny neck.

They played several rounds, and it didn't take long before Michael was sitting back and allowing Miss Fernside to take the reins. The waif was no slouch with the numbers.

Why was he surprised?

Thomas could tell that not only was she counting the cards, but she was also making rather accurate estimates of how likely a particular card would be to show up in a round. There was not much Thomas respected more than a decent card player, and a decent card player wearing a plummy pink dress and jiggling about in her chair with delight was almost more than he could take.

"You're swimming in buttons," declared Thomas to Miss

Fernside when the last hand had been played. "Some might call it beginner's luck."

She was flushed and happy as she pulled the pile of buttons towards her.

"Some might." She flashed him a smile. "I think I shall make a garland of them—a keepsake of the day."

She spared a glance for Patience, and Thomas could have sworn that she mouthed the words "thank you" in her friend's direction.

And that was that—a complete recovery from the night before. Thomas should have been thanking his lucky stars that the waif appeared neither upset nor saddened nor even terribly embarrassed by his behaviour with her in the dark. He *should* have been thanking his lucky stars, but instead, he spent the next several weeks willing her to look his way and feeling rather despondent when she did not.

That evening, as Thomas stood staring out the window over the front lawn which was slowly losing its colour to the growing darkness, Michael stepped up beside him.

"You shouldn't talk down to her," he said.

"Excuse me?" Thomas turned from the window.

"The songbird," said Michael. "You shouldn't talk down to her as if she's just some silly girl with a few shillings worth of pin money stuffed in her pocket."

"I wasn't talking down to her," said Thomas.

Michael made a noise in his throat.

"For one thing, she is extraordinarily clever and talented—"

"—I know that," interrupted Thomas with annoyance.

"She's also related to a Scottish marquess," said Michael. "The Marquess of Huntly is her uncle."

"Can't say that I know the man." Thomas affected not to

care.

Good Lord—she was proper nobility.

"And she is in no way beholden to anyone to decide anything on her behalf—not her mother and certainly not her stepfather," added Michael.

"Why is that?"

"This is just between the two of us—if word got out, she would be awash with fortune hunters. The fact is she's in possession of a modest inheritance," said Michael. "Her father bequeathed her and her sister's portions to them unencumbered by conditions of marriage."

Thomas stared at Michael without blinking. While he thought of Miss Fernside in his mind as 'the waif', in reality, she had both status and means.

"A forward-thinking gentleman, her father," said Michael with good humour. "She is free to do as she pleases . . . within reason of course." He paused. "You should see the look on your face, Thomas."

"Bugger off, Michael."

"Before I bugger off, I'd just like to say one last thing. It shouldn't take a noble title or an inheritance to treat a woman such as her with the respect and consideration she deserves."

James was right, thought Thomas. *Michael would try the patience of a saint.*

Cards became a nightly affair, which really was the only thing that kept Thomas from reaching for the whisky. He wasn't one of those men who *had* to drink. As long as he had something to take its place, he was all right—a little excitement such as gaming or flirting or even boxing could go a long way to distract him. Soon the buttons were replaced with pennies, and Miss Fernside appeared to be chomping at the bit all evening until dinner was done and the cards were dealt. It made him smile. He knew how she felt.

They did eventually attend church. All of them—even James came along despite his grumblings. It was a glorious Sunday, the kind that spends its time bowling fluffy white clouds across the sky as it kisses you gently with a warm summer breeze.

"She looks like a porcelain doll," said Michael of the vicar's wife as they all climbed up the small hill towards the church. "But I imagine she's survived quite a life—it's possible only the vicar could break her should he wish to."

"If it's true love," said Thomas, swinging himself forward on his crutches, "I imagine she could also break him with only a few words."

"Yes," said Michael, darting a glance towards James. "Love is a rather dangerous game all told, isn't it? To hold someone else's frangible heart in your hands."

"Frangible!" said James, turning his golden gaze on Michael. "That's not a word!"

"Of course it is," said Michael, pretending affront. "I'm a learned man, don't you know? And it's terribly bad manners to mock your betters, Mr. Winter."

James laughed as he put an arm around Michael's shoulder and pulled him in tight to his side. A quick squeeze before letting him go.

Glancing up at her husband, Patience slipped her hand in his. Miss Fernside kept her eyes on her feet as they climbed up the steep path. It was slow going, and her stride was not as long as that of the others, so she inevitably fell to the back of the pack.

The church itself was one of those ancient stone affairs, built at the top of a low green hill. Inside the church walls stood an enormous yew tree that bowed itself over the church and the assembling congregation like a sentry of protection. Several people were milling around outside the church in their Sunday best, and as a full-figured lady in an enormous straw bonnet stepped to the side, Thomas caught a glimpse through the gate of a familiar face. He immediately slowed his step, falling back until he was beside Miss Fernside. The other members of his party proceeded in through the church gate in front of them.

"I think I'll have to sit this one out," said Thomas to Miss Fernside.

She stopped to regard him as everyone else made their way into the church.

"Excuse me?"

"Probably not a good idea for me to go in," he said. "I'll meet you around back afterwards. I'm sure there's a bench in the yard where I can take a nap while you're all being regaled with tales of biblical derring do."

"But it was your idea to come," said Miss Fernside. "What's the matter?"

Thomas eyed the entrance to the church, then gestured with a tip of his head for Miss Fernside to join him outside of the churchyard wall where they were hidden from view. She drew her brows together suspiciously as she approached him by the wall.

"I know the vicar's wife," he whispered. "I can see her by the entrance."

"What? The former . . . . actress?" Miss Fernside peeked around the corner.

"I don't think she would be pleased to have a piece of her old life piercing through her idyll of love and contentment."

Miss Fernside narrowed her eyes.

"Did you . . . ? Did you and she . . . ?"

"We were amorously entangled on occasion," said Thomas. "It was never anything serious. More a comfort for the two of us than anything else."

A very long pause ensued.

"I see . . ." said Miss Fernside finally. She peered around the wall and through the gate a second time. "Everyone's already gone in, and they've closed the door. I don't mind sitting with you in the churchyard."

"It's not necessary," said Thomas. "Go on in. Apparently, you have much to atone for."

She gave him a slight smile.

"Yes, but I truly don't like drawing attention to myself like that—walking in when the reverend may already be speaking. I'll wait with you."

"As you wish."

They then quietly slunk in through the gate and made their way past the yew tree and towards the back of the church.

"It must be ancient," said Miss Fernside, tilting her face up to the boughs of the great tree as they passed under it.

"Older than the church," said Thomas, swinging himself up beside her on his crutches. "The heart of the tree is as red as Christ's blood, so there's some symbolism there. But it's a soldier's tree as well."

"I know," said Miss Fernside. "The wood used to be fashioned into longbows that stood as tall as a man and could shoot an arrow over 200 yards with the ability to pierce chainmail."

He darted a surprised glance towards her angelic profile which was still tilted up towards the heavens.

"So much for turning the other cheek," he added.

She turned to him with an appreciative smile.

"I imagine that was the slogan for the crusades as well," she said.

He laughed as a warm breeze lifted his hair and played with the leaves of the tree overhead. They meandered around back to the churchyard where they took a seat on a wooden bench overlooking the gravestones. Thomas propped his crutches up beside him, while Miss Fernside slipped sideways along the bench in order (he assumed) to keep a respectable distance between them.

"So much history," she mused. "So much blood."

"It's the way of things," said Thomas grimly.

"How do you do it?" Miss Fernside turned to him on the bench. "How do you . . . ?"

"Kill?" asked Thomas.

She didn't respond, but she was watching his face with a peculiar intensity. No one had ever looked at him in that way before . . . No one had ever asked him that question before either. He wanted to give her a proper answer, so he took his time, choosing his words carefully.

"In order to kill, you need to feel as if you're protecting something that is worth the forfeit of your soul," said Thomas simply. "It's not an act from which you can emerge spiritually unscathed."

"Oh."

Miss Fernside looked down at her lap for a few moments

then lifted her eyes to his once more.

"Sorry. I shouldn't have asked."

"No, it's all right," said Thomas. "Most people don't ask because they would rather not think properly about what we have done and what it has cost us. Instead, they host a parade and force feed everyone cake as if it were a birthday party rather than a mass funeral."

The silence that followed was filled with the tiny chirps of crickets floating up from the grass and the sweet twittering of birds drifting over from the yew tree out front. As Thomas looked out across the tombstones littering the churchyard, his view was replaced by a muddy battlefield, the blurred charge of cavalry bearing down on him, and the certain knowledge that he could not let them pass.

"She's extravagantly alluring," said Miss Fernside out of the blue.

Thomas had to drag himself back to the churchyard from the battlefield.

"Excuse me?"

"The vicar's wife. She looks like she might have stepped out of a painting."

Abigail gave Thomas a quick sideways glance before shifting her eyes back out to the graveyard. Then, speaking to the graves, she said, "You've never wanted for beautiful women, have you?"

The answer was 'no', but Thomas kept his silence. They were wading into dangerous territory with this line of questioning. He willed the waif to drop the subject, but she continued.

"Does it make you feel special?" she asked, still speaking to the graves with her hands clasped in her lap and her knees pressed together.

He kept quiet.

"I've always wondered what it would be like to have that kind of attention. I imagine it's a brief weightless feeling, like a hot wind lifting you up."

Thomas cleared his throat.

"You could describe it that way," he said. "But the wind always dies down, and then you find yourself on the cold, hard ground once more."

"Searching for another gust of wind?" she asked.

Thomas was beginning to feel rather exposed. He wondered if she would like him to strip naked and stand before her so that she could point out all the little imperfections of his body.

It likely wouldn't be enough, thought Thomas. *She would want access to my soul as well, and she'd probably go at it with a magnifying glass.*

He knew quite well what she would find—a killer, a rake, a coward.

They sat quietly together for a long time. A large bee lurched by and landed on a dandelion. As it nuzzled into the centre of the yellow flower, the waif shifted in her seat and turned to look at him.

"I like talking with you," she said. "Despite everything."

He wondered if she meant despite the fact that he was a killer, a rake, and a coward or despite the fact that he had hurt and disappointed her. He supposed it was all those things which made it a rather brave thing to say. He briefly wondered what it might be like to have that sort of courage.

"I always like talking with you, Miss Fernside."

She smiled in a way that suggested she didn't believe him.

"I think I shall go for a walk and stretch my legs," she said. "Feel free to take that nap you spoke of earlier."

As he watched her stand from the bench and walk away in her gauzy white dress, he thought that if anyone looked like they had stepped out of a painting, it was her.

What could her mother possibly have to complain about?

He imagined what it might be like if the tables were turned. How would it be if the waif was in the habit of receiving attention from handsome admirers? Just the thought of it heated his blood in a rather frightening way, and he tried not to think about why that might be.

Thomas spared a glance behind him to the stone wall of the church. He truly hadn't wanted to attend—it was really just a lark so that they could spend their Sunday luncheon gossiping about the vicar and his unlikely wife. Thomas had never felt entirely comfortable inside a church. There was a lot of cold judgment bundled up with doing unto others and loving thy neighbour, and he had more than once had his fill of the hypocrisy, though he supposed that perhaps this vicar and this church might be different.

No matter, he thought. *At least there is the yew tree standing outside, all red and bloody with the truth.*

The summer continued to roll out like a carpet under his feet, but Thomas was achingly aware that the warmth and the camaraderie and the quiet presence of the waif in his life day-to-day would soon be at an end. Avery House wasn't his home as much as he was welcome.

Sometimes, Thomas would pass by the drawing room and hear Miss Fernside playing the pianoforte. It was always apparent to him if she was playing something for the dowager or something for herself. And even if—especially if—it was a melody that pulled at every buried emotion in his body, he never stopped to listen, but rather forced himself to continue on down the hall until the music faded behind him and he was left with that odd, incomplete feeling that descends when one has heard the beginning of a piece of music but been denied its conclusion.

The physician came and went over the course of the summer, and Thomas's leg and neck continued to heal. Richard and James made sure that he exercised his leg as instructed by the doctor, and by the end of August, he had dispensed with his crutches and was limping around the estate. August brought with it a considerable heat and dark storms that broke over their heads in ominous rolls of thunder that shook the windowpanes in their frames.

It was on such a dramatic day that Thomas found himself in the orangery at Avery House. Lemon trees and flowering shrubs surrounded him as he sat on a small bench under the glass roof, listening to the loud smack of water and waiting for the occasional flash of lightning to illuminate the dark indoor garden. He imagined the room alive with birdsong as it had once been when Richard's father was alive.

Sitting on the bench, he could see Miss Fernside's golden brown hair bobbing behind the shrubbery as she approached. She didn't even see Thomas until she was practically upon him. So absorbed was she in the letter she was reading that if he hadn't said anything, she may well have sat down on his lap. She was wearing another one of those white dresses of hers. Pure and simple and bright against the gloom of the day.

Thomas cleared his throat before she actually did sit on his lap.

"Oh!" Abigail looked up. "I didn't realise anyone was here."

"The bench is yours." Thomas rose to his feet.

"Nonsense," said Miss Fernside. "I won't disturb you."

"There's nothing to disturb."

Her wavy hair was springing free of its pins again. A few tendrils hung loose against her face which made his hands itch to stroke them back behind her ear.

"My sister." Miss Fernside lifted the letter in her hand.

"Is this the perfect sister you spoke of once before?"

"Mm," said Miss Fernside still staring down at the letter. "She's married to a Mr. Evan Sharp, an elected member of Parliament, and they've been blessed with a baby boy who is just now starting to walk."

"Sounds blissfully perfect to me," said Thomas helpfully.

Abigail lifted her eyes to his and gave him a distracted smile.

"Apparently, Mother is expressing some hurt feeling that I have spent the entire summer away."

"Ah."

"Do you have siblings?" she asked.

"I . . . uh . . . just the one. A brother."

"Siblings can be complicated, can't they?" said Miss Fernside, sitting down. "I always feel so guilty about avoiding Harriet because the way I feel around her certainly isn't her fault. But then when I do see her, all the old useless feelings start rising up like a tide around my ankles, and I simply feel as if I'm going to drown."

Thomas found himself sitting back down on the bench. He knew something about siblings and useless feelings and drowning in tides.

"My brother Alexander and I are not the best of friends," he said.

"But don't you wish you could be?"

Thomas tilted his head to one side.

"I used to terrorise him. Worms down his breeches—that sort of thing."

Miss Fernside laughed.

"It sounds innocent enough, but I truly did resent him, and he in turn came to *loathe* me which really only made sense given my behaviour."

"Why did you resent him so much?" Miss Fernside folded her letter and placed it on the bench beside her.

Thomas hesitated for a few seconds. The rain continued to batter the glass room as if it were trying to break its way in, and Thomas had to raise his voice above the fray.

"When I was five years old," he said, "my parents introduced me to my new brother, and I could feel their attention and concern shift to the little squalling bundle in the nurse's arms. I was no longer the centre of their world, and as the years progressed, he continued to be the more favoured child. So taking the high road as I am usually wont to do, I spent the rest of our childhood putting dead mice in his bed."

"You didn't!"

"Being the elder (and quite the charmer as I'm sure you'll agree), I would often manage to convince him to take part in some mischief or other that would see him rather severely reprimanded when he was found out. But it never worked. He continued to be the chosen one as far as my parents were concerned."

"So you were a devil to him," said Miss Fernside. "And now . . ."

"And now he hates me. With good reason."

Thomas felt a familiar sadness wash over him—the sadness

of having to hide himself, of having to tell half truths, of having to always look over his shoulder. Not all Alexander's reasons for hating him were good ones, but he couldn't very well explain that to Miss Fernside. For all he knew, she might revile him for the very same reasons.

Her beautiful hazel eyes moved over his face as her mind worked to slot the information he had just given her into a place that made sense. She drew her gaze back down to her lap for several long moments.

"How is it now with your parents?" she asked before darting her eyes his way once more.

"My father passed some time ago, and from what I've heard, my mother has lost most of her faculties."

"From what you've heard? You don't see her yourself?"

Thomas shook his head sadly.

"She doesn't want to see me anymore. She only wants to see Alexander."

"Oh," said Miss Fernside. "I didn't realise it was like that."

"It's been like that since I was sixteen. I told you, Alexander was the favoured son."

Miss Fernside looked as if she was struggling with some confusion, and Thomas didn't blame her. He had only told her part of the story.

"Do you think," she asked somewhat hesitantly, "that . . . you and I . . . that we are the way we are because we feel *less than?*"

Her simple question pierced him clean through. He forgot to take a breath, and when he opened his mouth, found he could not form the words. A flash of sheet lightening lit up the orangery and made the lemons dangling from the trees gleam like so many incandescent bulbs.

Abigail had enjoyed the summer of her life at Avery House. The embarrassing nocturnal incident with Thomas had happened what seemed like a lifetime ago, and Abigail did not regret it in the slightest. It had forced her to open her eyes, to take stock of herself, her situation, her life.

Was the soldier sitting on the bench beside her handsome? Yes. Charming? This could also be answered in the affirmative. Clever, kind, funny, brave? The answer to all those questions was 'yes'. But he didn't think she was special, not enough to imagine an ending beyond tears and resentment, so . . . so she had put him out of her mind. It had been surprisingly easy to do after all. Just lift him up and put him down in a corner out of the way somewhere. Of course, he was still physically present day-to-day, but he did not affect her in quite the same way anymore.

Patience had certainly helped her work through her feelings. They had spent the summer talking about art and music . . . and muffins. Patience had a great deal to say about muffins. And amorous congress! Good Lord, Patience was not at all shy when it came to explaining the potential for pleasure in that regard. Her diagrams themselves were worthy of any of the more salacious publications that circulated around London, and Abigail found herself blushing just to think of them.

"You don't need a muffin to do it," Patience had said as she dabbed at the portrait she was painting of Abigail.

"I should hope not," laughed Abigail. "There would be crumbs everywhere."

Abigail was posing seated on a chair in one of her white dresses, her body tilted slightly away from the canvas.

"You know what I mean." Patience gave her a look. "You can experiment on your own."

Abigail had done so on occasion, but she had been hindered by a sense of wrong-doing and the thought that perhaps, if she went too far, she would no longer be a virgin, and no one would want her.

"I lost my virginity to a horse," said Patience quite cheerfully as she mixed a new colour on her palette.

When she saw the look on Abigail's face, she clarified.

"No, not like that! What I meant to say was that all the bouncing around riding horses did away with, well, you know."

"Oh," said Abigail. "And Lord Winter . . . he didn't . . . did he think . . .?"

"He wouldn't have minded if it hadn't been due to the horse-riding. Although, no, that's wrong—he would have minded, but he did say he could have moved beyond it.

"Abigail," she said, "you must never think that is all you are worth. You have so much more to give. You are an entire person. Not just an idea of modesty and decorum."

These were the kind of words Abigail needed to hear. They made her feel . . . well, a little rebellious actually. A little as though she might be able to come out of hiding and take part in the world some day soon. If she tried. If she was brave.

She had spent the summer working on her music. The composition she had played for Thomas that first evening was now complete, and it was with some pride that Abigail performed it for herself. It still wasn't enough, however. She wanted to do more, to *be* more. There was one particular piece she had been working on that made all the others pale in comparison, and she had an idea to perform it for a proper audience, not merely a handful of friends. It had been a year since she had performed in public, and though it had been a success, her bubble of joy had been pierced by the sharp prick of her mother's incomprehensible discontent. She had neither congratulated Abigail nor even smiled in her direction after the performance.

Her one compliment had been handed over like a rose with a thorn: "You have some talent, my dear. It's a shame your complexion is so pallid. Pinch your cheeks."

It seemed to Abigail that there was very little she could do to please her mother, and she wondered if it was even worth the effort anymore.

Sitting on the bench beside Thomas in the orangery, Abigail lifted her face to his.

"You could do with a little more confidence," she said.

The look on his face—it was one of sheer incredulity.

"Hah!" he laughed.

Abigail had noticed over the summer that he always found a way to laugh when a conversation took a more serious turn. She had imagined that he was so much older than her, so much more experienced and worldly . . . but in this respect at least, he seemed a young boy, quite unwilling to engage with the subject matter of adulthood.

As the rain continued its assault on the glass roof, Abigail decided that it was time for her to leave Avery House.

Six

Peachy-Pink Nonsense

"But the summer is not quite over," said Patience as Abigail handed her maid Betsy a dress from the closet.

Betsy laid the dress out on the bed and proceeded to fold it for packing.

"It's been over two months," said Abigail.

Patience made a disgruntled sound in her throat, but she didn't argue.

Abigail paused with a lacy white shawl in her hand, then threw her arms around her friend and gave her a kiss on the cheek.

"Thank you for everything, Patience. It's been . . . You can't know what this summer has meant to me . . ."

Patience took Abigail's face in her hands and planted a wet kiss on each of her cheeks.

"You're always welcome here."

"It's the best kind of house," said Abigail. "The kind that makes you feel free to dream a little."

"And we'll see you soon in town," said Patience. "There's been talk of our cousins coming to London for the Season—Samuel and Arabella Pemberton. I'll have to introduce you . . . especially to Samuel. I imagine you've never heard a voice like his."

"Does he sing?" asked Abigail.

"No." Patience tossed her a sultry look. "He purrs."

Abigail and Patience fell into laughter, and even Betsy was hard-pressed not to descend into giggles.

"You should see him as well," said Patience. "He's big like Richard. A gentle giant." She lifted her eyebrows and added, "Blonde."

"Why do I feel as if you're trying your hand at matchmaking?" asked Abigail.

"All I'm saying," replied Patience, "is that he'll be in London for his sister's coming out. And we'll be in London . . . and the two of you will have to meet."

"How exactly are these cousins related to you?"

"My father's first cousin's children . . . so they are my second cousins if we want to be technical."

Abigail waved a hand.

"No need. 'Cousins' will do."

"George is hosting them for the Season," said Patience.

"George! I thought your brother wanted you to call him 'Lord Pemberton' or 'His Lordship' now that he's the baron," teased Abigail.

Patience blew out a breath and rolled her eyes.

The breakfast before Abigail set off was a rather awkward affair in so far as Thomas remained silent throughout. James and Michael, on the other hand, were their usual witty selves, verbally sparring with Patience and setting Lord Winter laughing into his teacup.

"You'll be missed," said James when the breakfast was nearly at an end. "We should make a habit of it—you should always come for summers at Avery House."

"As the actual owner of the house," said Lord Winter in a rather ominous tone, ". . . I concur."

Everyone laughed at that—everyone except Thomas.

"Thank you, Lord Winter," said Abigail. "You've been most kind."

After breakfast, Abigail's trunks were loaded into the carriage by a couple of footmen, and there was only the matter of checking her room one more time to make sure she hadn't left anything behind. When she emerged from her bed chamber into the hall, Thomas was standing there leaning against the wall with her spectacles in his hands. His cravat was loosely tied, and his hair was falling forward into his face like an unkempt schoolboy.

"I was thinking of hiding them," he said. "You might not leave if you couldn't find your spectacles."

Abigail smiled.

"But it's time to leave, Lieutenant Colonel Walpole."

He winced briefly at the form of address she had chosen.

"Miss Fernside."

"Yes."

"Miss Fernside," he began again. "I wanted to apologise for the upset I caused you during your stay."

"Not at all," said Abigail.

"And I wanted to say how very much I admire your . . . your perspicacity."

"My perspicacity?" said Abigail. "What's that when it's at home?"

Thomas laughed, but after a moment his laughter died away.

"It's a wee bird," he answered softly, "with a sharp beak and a rather beautiful song in its breast."

"Oh."

She honestly didn't know what to say to that.

"I don't know if you know this, but Richard's father used to keep birds in the orangery," said Thomas.

"I didn't know."

"The former viscount liked to go and sit on the bench among the lemon trees and hear them sing. James says that what their father liked most was not the birds so much as the fact that they were his—kept under glass, their flight paths limited to short hops between trees. When Richard came home from the continent to find his father dead, he opened up all the windows of the orangery and let the birds fly free."

Why was he telling her this?

Thomas was standing in front of her with a rather forlorn look on his face, and she had to fight the very feminine urge to make him feel better. He stepped towards her, and the slight limp in his leg made her breath hitch. He offered her the spectacles, and she took them in one hand. Her other hand he took in his, examining it one way, then turning it over.

"Rather small, don't you think? As far as hands go," he said. "I wouldn't think you could do much with it."

"I get by."

"You do, don't you?" He had not released her hand. "Goodbye, Miss Fernside. Perhaps I will see you in London when

90

the Season begins."

"It's likely."

"We probably shouldn't dance," said Thomas.

"Probably not."

"But we might." He squeezed her hand ever-so-slightly in his.

Abigail's heart started to flap, stupid little thing that it was. She pressed it back down with a firm hand.

"No," said Abigail. "I don't think that we will."

She pulled her hand from him and folded her spectacles in front of her.

"I wish you well," she said before stepping past him and striding with some purpose away from the darling man.

The waif is gone, thought Thomas, *which means that I can have a drink . . . or two . . . or five!*

He felt unshackled, and he determined to make the most of the situation.

A week later, Richard stepped into the drawing room to see Thomas with yet another drink in his hand.

"You are consistently back at it, I see," said the viscount.

"It's time for me to live, Richard." Thomas lifted his glass. "To really live! Bonaparte is defeated. My leg is almost completely healed . . ."

Richard smiled at his friend. Thomas felt it was a condescending kind of smile, but he didn't remark upon it.

"You're young and pretty," added Richard. "There's still much you might take from this world."

"Exactly!" Thomas knocked back his brandy. It was sweet and rather cloying, but he decided that he liked it anyway. "Cherry," he said, lifting his glass once more. "A nice choice."

Richard shook his head in a subtle movement. The man was always such a stick-in-the-mud—a loveable stick-in-the-mud, but a stick-in-the-mud nonetheless.

"I think I shall be returning to London," said Thomas. "Country life doesn't suit me."

"Now that Miss Fernside has gone."

"No," said Thomas quickly. "It never suited me. But we invalids must take succour where it is offered. And I've appreciated all the lovely succour that you and yours have provided this summer. Here. Have a brandy. Let's toast to succour!"

"Stop saying that word," said Richard, but Thomas could see that his friend was having trouble hiding his smile.

Just then, Michael stepped into the room with a book under his arm.

"We're toasting to succour," said Thomas.

"Suck what?" aked Michael, pretending confusion, and even Richard couldn't withhold the bark of laughter that escaped him.

"Don't be so rude," said Thomas. "You'll embarrass her ladyship."

They all turned to see Richard's mother enter the room.

"Why do I feel as if I've just stepped into the gentlemen's smoking parlour?" asked the dowager.

"Thomas is leaving," said Richard.

His mother pressed a hand to her heart.

"So soon?"

"My lady." Thomas stood to take her hand. "You will be ever

in my thoughts."

"Take care of yourself, Thomas, won't you?"

"Of course. And I will see you in London in a couple of months when the viscount here takes his seat in Parliament."

"Yes," said the dowager. "Yes, you must come for dinner."

"It would be a pleasure," said Thomas, bowing down to kiss her hand.

As he did so, he couldn't help but imagine that dinner with the Winters would be the least of the many pleasures London had in store for him.

As Thomas's carriage trundled into London, he heaved a rather large sigh into the empty seat in front of him. He had to repress with some force a sudden sensation of aimlessness that threatened to engulf him. For a moment, he saw the waif sitting in the seat opposite him in one of her plain white dresses, knees pressed together, her gaze aimed down towards her lap. How many times had he seen her sitting like that? He had always taken the opportunity to study her unobserved. The way her ear curved around in a pink swirl, the delicate line of her nose. Her lips which seemed so innocent but would likely momentarily part to say something rather unexpected.

"Alive will have to do."

"Perhaps I would not be so shy."

"Don't be obtuse!"

"Do you think that we are the way we are because we feel *less than*?"

It had been over a week since he had last seen Miss Fernside, and her absence was now clinging to him like the sticky mud of the battlefield. It felt as if he would never be able to wash it off. It was one thing to have danced the occasional dance with her last year—even then he had known he was flirting with danger—but it was quite another to become accustomed to having her company each and every day. Thomas let out a groan and banged his head against the back of the seat. He needed a plan—a plan for the evening. A laugh, a dose of fun, and with any luck, some physical attention.

What's the point of surviving death if you don't really live?

An hour later, Thomas stepped through the door of The Horse and Dolphin with money in his pocket and a smile on his face. The public house was just as he had left it—dark wooden tables polished to a shine and a clientele that was neither too rowdy nor too refined.

"Well, if it isn't the ghost of an old blighter!" said his friend William Robins from behind the bar. "I hear you gave old Bonaparte a smack on his tiny backside!"

"Turns out he likes that sort of thing!" said Thomas which set the entire place roaring. Several men banged jovially on the tables.

William poured a pint of ale and set it down in front of Thomas who pulled up a stool.

"It's good to see you," said William, his brown eyes shining. "I've heard some stories. Was wondering when you'd make an appearance."

"It was me leg, Willy," said Thomas, stretching his injured leg out long and pulling his face into his most comical woe-begotten expression. "I was forced to convalesce . . . in the country no less. Can you imagine?"

William shook his head.

"Sounds terrible," he said. "You missed a match last night."

94

"Well, I won't miss another." Thomas took a sip of his foam-topped ale and wiped his mouth with the sleeve of his jacket. "How's Mary?"

"She's fine," said a petite blonde lady, stepping up to the bar.

William's shirtsleeves had been rolled up, and Thomas watched Mary place a pale hand to her husband's dark brown forearm.

"You can't go out tonight," she said to her husband though she was eyeing Thomas. "I need you to watch Johnny."

William placed a hand atop hers. "I'll be there. Don't worry."

As Mary left to see to a customer, Thomas said, "Your wife doesn't like me."

William didn't say anything to that.

"The boy's been poorly. Nothing to worry about. He's getting better, but Mary has to see to some errands tonight, so . . ."

"So you can't come out with me," groaned Thomas. "Willy, you're killing me. And I don't say that lightly. I've been through a war."

"Don't be so dramatic," William laughed. "What would I do with you, anyway? I'm a married man, so no women. And I've a business to run. Mary wouldn't speak to me for a month if I gambled away the week's earnings."

"Just a month?" asked Thomas playfully.

"That's not all she wouldn't do for the month." William slid his gaze across the room to find his wife once more.

Thomas knew that theirs had not been an easy marriage, but their love for each other was all the more steadfast for having had to stand strong against a rather vocal and sometimes violent opposition. William was a former American slave, a talented carpenter, and a retired championship prizefighter.

The man had a great deal of patience, but he knew when he needed to stand and fight. Thomas had seen him fight for Mary, so he understood why his friend would not be joining him that evening.

"Responsibilities," said Thomas into his pint.

"That's a word you could use," said William as he wiped the counter. "I would use the word 'blessings' myself."

"I didn't come to hear you philosophise." Thomas took another sip of his ale.

William gave him a strange look.

"Men who've returned from Europe have been telling stories about you."

"Have they?" Thomas glanced around the pub.

"Tall tales," said William.

"Likely." Thomas shifted in his seat.

"You've been hiding," said William, placing his forearms onto the counter and leaning in.

Thomas thought that was an odd thing to say, and his heart gave a strange lurch, as if he had just been found trousers down in the woods with a Portuguese farmer.

"Hiding under the rank of captain," added William.

Thomas let go of a breath he had been holding.

"What's a captain?" asked William. "Second in command to a group of one hundred and fifty men? Stories I've heard have you commanding over a thousand, maybe fifteen hundred men to defeat eleven cavalry charges—eleven!"

Thomas regarded his friend in cold silence.

"That's what I thought," said William, pushing himself back up to his full height.

"What's what you thought?" asked Thomas before he could stop himself.

"Your own competence scares you."

"Don't talk shit, William." Thomas finished up his pint. "If I wanted to hear someone talk shit at me, I would have stayed in the country with Richard."

"Where are you off to tonight?" asked William. "A party? Crockford's? The usual?"

He managed to make it sound so . . . so pointless.

"There's nothing *usual* about it," said Thomas. "It's a different adventure every time."

When Thomas emerged from The Horse and Dolphin and out into the late afternoon sunshine, he felt tired, as if there were something weighing him down, dragging at his ankles. He walked on rather aimlessly for some time, his head in a daze as he grappled with a heightened level of irritation after his encounter with William. Everyone seemed to be prodding at him these days—they were like children poking a hedgehog with a stick. It made him feel like curling up into a prickly ball and injuring someone, albeit passively.

As he continued down the street, he caught sight of a slim lady in a white dress stepping into a modiste's shop. She was followed closely by a lady's maid.

Did his eyes deceive him? Was it the waif? Could she be in London this early? The Season wouldn't begin for another couple of months.

Thomas had to wait for some time before an opportunity presented itself to cross the road. He tried to slow his step as he casually sauntered down the pavement, his heart picking up its pace as he approached the modiste's shop.

Peering in through the window, he saw that it was, in fact, the waif. She was stepping up onto a block, and the modiste's assistant was pinning her body in a rather suggestively draped peach-coloured silk. Thomas pressed the tremor of his hand into his thigh as he watched the assistant tuck and pin the fabric in a way that revealed every curve that was usually hidden under a smock-like dress of whitest white. A surge of emotion that was altogether alien to him swelled in his breast like a beast gaining strength.

Surely, her mother won't let her out of the house in that! thought Thomas.

The colour alone made it look like she was wearing nothing at all.

He watched as she spoke a few words to the modiste and then protested as a pin sank in a little too far. He cringed on her behalf. She turned and, Good Lord, with the fabric cinched at her waist and the peach silk flaring out to hug her hips and her round little bottom, Thomas couldn't tear his eyes away. The modiste said something to her, and she slowly turned on the block to face him once more. Then without any warning, she lifted her hazel eyes to the window to find him watching her through the glass.

Hell.

He felt like the worst kind of peeping Tom.

There was nothing for it. He was simply going to have to bluster through. Flashing her his most cheerful smile, he gave a little wave and then came around to enter the shop.

"Miss Fernside, I did not realise you would be in London so early."

"You're not at Avery House," said the waif, brow furrowed.

"Country life is a bit of a snooze." Thomas took a confident seat on a pink upholstered chair and made an effort to look her in the eye.

It took an inordinate amount of willpower to prevent his

eyes from dropping down her body, to follow the sweep and tuck of the silk. Belatedly, he noticed that the waif's gaze was to his left hand which—*fuck it all*—was shaking again.

"Are you sure you are well enough to be on your own?" she asked as she stepped down from the block.

Christ.

She stepped up to him in her peachy scandal of a dress, and it took every ounce of his control not to place his hands to her waist to feel the slide of the silk over her skin.

Other men would see her in this dress and feel the same.

Something about this realisation coupled with his residual annoyance at William made Thomas decide that the best course of action at that point was to be a complete arse. He reached out and took a fold of the fabric between his fingers.

"This colour," he said, lowering his voice, "does not leave much to the imagination. Does your mother know you're here?"

Abigail opened her mouth, but she was initially too shocked to form any words.

The nerve of him. Interrupting her day with his conde-scending words. A day in which she was trying to be brave. The dress was symbolic: she would not hide herself any longer. No more shrinking, no more sliding into the background.

"How old do you think I am . . . Lieutenant Colonel?"

Thomas made a show of leaning back and placing his hand to his chin as if he were pondering the question.

"Not a day over seventeen," he said playfully, "though I've been known to be wrong on such matters."

"I'm twenty-one," said Abigail without matching his playfulness. "And I like this colour. My mother does not have a say in the matter because I am a grown woman."

Thomas's face registered her words, but there was more going on behind his eyes than she could comprehend in the moment. He stood from the chair.

"Get dressed," he said. "Now!"

Abigail had never heard him speak in that tone of voice before. It was commanding and forceful and carried not a single hint of his usual humour. There was something about it that intrigued her in a complicated way. She glanced about the room to see that the modiste and her assistant were making a show of rearranging the bolts of cloth on a shelf, and her maid was thoughtfully fingering a coil of blue ribbon. Everyone was pretending not to be listening.

Patience would say "No!" thought Abigail. *I should stand my ground and say no.*

Yet she was curious about this side of the man. She wondered what might happen next if she obeyed.

"Very well," she said to him. Then turning back to the modiste, "Miss Beauchamp, if you will excuse me, we will have to continue the fitting another day."

"Of course," said the modiste, rushing forward.

Abigail was ushered into the back room to change, and she took the opportunity to have a word with her maid Betsy.

"Hang back."

Betsy lifted her eyebrows.

"The lieutenant colonel is completely trustworthy. A consummate gentleman. I only want to have a private word."

Betsy's eyebrows remained where they were, up by her hairline.

"And not a word about this to anyone," hissed Abigail. "Especially not Mother."

Betsy nodded seriously, but Abigail noticed she was having some difficulty hiding a smile.

By the time she and Betsy emerged from the backroom, Thomas was looking decidedly thunderous. He took her firmly by the elbow and led her out of the shop and into the street.

"Does she follow you everywhere?" he asked, tossing a glance at Betsy over his shoulder.

"It's the done thing," said Abigail. "Where are we going?"

"I'm taking you home."

"Ah," said Abigail. "And you're doing this because . . . ?"

"Do you know what kind of attention you will draw to yourself in that dress?" said Thomas angrily.

"I have some idea." Abigail snuck a glance at the side of his face.

"You have *no* idea," said Thomas, the volume of his voice rising.

A lady carrying a basket of shopping gave him a rather judgmental look, and he lowered his voice.

"Men will get the wrong impression."

"What wrong impression is that?"

Thomas stopped walking and turned to her, taking her by the shoulders.

"Do you know what I wanted to do when I saw you cinched into that flimsy piece of peachy-pink nonsense? Your dress is entirely improper!"

"What's improper about it?" asked Abigail as calmly as she could.

"The colour for one." Thomas was still holding her by the

shoulders. "It looks like you're . . . naked."

Abigail rolled her eyes which made his cheeks flush pink.

"Is that all?" she asked.

"No," said Thomas as his eyes bore furiously into hers.

"Well?"

He didn't seem to want to explain any further, but eventually, he spoke again, this time squeezing her shoulders just a little more firmly than he had been before.

"The fabric is hugging your body in a way that . . . in a way that . . . "

"Yes?"

"Trust me," said Thomas with some agitation. "It's improper. Full stop."

"I've seen many a lady wearing a dress like that as she hung off your arm," said Abigail. "I don't suppose you told them how improper their dresses were at the time?"

He stared at her, jaw clenched.

"Bloody hell, you're difficult!" He took her by the elbow and steered her at a limping clip along the pavement.

He looked back just the once, and Abigail followed his gaze to see Betsy stranded on the far side of the street waiting for a large convoy of horses and carts to pass. Thomas quickly turned a corner and pressed Abigail into a narrow alley. He was breathing hard, his face a confusion of fury and . . . something else.

"Shall I show you?" he said in a fierce whisper, a hint of red flushing across his handsome face. "Shall I show you what I wanted to do when I saw you in that dress?"

Abigail felt her legs lose their integrity as heat flared within her. She stepped back and leaned her weight against the wall.

"Show me," she whispered.

Thomas's eyes grew dark as he leaned over her, pressing a hand to the wall beside her head. He brought his fingers up to touch her lips lightly, brushing them back and forth and sending a tingle of sensation through Abigail that had her blooming between her legs. As he swept his fingers over her lips once more, Abigail couldn't help herself—she parted those lips and took one of his fingers into her mouth.

"Jesus," he whispered, leaning down to kiss her with his finger still in her mouth.

His mouth came over hers, and it was so warm and inviting, Abigail thought she might very well melt into a puddle in the alley. His tongue tangled with hers and licked up against his own finger just as she did the same. Then he took his wet finger from her mouth and slipped it down her bodice to brush up against her nipple. The sensation was excruciating. It sent a pulse of need through Abigail that was so violent she found herself pressing up against him with some force as she let out a small cry. He pressed back, the hard length of him rocking against her.

Despite the cloth between them, there was no mistaking his desire for her, the knowledge of which was a rather heady potion as far as Abigail was concerned. Her confidence surged, and she reached for the sides of his face, pulling him down for another kiss. Groaning into her mouth, he continued rhythmically rocking up against her as he slipped a hand behind her to squeeze and lift her bottom. He was pressing himself between her legs quite hard, and as her pulse quickened and her breath came fast, Abigail could feel herself reaching for her release. There was a quiet desperation to her struggle as she clutched frantically at Thomas's arm, her fingernails digging in as if she might claw her release from his very skin.

And then, in the middle of it all, he pulled away with a low guttural sound, took two steps back, and brought his palms together and up to his mouth with a look of such sheer bewilderment that she half expected him to burst into tears.

"I'm sorry," he said. "Oh God."

It took a moment for Abigail to catch her breath and climb down from the cliff upon which he had left her. They stood staring at each other for several long seconds, chests rising in tandem.

"I asked you to do it," she said.

"I don't know what's wrong with me," said Thomas.

He swore an oath under his breath before reaching over and very hesitantly tucking a strand of hair behind her ear. Then he took her by the arm and led her back out into the street.

"Where's that maid of yours?"

"She may have passed us by already."

"I'll have to see you all the way home then." He made it sound like such a chore.

Thomas guided her at a brisk pace down the street only slightly hindered by the faint limp in his step. Abigail turned her head to look at his profile, but he was staring straight ahead, his face a mask of guilt and impatience.

Seven

A Dream and a Black Dagger

Having semi-ravished Abigail up against a wall in an alley, Thomas was all business as he walked her home and deposited her on the doorstep like a package he was glad to be rid of. She watched him as he took off down the street without so much as a fare-thee-well.

Betsy was waiting for her just inside.

"We lost you," said Abigail.

"The streets were very busy," said Betsy as if nothing suspicious or untoward had happened. . . as if a ranking officer in His Majesty's army had not scolded Abigail at the modiste's and commandeered her from the shop. . . as if the two of them had not purposefully lost her maid and then reappeared some time later looking rather rumpled.

"You'll want me to redo your hair," said Betsy, "before your mother arrives home."

"Oh." Abigail put a hand to her head. "Yes, thank you."

She placed a hand to the bannister and began to slowly and thoughtfully climb the stairs with Betsy at her heels.

As she sat in front of her vanity mirror, Betsy stood behind unpinning her hair and brushing it out.

Abigail looked her reflection in the eye. She had a lot of explaining to do . . . to herself. Thomas did not think she was particularly special—he had implied as much when he had said it would end in resentment and tears. And he had been so incredibly patronising at the modiste's that she had wanted to slap him across his lovely face. So why had she followed him out like a good little girl? And then why had she asked him to take liberties with her like . . . well, certainly *not* like a good little girl? What had happened to picking him up and putting him out of the way in a corner somewhere? That had worked at Avery House, but she had been blind-sided by his appearance at the modiste's.

The way he had dumped her in front of the house afterwards made the whole incident seem rather sordid, so why did she want to do it again? *What was wrong with her?*

Abigail decided that there was no need to give in to her baser impulses should the opportunity arise again. She had a little more self-respect than that. The whole point of coming to London early had been to set herself up—to order some nice dresses and make a few forays out into society in order to build her confidence before the Season began. Patience had given her so many intangible gifts this summer, and she wanted to put them all to good use. No more hiding. That went for both her person and her talents. What Abigail sought most of all was the freedom to be herself and to pursue her passions without apology, just as Patience did.

Betsy twisted her hair up and back, pinning it away from

her face.

"That should do it," she said.

Abigail reached towards her head and took the maid by the hand, giving her a gentle squeeze.

"Thank you, Betsy. You're so good to me."

The events of the day had occupied a rather large portion of Abigail's mind, and she was still considering her situation when she sat down to dinner with her mother and Mr. Anderson.

Wine was poured, and cutlery clinked.

"My dear," said her mother, piercing her with a look from across the table, "did you lose all your manners over the summer? You'll want to sit up straight at the dinner table."

Abigail sat up a little taller and in doing so felt a small piece of herself slip away.

"I was just telling Lady Crampton what a wonderful summer you had at the Winter residence," said her mother much too brightly.

Abigail looked up from her peas.

Here we go, she thought.

"I told her how lovely it was that the dowager and Lady Winter were present to chaperone you, there being *three* bachelors in the house as well. She wondered if there had been a proposal made by any one of those gentlemen. I told her, 'Time will tell, time will tell. We mustn't rush these things. My Abigail is a highly discerning young lady'."

Abigail looked down and shifted her peas around her plate as her mother eyed her from across the table.

"Should I have said something different?" Her mother placed her fork on her plate.

Abigail refused to lift her gaze from the peas.

"Twenty-one," said her mother as if the word were a sentence. "An entire summer with three bachelors and not one proposal. Tell me you at least tried, my dear."

One would think she would be accustomed to this sort of verbal assault by now, but it always felt as fresh as a slap.

"I tried," said Abigail. She hated herself for saying it, and a brief burst of anger flared inside her.

"There you have it," said Mr. Anderson in an attempt to come to her rescue or perhaps simply to have done with the conversation. "The little bird tried. There's not much more one can ask."

"One can ask for a trifle more persistence," said her mother to Mr. Anderson. "I worry about the poor girl, about her future." Then turning back to Abigail, "Your sister always turned out well for an evening affair. Every eye in the room would be drawn in her direction."

Abigail stilled an urge to roll her eyes to the ceiling, but she couldn't help the retort that broke past her lips. As she spoke, she felt something shift inside her.

"Harriet didn't marry until she was twenty-five."

Abigail's mother brushed the sentence away with her hand as if shooing a fly.

"But she was never on the shelf, my dear. She was merely biding her time."

Of course. Harriet could do no wrong.

"I saw five throstles today," said Mr. Anderson apropos of nothing. "Five."

Abigail's new step-father liked to count birds, but more

importantly, he liked to inform them that he *had* counted birds—which kinds and how many.

"Is that right?" said her mother. "Did you record that in your book?"

"My naturalist's diary," corrected Mr. Anderson. "Of course. Time of day, location, surrounding environment, all the details. The devil is in the details," he said, chuckling.

Abigail was not entirely sure that the devil was in those particular details . . . unless, of course, he was trying to bore them all to death so that he could snap up their souls. Despite the tension that had settled over her shoulders, she smiled to herself.

"That's a rather enigmatic smile," said her mother.

"I've been practising," said Abigail in a momentary flight of irreverence. *Something really had shifted inside her.* She imagined Patience sitting with her at the table, and she knew she would approve.

"Practising what?"

"My enigmatic smiles. What do you think?"

"I think," said her mother, "that young ladies do not find themselves a husband by being enigmatic. Pretty and sweet and open. That's what the gentlemen are looking for. You don't want to go taxing them with riddles or opinions or mysterious smiles, my love. It will only put them off.

"Isn't that right, dear?" She placed a hand beside her husband's on the table.

"You were never enigmatic," said Mr. Anderson. "That was something I very much appreciated."

Good Lord.

Abigail had a brief vision of her mother taking Mr. Anderson's finger in her mouth before he leaned in for a kiss.

They couldn't, she thought. *Not like that.*

In bed that night, she reimagined the entire afternoon with Thomas. The way he had shifted from fun-loving to furious, the way he had pressed himself up against her in the alley . . . If she could have that effect on him simply by wearing a silly peach-coloured dress, she could certainly have that effect on another man—perhaps someone who might take her as a more serious prospect. Perhaps someone who could come to love her and she him.

Abigail rolled over onto her side and tried to ignore the hurt. While the whole incident had left her feeling alive in a searing kind of way, she had been more than a little burned by the way Thomas had treated her at the end.

She closed her eyes, and sleep took her. She dreamed that she was seated on a green plaid blanket in the middle of a battlefield shrouded in mist, or perhaps it was smoke. Dead soldiers, French and English, lay haphazardly where they had fallen, limbs thrown out at odd angles. Her mother was beside her, opening up a wicker hamper.

"Spice buns!" she said. "Oh Abigail, you remembered."

Abigail turned her head when she heard the horses, a whole charge of cavalry heading towards the picnic. Hooves beat the earth, sending clods of dirt flying. There was no time to run. Abigail closed her eyes as the horses descended upon them, cringing in anticipation of the impact. But the horses flew by, creating a wind over her face, and when she opened her eyes, she saw that Thomas was sat upon the last horse charging through. One of his legs was injured and coursing with blood, but he had his eyes on his destination and did not once glance down at her. As he passed her by, she stood and shouted.

110

"Thomas! Thomas! Over here!"

He briefly glanced back. She knew that he saw her. But he turned his head and continued on his way. Abigail felt a sharp pain in her sternum as she watched him disappear into the mist. She couldn't help but feel that she was rather unimportant—a silly girl at a silly picnic.

Her mother bit into a spice bun.

"That's what you get," she said, "for being enigmatic."

Thomas had played a few rounds of baccarat at The Black Dagger where he had lost some money and gained some friends in the process. He had engaged in the usual drinks and banter, but it was all feeling rather hollow, and he was now sitting in a corner with a glass of gin as he watched the evening unfold around him.

The Black Dagger was not as seedy a place as one might imagine. It was a gaming hell that rested somewhere on the continuum beneath the respectability of Brook's or Crockford's and above the squalid reputation of, say, Coaxing John where a night out was not complete without at least a few rounds of drunken brawling (and that went for the ladies as well).

"Will you not play another round?" asked a rather striking man with the greenest eyes Thomas had ever seen.

The man was smartly dressed in a dark green jacket and a bronze-coloured waistcoat. He sank himself casually down into the armchair beside Thomas.

"Not my night," said Thomas, trying to ignore him.

"When it's not your night, it's *my* night." The man smiled. "Grave's the name." He offered Thomas his hand. "Christopher Grave. I'm the owner of this fine establishment."

"Fine, is it?" said Thomas.

"It pays the bills," said Grave. "May I ask . . . have you returned from abroad recently?"

"I was holidaying in the Low Countries." Thomas took a sip of his gin. "A short stay on a farm."

Grave leaned back in his chair and gave Thomas a wry look.

"Only, the lady over there says she knows you as an officer in His Majesty's infantry. If that's the case, drinks are on the house."

Thomas looked across the room to see a beautiful golden-haired woman he knew well—Penelope Roberts. She raised a hand and made her way over.

"It's him all right," she said to Grave. "Thomas, it's so good to see you."

Grave relinquished his seat to her, and she perched herself at the edge of the chair. Thomas couldn't help but notice that she was wearing a dress of a nearly transparent red muslin that made Abigail's peachy number look rather modest in comparison. Her breasts were full and pert (he remembered them well), and she was smart and sassy which he particularly liked. Despite being an aspiring artist in her own right, she modelled for the gentlemen artists at The Royal Academy during the day and played the muse to her benefactor at night. What was his name? Thomas couldn't remember. Regardless, he was not a particularly possessive man, and Penny was a rather generous woman—at least she had been with Thomas.

Her improper dress, he noticed, did not make him the least bit furious.

"You are a vision, as ever," said Thomas, sliding back into his old habits. "I was just telling your friend Grave over there about my little holiday in Europe."

Penny cast a glance across the room to the owner who was now loudly berating a man in a black cap. She turned back to Thomas.

"Why are you trying to be funny?" she asked. "We've all heard the stories. It was a massacre."

Thomas downed the rest of his drink, but she didn't take her eyes off him.

"Eleven cavalry charges, they say. How did you manage it?"

"Luck," said Thomas. "The French were low on artillery."

Penny shook her head. She stood up and came to sit herself down on his lap.

"I've always had a soft spot for you, Thomas. We could pick up where we left off."

Thomas curled his arm around her waist and felt the slide of the fine muslin over her skin. This was what he needed, what he had been waiting for. No strings attached. With a woman he respected and liked, someone who would expect nothing from him afterwards. As she shifted against his lap, however, Thomas noticed with a rising sense of distress that his body was not responding in the usual manner. As she leaned down for a kiss, he instinctively (though it had never been an instinct of his before) turned his face to the side.

"Are you trying to be coy?" laughed Penny.

"I don't think . . ." said Thomas. "I don't think I'm up for it tonight."

"Your injuries? I'll be careful."

She stroked a hand up the side of his face, and he found himself taking her gently by the wrist and removing her hand from his person.

"Sorry," he said. "Not tonight. How about we have a game of baccarat instead?"

She stood and gave him a quizzical look.

"It's nothing," said Thomas. "I just . . . can't right now."

"Baccarat it is then," said Penny.

Christ, thought Thomas. *What's wrong with me?*

At the table, he found himself eyeing the perfect lines of Penny's profile as the dealer turned over the cards. She was a sought-after model for a reason.

"On your own tonight?" he asked.

"Yes, isn't it wonderful? Christopher has no tolerance for the harassment of ladies in his establishment. He's managed to double his clientele while giving girls like me a place to spend our hard-earned money." She leaned her body into Thomas's side. "And have a little fun."

Thomas looked around. She was right. The place was hopping with ladies placing bets. And while none of them were gently bred ladies of the beau monde, not a one could rightly be deemed a lady of the night as would be the case in any other gambling establishment. The gentlemen didn't seem particularly put out by their presence either. If anything, they seemed to be on their best behaviour. A few appeared to have even brought their wives with them.

"How did he do it?" asked Thomas.

"Rumour has it the first incident of bad behaviour saw a cricket bat cracking into the man's face," said Penny, turning to him with wide eyes. "The second and third, well, they would have been happier for the cricket bat. No one's tested him since."

"A violent man, is he?" Thomas searched the crowded room

for Grave's green jacket.

"Nah," said Penny. "He's really just a kitten."

Thomas gave her a look.

"Have you two . . . ?"

"Oh, God, no. The man's as tight with his affections as the Archbishop on Sunday."

"I suppose that might explain the violence," said Thomas with a cheeky grin.

Over the next month, Thomas found himself spending quite a lot of his time at The Black Dagger. He liked the atmosphere. It didn't have the reek of privilege that White's or Brook's did, nor did it have the depressing air of desperation that settled over most gaming hells like a cloud of smoke growing thicker and heavier as the evening wore on. Thomas would like to have said that he had come to know Christopher Grave over this time. The man certainly had his appeal. But Thomas had tried his charming best, and Mr. Grave could not be enticed into sharing anything at all about himself. Of course, this made him all the more intriguing.

Thomas's only problem in the evenings was the ladies. He was so damn appealing, he drew them in like butterflies to a flower. The difficulty he had initially noticed with Penny had persisted. Unfortunately, the ladies found him all the more attractive for being coy . . . though he thought 'evasive' was perhaps a better word to describe his behaviour.

Regardless, he had been living like a fucking monk, dragging his lonely body back to his bachelor apartments each evening to flop himself onto the bed and sink into a solitary slumber.

He knew the problem wasn't physical, for he'd wake every morning with a raging erection and the shadow of a dream he had forgotten resting lightly over him like a mist.

This evening was different from the others in that he had been invited to "An Evening of Poetry and Music". Thomas stepped from his carriage onto the flagstones outside a stately London home. The night was unseasonably warm, and the glow of the streetlamps seemed to add an additional layer of heat. Thomas felt damp beneath his cravat.

The invitation had arrived five days earlier on a gilded card. It was from the most distinguished and elderly Lady Leveson-Gower whom Thomas knew would not take no for an answer. In fact, her invitation read more like an order from a commanding officer.

Dearest Lieutenant Colonel Walpole,

Where have you been hiding yourself? I had to hear of your return from a friend of a friend of a friend no less. You will attend the evening of poetry and music I am hosting Saturday night. You will not make excuses.

I look forward to seeing you again.

Yours in greatest affection,

Lady Leveson-Gower

Stepping lightly up the steps to the house, Thomas was greeted by a footman.

"This way, Sir. The entertainment has already begun." He was late. Lady Leveson-Gower would not be pleased.

Before the footman even opened the door to the drawing room, Thomas could hear a complex pattern of notes being played on the pianoforte. It sounded like a waterfall, then a

116

singing brook, before he imagined a flock of doves climbing up into the sky. He stepped quietly into the room which was lit with low candlelight and packed with gentlemen and ladies seated in chairs, spellbound by the music. Since it was such a crush, he had to pay attention to his feet so as not to trip over a chair leg or a dangled shawl. When he finally found a corner in which to stand at the back of the room, he lifted his head to see the most arresting sight of his entire life.

Abigail Fernside was playing the pianoforte at the front of the room. She was wearing her peachy-pink silk dress, and it fit her to divine perfection. The gently curved silhouette of her slender body in profile brought him back to that alley—the taste of her mouth, the feel of her breath against his cheek. Her golden brown hair was done up and decorated with a spray of white baby's breath, and she was playing the pianoforte as if there was no one else in the room. She was playing for herself.

Thomas's heart fairly stalled in his chest, and within moments he had broken out into a cold sweat under his jacket. He needed to leave, but he was frozen in place.

As she continued to play, the doves that he had imagined taking off into the sky came crashing down into the audience. A lady in the back row gasped and placed a hand to her breast. Thomas blinked, and in the moment he closed his eyes, he could see the smoke rising up over the battlefield and hear the cries of his men as bayonets clashed with sabres. He felt the terror of his own authority and duty as he threw himself forward towards death with the knowledge that he would fail the brave men under his command.

Thomas opened his eyes, and there was the waif slamming her fingers into the keys, bringing the whole world down around him. And then abruptly, there was silence—an emptiness that was almost a relief if it were not so hollow and so lonely. It was such a long pause that one gentleman began to hesitantly clap, but Thomas could see that the waif wasn't finished. She placed her hands to the keys once more, and the plink, plink, plink of dripping water filled the room, growing louder and louder. Soon it was a singing brook, a rushing waterfall, and then the doves had taken off once more into the sky with a flutter that was more hopeful than happy.

Choking back a tangle of unwanted emotion, Thomas pressed his tremulous hand to his thigh and turned to leave.

"Not so fast, Lieutenant Colonel."

Lady Leveson-Gower had him by the arm, and her grip was like that of a vice.

Eight

Demons at the Gate

Abigail lifted her head from the pianoforte as she slowly emerged from her trance. The room swam back into view. The flicker of the candles in their sconces on the walls, the audience applauding their approval . . . of her! She had worn the peach dress, and she had been brave—so bloody brave (that's right—she was so brave she was swearing in her thoughts today). It was the first time she had ever played one of her own compositions for strangers. It had been an intimidating and vulnerable prospect but one she had forced upon herself.

Here I am, she thought, and in thinking it, she smiled to herself.

She turned her head to scan the room. There was her mother applauding politely as she glanced to the left and right of her to assess the level of audience approval. Abigail lifted her eyes to the two people standing at the back of the room, and that was when she saw Thomas shift his eyes to hers as Lady Leveson-Gower held him by the arm. By the time she had stood and stepped into the crowd, her view of Thomas was blocked by a host of well-wishers who were congratulating her on the performance.

Drinks were being served in the next room before the poetry readings would commence. As the crowd dissipated to find refreshment, a gentleman with a pleasant face and curly brown hair lingered by her side.

"It's not often one experiences a talent such as yours," he said. Extending his hand, "I do believe your mother introduced us last Season. Mr. Andrew Banfield."

She placed her hand in his, and he politely bowed over it. Abigail remembered him doing the same last Season but with decidedly less eagerness. They had been introduced, but he had not bothered to ask her to dance, making his excuses as soon as her mother had left the vicinity.

"That is a rather fetching dress you're wearing," he added. "You look very grown-up."

Abigail narrowed her eyes.

"That is because I *am* grown up." She could feel her face heating, not with embarrassment but with annoyance.

"Of course," said Mr. Banfield.

"If you'll excuse me," said Abigail before making her way to the reception room.

A bubbling glass of champagne was placed into her hand, and she sipped at it gratefully. Thomas was nowhere in sight, but she did not have time to wonder about him as she found herself spun from one group of ladies to another. It was as if having been exiled from the bright bubble of social engagement all her life, she had finally been permitted inside.

They all wanted to know which modiste she had used and whether she had any recommendations for music teachers in London. The gentlemen were no less engaging—asking her questions and actually listening intently to her answers.

When she stepped away from a group of well-wishers, her mother took her arm and pulled her close.

"Gentlemen don't want to hear your opinions, dear heart. You must ask about theirs. It's all very well to have some talent, but nobody likes a show-off."

Abigail felt herself sinking down into the carpet—a familiar feeling, so she thought nothing of it until Lady Leveson-Gower stepped up beside them.

Their hostess took both of Abigail's hands in hers and said, "You were absolutely wonderful, my dear . . . but I suppose you know that already."

Abigail found herself buoyed by the words, and she smiled. When Lady Leveson-Gower left them, her mother leaned in.

"There's nothing a gentleman despises more than immodesty. Trust me, dearest. School your face lest you offend any potential suitors that might be attending tonight."

Abigail affected a neutral expression to appease her mother. It didn't matter. The evening had been a success. She was quietly elated.

Some time later, when she had excused herself to go to the lady's retiring room, Abigail was still reflecting on what a success the evening had been. She turned a corner down one of Lady Leveson-Gower's lengthy hallways and charged straight into Thomas's arms.

"Oof!"

"Excuse me," said Thomas, setting her to rights by her shoulders.

As recognition descended over his features, he withdrew his hands so quickly from her person, it was as if she had scalded him.

"Thomas, I didn't realise you would be here."

"Nor I you." His eyes fixed on hers. "I was just leaving."

"Oh."

There was something about the way he was looking at her . . . His eyes were rimmed in red, and he did not seem himself at all. She shifted her gaze to his left hand, and he pressed it against his leg but not before she could see it trembling.

"Miss Fernside . . . I would like to apologise," he said. "For the things I said to you the other day. Your dress is absolutely lovely. You look—"

"—all grown up?" supplied Abigail.

Thomas furrowed his brow.

"That's not what I was going to say."

"What were you going to say then?"

Thomas rubbed a palm up over his forehead. He suddenly looked to her quite bone weary, as if he hadn't slept properly in weeks.

"I was condescending towards you that day at the modiste's. I lost . . ."

". . . lost what?" asked Abigail.

"What I was going to say," said Thomas, his eyes sadder than ever, "was that in that dress . . . you look . . . like yourself. You are one of a kind."

"Oh."

The compliment struck deep, plunging down into the darkest corners of her soul like a flaming arrow lighting up the caverns as it descended.

"Good evening, Miss Fernside." He made to pass by.

"Thomas." She reached for his hand, but he pulled it just out of her reach. "Are you . . . ? Are you well?"

"Why wouldn't I be well?" Thomas forced a smile. "Good evening, Miss Fernside."

She watched in silence as he moved past her and down the hall, noticing that he was no longer walking with a limp. It had been at least a month since she had last seen him, and time had worked its magic. For a second, she thought to continue on her way to the lady's retiring room, but a moment's hesitation, and she had turned to follow him through the front door like a concerned nurse trailing a patient who had wandered too far from his bed. There was something about his demeanour that cast a sense of foreboding over her like a net, and she could not shake it off. From the open door, she saw him descend the last two steps to the pavement and hail a hack.

"The Black Dagger," he said to the driver before pulling himself up to the carriage and disappearing into its dark interior.

Abigail watched the hack pull away. As it disappeared around the corner at the end of the street, she drew her eyes up to the night sky. A swollen orange moon hung over the city like an enormous lantern.

"What should I do?" she asked the moon.

She responded as if the moon had answered.

"I know. Be brave."

Well, she thought forty minutes later, *it is one thing to be brave, but it is quite another to politely extricate yourself from an evening of poetry and music.*

"You can't leave now," said her mother. "The evening is only getting started. That Mr. Banfield hasn't taken his eyes off you all night."

"Mr. Banfield can suck eggs for all I care," said Abigail in a moment of impatience. "He wasn't particularly minded to ask me to dance last Season, and if his mind changes with something as superficial as my dress, then I don't particularly care to know him."

Her mother looked at her with all the wisdom of an old owl who did not bat an eye at the phrase 'suck eggs'.

"Gentlemen, you'll find, are rather simple in that respect," she said, "and there's nothing one can do about it, Abigail. Why do you think everyone is asking after the modiste that you employed? They want Mr. Banfield to be looking at them. They don't particularly care if it's because of the dress that they're wearing and nothing else."

"I have to leave, Mother," said Abigail. "I'm not feeling well at all."

"You look fine to me. It's just nerves, my dear."

"I'm not well," said Abigail, clutching her stomach. "The river is flowing unexpectedly tonight," she added in her best cryptic.

That should do it.

"Oh heavens!" said her mother. "You will ruin your dress. Have you spoken to one of the maids?"

"I think I should just go home," said Abigail.

Her mother tutted.

"Yes, that's probably for the best. You know, Harriet was never this unpredictable. Everything was like clockwork with her. I imagine that was why it was so easy for her to conceive. She has wider hips as well." Her mother cast a glance down Abigail's narrow frame. "I worry that child-bearing will be difficult for you, my dear, if indeed you ever find a husband."

Abigail was already walking in the direction of Lady

Leveson-Gower ready to present her with a bouquet of polite excuses.

"Well," said her host with some disappointment, "there must be something in the water. That makes two of you tonight."

"Two of us?" said Abigail.

"Lieutenant Colonel Walpole was feeling poorly as well. I've never seen him quite so exhausted. I imagine the toll of war is one that is paid over time." She shook her head. "Not that anyone cares to notice."

By the time Abigail had taken her family carriage home, entered the house so that the driver would not report anything amiss to her mother, had a word with Betsy, and then snuck back out to hail a hack, a great deal of time had passed. She had stuffed a purse filled with coins into her reticule—it's not like she had any idea how much a ride in a hack cost as she had never taken one before.

"The Black Dagger," said Abigail, and the driver lifted his cap as if it was a regular evening, and no one was being brave, and The Black Dagger was a perfectly respectable destination for a young lady who had just stepped out of her house in Mayfair.

When they arrived, Abigail paid the driver double his fare to wait for her in the street and turned towards the open door of the gaming hell—for a gaming hell was what it was. The Black Dagger was hardly the name of a restaurant.

Inside, she was surprised to find both women and men engaging in an evening of merry revelry. Glasses clinked as dice rattled, and the roar of conversation was sprinkled liberally with laughter. She stepped into the fray, squeezing her way past a crowd of on-lookers who were cheering over a game of hazard and walking slowly by a couple who were kissing on a settee. The open display was a little more than she had bargained for, and she had to force herself to keep moving rather than stand and gawp.

Searching for Thomas in the crowd, she finally found him at the back of the room, head slumped forward and an arm around the shoulder of a rather handsome man who flashed his startling green eyes her way as he hoisted Thomas up to standing. Her entire body began to sing an ominous note that set her skin vibrating and her stomach churning.

"Thomas!" she cried, rushing forward.

"You know him?" said the man with green eyes.

Up close, Abigail noticed that though the emerald-eyed man was alarmingly handsome, his features were hard, as if he had been chiselled in stone before coming alive.

"Yes," said Abigail as Thomas lifted his head slightly before dropping it down once more.

"I suppose I shouldn't have told him drinks were on the house," said Mr. Green Eyes. "But I can't exactly let him leave. He owes me a good deal of money."

"How much?" asked Abigail.

"For fifty pounds, he can be yours," said Mr. Green Eyes.

"Only fifty?" said Abigail.

As the words left her lips, she was as startled by them as Mr. Green Eyes appeared to be. His face softened ever-so-subtly.

"If you would be so kind as to help him out to the carriage, I shall have my man of business call around tomorrow," said Abigail.

"Hah!" laughed Mr. Green Eyes, eyeing her up and down as he shifted Thomas's weight in his arms. "Your man of business?"

Abigail gave him a frosty look. She pulled out her purse.

"I can give you ten guineas now," she said, "and my name—Miss Abigail Fernside. Now that's ten more guineas than you had five minutes ago and a promise that the balance will be made up on the morrow."

"Christopher Grave," said the man with his eyes on her fist full of guineas. "I'm the owner of this establishment, and you, my lady, are welcome here any time."

"How do you do?" said Abigail. "Are we in agreement?"

"I think you'll find," said Mr. Grave as he manoeuvred Thomas slowly through the crowd, "that you've got your money's worth. The man's a war hero no less and rather good company when he's conscious."

When they arrived outside by the carriage, Abigail realised that she didn't know where she was taking him.

"Thomas." She smacked his cheek gently as Mr. Grave held him up. "Thomas, where do you live?"

He lifted his head.

"The waif!" he said. "What's *she* doing here?"

"I know where he lives!" called out the driver. "Lieutenant Colonel Walpole is a regular customer of mine."

"There you have it," said Mr. Grave, helping Thomas into the carriage. "Just an ordinary Saturday night for you Miss, isn't it?"

He gave her a look that suggested he was not displeased with the way events had turned out.

Abigail climbed in after Thomas, and the driver pulled the hack away from the pavement with a sudden lurch followed by the steady clip-clop of hooves. Abigail had sat herself down opposite Thomas, but when she saw him slump forward and nearly fall off the seat, she shifted to sit beside him, pulling him back up and against the backrest. She wondered if a man weighed more when he was drunk than when he was sober, for Thomas was as heavy as a sack of rocks.

"Try not to fall on the floor," she said, holding him by the arm.

Thomas leaned down towards her and kissed the top of her head.

"You're always such a little nag," he mumbled. "I like it."

The words of a drunk should not have warmed her quite as they did. She looked up at him and placed a hand to the side of his cheek.

"What are you doing to yourself, Thomas?" she whispered.

"That's . . . not the question," he said, raising a wavering finger. "The ques . . . question is . . . what are *you* doing . . . to me?"

"I'm taking you home," said Abigail.

"The waif's taking me home." Thomas leaned into her and rested his head atop hers. "She will guard me from the demons at the gate . . . with her tiny dagger . . . and her sharp little tongue."

As the hack bumped along, Thomas remained leaning heavily up against her as she held his arm to keep him in place.

"I'm glad you're here," he said after some time had passed. "You're the only . . . the only . . ."

"The only what?" Abigail shifted her grip on his arm.

"Never mind," said Thomas as he gave her head another clumsy kiss.

Once they arrived, the driver helped Abigail steady Thomas until they had reached the front door to his apartments and he was propped up against the wall.

"I can manage from here," said Abigail.

128

The driver doffed his cap.

As she banged the knocker on the door, she could hear the hack pulling away. She waited, but no footman appeared. Apparently, bachelor apartments weren't stocked with footmen in the dead of night. It was turning out to be quite the evening.

"Your keys, Thomas. Where are they?"

He tilted his head at her, and a lock of brown hair fell forward into his face, but he didn't respond.

"Really," she said with some exasperation as she patted at his breast pocket.

"Cold." He leaned his forehead down to hers. "Very. Cold."

"What are you talking about?" Abigail moved on to pat at his jacket side pockets.

"Warmer," said Thomas.

She looked up to see him smiling at her with a rather mischievous glint in his eye.

"I hear the southern parts are even warmer," he said.

Abigail fixed him with a glare as she pressed the front of her body up against him and slid her hand down deep into one of his trouser pockets.

"You're burning up now," said Thomas, his arm coming around her waist to hold her close.

"Oh do shut up!" Abigail pulled forth his keys from his pocket and untangled herself from his embrace.

Inside, she found a lamp to light and managed to support Thomas to his bed chamber. With his arm around her shoulder and due to the sheer bloody weight of the man, she ended up stumbling and collapsing onto the bed with him. For a moment, she lay beside him, chest heaving with her exertions. As she made to get up, he tugged her back down.

"Don't leave me." There was not a trace of humour in his

tone.

"I'm just going to remove your boots," said Abigail, "and help you out of your jacket."

The boots were easy, but the jacket was rather more difficult to remove since it required Thomas's cooperation. It didn't help that he was staring at her the entire time. It also didn't help that she was forced at one point to straddle him as he lay on the bed in order to manoeuvre the jacket from his shoulders.

"You are the most . . ." he said as she yanked at him, ". . . the most . . ."

"The most what?" asked Abigail distractedly as she tugged him free of one jacket sleeve.

"The most exquisite creature . . . ever to walk the face of this earth."

That made her pause.

"You are quite foxed, aren't you?"

"The liquor has a way of liberating the truth," said Thomas in a remarkably sober-sounding rebuttal.

"If that's so," said Abigail, forcefully tugging him free of his second sleeve and sliding his jacket out from under him, "tell me this: why are you drinking so much in the first place?"

"The waif has questions." Thomas reached up with strong arms and pulled her down on top of him.

"Thomas!" Abigail rolled off him and onto the bed.

He turned to face her in the lamplight, looking suddenly quite solemn and reached a hand up to stroke a lock of hair behind her ear.

"It was so quiet," he said. "After.'

"After what?" she whispered.

"After the killing," said Thomas. "You were right. The piece

130

you played tonight."

"Me? About what?"

"About how lonely it was . . . Victory is a hollow thing when there are corpses strewn as far as the eye can see, and you're being dragged from the field with a useless leg . . . a useless body. . . I couldn't even help to bury them."

A tear rolled down the side of his face and into his hair.

"There were thousands of them, Abigail. Thousands," he whispered. "I was responsible for keeping some of them alive, and I couldn't do it."

"Oh Thomas." She reached for him.

He slipped down into her embrace and buried his face in her chest. She felt him shudder as the sobs began to wrack his body, and with her heart breaking for him, Abigail's own tears fell as she held him close.

Nine

Guardian Angel

Thomas woke the next morning with an unaccustomed air of peacefulness resting over him like a warm blanket. A blanket with a small thorn—there was something poking him in the eye. Reaching up to his face, he lifted a sprig of baby's breath. He looked at it with some confusion, twirled it in his fingers, and then as his hand came down, so did his eyes, and he saw the waif sleeping beside him with an arm flung out over his chest.

Holy hell.

Thomas squeezed his eyes shut and tried to resurrect the previous evening. He remembered Abigail's concert, and he could see dice being tossed to a felt-covered table. After that, all he could remember was some game over finding his keys and then pulling Abigail down on top of him.

Oh God.

He opened his eyes and took a quick scan of her body.

Fully-clothed, thank the sweet Lord Jesus.

But why was she here? How was she here?

She moved against him, and he froze as if she might not notice his presence if he remained as still as possible. An audible sigh escaped her lips, and he felt it as a small puff of breath against his neck. Her hand then slid slowly up over his chest to rest at the base of his throat as she shifted closer into him, and when she did so, he felt as if he'd been stabbed in the groin. Looking down, he could see the unmistakable tenting of his trousers under a painfully insistent erection.

He rested his head back down on the pillow and stared at the ceiling, willing the white expanse of it to come up with some answers. He was no further along in his understanding of the situation when she finally opened her eyes and sat up.

"What time is it?" she said.

"A good morning to you too," said Thomas, ignoring the dull ache in his head and trying to sound as unflustered as possible.

"Mother will have a fit if she realises I'm gone," said the waif, crawling over the bed to find her slippers.

Thomas lifted himself on his elbows to watch her pretty little rear end sway beneath the thin peachy silk of her dress as she reached down to the foot of the bed and untangled a slipper from the blanket.

"You'll want to fix your hair," he said as she stood from the bed. "Here, I found your baby's breath. It was lodged in my eye."

The waif reached out to take the little sprig from his hand, twisting her mouth in an effort not to smile.

"My housekeeper arrives in about half an hour," said Thomas. "And she's a big old gossip, so . . ."

"How are you feeling?" asked the waif.

"Grand. Never better . . . Can I ask . . . ? What did we . . . ? Did I . . . ?"

"You don't remember." She shook her head. "You were falling over drunk at The Black Dagger. I brought you home, but I must have fallen asleep after . . . after . . ."

"After what?" asked Thomas slowly, cringing in anticipation of the answer.

"After we . . . talked." She put two hands to her hair and attempted to tease out the dangling pins. It was rather a mess.

Talked, thought Thomas. *Excellent. Talking was excellent. How very gentlemanly of him.*

"Sit on the bed," said Thomas. "I can help."

She sat quietly in front of him and allowed him to remove the pins one by one. Her thick wavy hair was a cascade down her back, and he untangled it with his fingers, resisting the urge to lean in and bury his face in the soft mass. He then took it all together in his hand and twisted it up into a knot at the nape of her neck.

"Stay still," he said, reaching down for a pin.

When he was finished, he had three pins left over, and he handed them around from behind her.

"You may want to take these with you," he said, leaning his face down just over her shoulder.

To his surprise, she took the pins with one hand and then lifted his empty hand to her mouth with the other. She kissed him, just the one soft kiss on his hand, and then without looking back, she fled the room.

He stood to follow her out, but the room was spinning, and he had to sit back down again. Eventually, he made his way to the window where he watched her wave down a hack from the pavement.

Her words came back to him then: "You were falling over drunk at The Black Dagger. I brought you home . . ."

What in the hell had she been doing at The Black Dagger?

Thomas would have to wait until the afternoon to investigate as the place didn't open until well after midday, and he couldn't very well go chasing after Miss Fernside. The question of *why* he couldn't go chasing after Miss Fernside was carefully side-stepped. Down that path lay dragons Thomas had been avoiding his entire life.

A memory came to him of the night before. He had seen Abigail's mother speaking to her at Lady-Leveson Gower's evening of poetry and music. Abigail had been flushed—eyes bright and mouth smiling with the success of the evening. Thomas had watched through the crowd as a few quiet words from her mother removed the smile from her face and dulled the light in her eyes. He had seen her mother have this effect on her last year on more than one occasion. A small word from the woman, and Abigail's flame would flicker and dim. The young wallflower had seemed to him somewhat neglected, at least emotionally, and it was perhaps for this reason that he thought of her as 'the waif'.

He recalled Abigail having a dream at Avery House. What had she said of her mother's behaviour in that dream?

"She was doing a lot of complaining . . . mainly about me."

Thomas knew a thing or two about being a disappointment. It wore you down.

He stood and walked over to a washbasin that rested in front of an oval mirror hanging from the wall. Peering into the room that lay beyond the glass, he saw himself staring back like a haunted man. He looked like hell. His eyes were all puffy and red in their darkened sockets, and his hair was stuck to one side of his face, crusty and stiff. He traced a faint pale line that lay like the silver trail of a snail down his cheek.

Had he been crying?

Thomas turned towards the door as if he expected to see the waif standing there in her crumpled peach silk with her slippers in her hand.

What had they been talking about?

This was the second time he had nearly compromised Miss Fernside—the third if he counted their tryst in the alley. But he didn't allow himself to think about the way he had behaved at the modiste's and in that alley because when he did, he found he couldn't take his next breath. He had a brief glimpse of himself as one of those men who so lost his mind over a woman that he flew into a jealous tantrum if anyone so much as glanced at her. The thought frightened him—he never wanted to be anyone's gaoler.

Thomas picked up a pitcher of water, bent himself over the basin, and gave his head a good dousing. The shock of the cold water did nothing to bring back his memory of the previous night, but it did wake him up.

Despite the mystery that lay over the morning and despite his headache and despite the fact that he looked like death warmed up, Thomas was feeling disconcertingly calm. The sense of peace with which he had awakened hung in the air like the cool shade of the woods on a hot day.

When he was finally washed and breakfasted and dressed, he went shopping for a shawl. The idea had come to him over coffee, and he could not let it go once it had wriggled its way into his mind. As he stepped out into the street with a spring in his step, he felt almost whimsical.

This is what it's like shopping for accessories, he thought. *I should do it more often.*

At the haberdasher's, he chose a pale blue cotton shawl bordered with a motif of white birds.

They might be doves, he thought and smiled to himself as the man behind the counter packaged it up in a flat box tied with a piece of string.

"Might you tie it with a ribbon?" asked Thomas. "Blue."

"That'll be extra," said the man.

Later that morning, with the box tucked under his arm, Thomas pushed his way in through the door at The Horse and Dolphin. A few heads turned his way, and William greeted him cheerfully from behind the bar.

"He's back, and he's brought me a present!"

"It's for your wife." Thomas stepped up to the bar and placed the box on the counter.

"Hold your horses," said William with mock affront. "She's not in the habit of accepting gifts from handsome men who aren't me."

"It's a peace offering. I can't stand that she dislikes me."

"She doesn't dislike you," said William.

"How's Johnny?" asked Thomas.

"Right as rain. He's back to bouncing off the walls and terrorising pigeons."

"Excellent." Thomas pulled up a stool.

When he looked up, he found William examining his face with shrewd eyes.

"Not meaning to insult you, Thomas, but you look a bit shit."

"It was a night," said Thomas. Then, as William pulled a pint glass from a shelf, "No, I'll not be drinking this morning.

Unless you have some tea . . . I'm actually quite parched."

William raised his eyebrows.

"Do I look like a scullery maid?"

"It's not hard, Willy. Hot water and some leaves will do it."

William laughed and leaned forward on his forearms the way he always did when they talked.

"What kind of a night was it?" he asked.

"Well, that's the thing," said Thomas. "I don't rightly know. There was definitely some drinking—to the point of memory loss, obviously. And I remember gambling at The Black Dagger, but . . ."

"But . . ." said William, trying to help him along.

"I woke up this morning with a lady in my bed."

"Sounds about right." William grinned.

"No, not like that," said Thomas, struggling to find the words to explain the situation. "A lady I know . . ."

". . . biblically," supplied William.

Thomas bristled.

"Be serious, William. I'm trying to tell you something. I'm fucking *sharing* things, so give me a minute."

"All right, all right," said William, lifting his hands and standing back. "Take your time."

"I woke up with a lady in my bed . . . a lady like Mary." Thomas hoped his friend would take his meaning without him having to spell it out.

"Blonde?" asked William. "Small? Antagonistic? Clever? Beautiful?"

He was watching Thomas's face as he worked through the list. Finally, he leaned forward over the counter once more.

"Special?" he asked.

"That's the one," said Thomas quietly.

"I don't see the problem," said William.

"The problem is that I don't know what happened. I was three sheets to the wind, and somehow she brought me home and manhandled me onto the bed. Apart from my jacket and boots having been removed, we were both fully clothed in the morning, so nothing happened. It's just . . . It feels as if *everything* happened. She fled when she woke."

"There's something you're not telling me," said William.

Thomas gave his friend a look he knew must reek of guilt and shame.

"She's a Mayfair lady," said Thomas. "An innocent."

William audibly choked back a comment.

"Twenty-one years old," added Thomas. "What was she doing at The Black Dagger?"

William whistled and shook his head.

"Well," he said. "I have to hand it to you. That was not how I was expecting this story to go."

Thomas just sat there staring at his friend and waiting. For some reason, he couldn't bring himself to take charge of the situation. It seemed too important to be left to him.

"What?" said William with some irritation. "You want me to tell you what to do? You should bloody well know what to do, you idiot." He shook his head. "It's like you took a musket ball to the head or something. I can't believe you thought it was reasonable to get up and spend the morning shopping for a present for my wife. Not that I'm returning the gift or anything." He pulled the box across the counter. "I'm sure Mary will be delighted."

Thomas left The Horse and Dolphin with a less sprightly gait than when he had entered. William had been no help at all. . . although it *had* felt good to lay the whole situation out on the counter. There was a warmth in sharing even if William wasn't forthcoming with his advice.

You should bloody well know what to do!

Well, thought Thomas, *I don't.*

He arrived at The Black Dagger just as one of Grave's formidably-built employees was propping open the door.

The place was empty, and Christopher Grave was going over some correspondence at a corner table.

Damn, he was dangerously handsome. The kind of handsome who looked like he might snap your neck if you spoke out of turn. He lifted his green eyes to the lone visitor in his "fine" establishment.

"Back for some more," he said with a stealthy smile. "You'll forgive me, but the offer of free drinks has been withdrawn for the time being."

He lifted a handful of banknotes from the table.

"She wasn't a liar," he said. "Your guardian angel. Her man of business settled up your account not one hour ago."

"Excuse me?" Thomas took a step forward.

"War hero or not, I would have had Paul over there sit on you until morning if you hadn't paid up."

Thomas spared a glance to the hulking shadow of a man arranging stacks of cards at one of the tables.

"Whose man of business?" asked Thomas, completely nonplussed.

"The tiny lady with the nerves of steel—a Miss Abigail Fernside."

Thomas opened his mouth.

"Not to worry," said Mr. Grave, "I am the soul of discretion. It's not everyday that a drunken officer is taken off my hands by a wee girl in a silk gown. I'll not be party to gossip. It's bad for business."

Thomas sat down in the chair opposite Grave. He was having trouble holding himself upright.

"And how much was my account?" asked Thomas in a small voice.

Grave gave him a look that was both dark and sparkling at once.

"Fifty pounds," he said. "She paid ten in guineas on the spot if you can believe it."

Guineas? thought Thomas. *Man of business? What had Michael said? She had an inheritance. . .*

"Jesus," said Thomas, placing his elbows on the table and leaning his forehead down into his hands.

He felt like the lowest form of human wastrel. Not only had he burdened Miss Fernside with his inebriated person, but he had cost her fifty bloody pounds. That was a full month's wages on his officer's salary. And she hadn't said a word. Instead, she had kissed his hand as if he had done her some sort of favour. Thomas suddenly felt quite sick to his stomach.

"Paul!" said Grave. "Bring us a bucket, would you? The lieutenant colonel is looking a bit green."

Abigail did not enter the house by the front door that morning. Instead, she crept around back to the servants' entrance and knocked. Betsy opened it within the span of half a heart beat.

"Miss!"

Abigail put a finger to her lips.

"You weren't at breakfast, and I didn't know what to do. I told your mother you were feeling poorly on account of your

141

courses. Mr. and Mrs. Anderson are just finishing up their toast now."

"Betsy, you're an angel." Abigail stepped inside. "There was an . . . incident . . . I had to take care of . . . Anyway, it's all over now. No harm done."

Betsy followed her mistress up the servants' stairs with the eagerness of someone who suspected that harm had indeed been done and that the juicy details may be forthcoming. They were quick and quiet as Betsy very efficiently stripped Abigail of her dress, put her in a nightrail, and plaited her hair.

"Quick," said the maid, pulling back the covers. "Get in."

Abigail slipped into bed, and as she placed her head on the pillow, her mother strode into the room without so much as a cursory knock at the door.

"I'll fetch her some raspberry leaf tea," said the maid with a brief curtsy to the lady of the house. "It will help with the cramps."

"What's all this?" asked her mother. "Horace was quite worried when you did not turn up for breakfast, and I can't exactly explain the situation without embarrassing him."

Her mother eyed her suspiciously.

"You've never taken to your bed before over a monthly complaint."

I'm a grown woman, thought Abigail miserably. *I should be able to do as I please without having the Spanish Inquisition breathing down my neck.*

"I'm sure the tea will make a difference," said Abigail, sitting up in bed.

Her mother leaned down to give her a kiss but instead paused and gave the air by her head a little sniff. She inhaled once more for good measure but made no comment.

"Right," she said slowly as she stood back up to her full height. "Right."

She glanced about the room, her eyes resting on the peach gown that Betsy had hung over a chair. Abigail noticed that the dress was rather crumpled—more crumpled than could be explained by an evening playing the pianoforte and a ride home in a carriage. She tried not to hold her breath.

Her mother took several strides for the door, placed her hand to the doorknob, then paused and turned back to Abigail.

"Abigail . . . sometimes, when one is not used to being noticed . . ." She took a breath and let it out. "Sometimes, a little kind attention can inflate one's sense of worth in a misleading manner. Not all attention is good attention, my dear. I hope—for your sake and for this family's sake—that you will not have to find that out through experience."

When her mother finally departed, Abigail whipped back the covers. She walked up to the peach dress, lifted it to her face, and inhaled. It smelled like Thomas—all smoky and sad. *She* probably smelled like Thomas.

Her mother suspected.

Abigail lay back down on the soft bed and in sinking back into the mattress, was enveloped in a memory of the night before—the way it had felt to hold Thomas as he cracked open his heart to let the contents pour out on a tide of tears. She had wept for him and stroked his hair, murmuring soft words of comfort and hope.

"Just a little longer," he said when the tears subsided. "I won't keep you much longer."

He had fallen asleep against her breast, the two of them tangled in the fiercest embrace Abigail had ever known. She had felt his heart beating against her belly, the slow thud-

thud of exhaustion and surrender, and though she knew she should leave, she had found she could not. Just to contemplate releasing her embrace felt as if she were leaving him to drown. Lulled by the beating of his heart, she had rested the weight of her head on his pillow and closed her eyes.

Ten

A Roll of Thunder and a Rainbow

A bigail did not hear from Thomas for two days, but on the third day, a letter was delivered.

Miss Fernside,
I would like to apologise in person for the regretful and shameful events of the other day. I would have come calling, but I imagined we would not be able to speak privately if your mother was present. Let me know a convenient time, and I shall come by.
Sincerely yours,
Lieutenant Colonel Walpole

Included in the letter were several bank notes, all of which added up to fifty pounds. Abigail tossed the money aside and reread the letter. The formality of it all struck her as inconsistent with both Thomas's character and her experience of having him weep against her chest as they lay together in his bed. The letter left her feeling cold, but she nevertheless sent a footman to deliver a reply.

Lieutenant Colonel Walpole,

No apology is necessary. Nothing was regretful. Nothing was shameful.

Sincerely yours,

Miss Fernside

His response arrived within an hour of hers, sent over with her own footman.

Miss Fernside,

I must insist on making a proper apology.

Also, I can't even imagine what you were doing at The Black Dagger unescorted in the middle of the night. Is this the sort of thing you usually get up to of an evening?

Sincerely yours,

Lieutenant Colonel Walpole

Well.

Lieutenant Colonel Walpole,

I think you will find that what I "get up to" of an evening is none of your business or concern. If I fancy trying my luck at cards in a setting that risks money instead of buttons, then I shall. Sometimes I like to wash the evening down with a glass of whisky as well. Mr. Grave has said that I am welcome anytime.

(No need for apologies.)

Sincerely yours,

Miss Fernside

Abigail sealed the letter with an angry flourish and sent it in the actual post. The nerve of him. Perhaps she *would* go out for an evening of gambling at The Black Dagger. She had seen plenty of ladies there—ladies who looked perfectly respectable. Actually, now that she was seriously thinking about the prospect, she noticed an excited flutter in her belly . . . as if she might actually be brave enough to do something like that. *Was she?* She wavered over it for all of a few days, until Thomas's next letter arrived.

Don't test me, Abigail. I'll not stand for any foolishness.
   Yours,
   Thomas

Abigail had the sudden perverse urge to test the man. Her next letter consisted of only one line: *I'll be at the card tables Thursday at midnight if you want to make your apology.*

Thomas read and reread Abigail's last letter with mounting incredulity. The waif had been full of surprises, but this was one surprise he didn't particularly like.

How had his offer of an apology gone so terribly wrong?

On Thursday, he arrived early at The Black Dagger with the intention of intercepting Abigail on her way in and escorting her home. Christopher Grave greeted him with an outstretched hand and a clap on the back.

"Always appreciate new patrons," he said. "The lady has rather deep pockets."

Thomas registered the man's words with a stab of panic and

looked frantically about the crowded room. His eyes came to rest on Abigail who was playing Vingt-et-un with one of the dealers—the massive Paul who had been so kind as to fetch him a bucket the other day. She was wearing her green shimmering dress, and a couple of gentlemen stood to her side watching the game and smiling. They applauded heartily (and Thomas thought, condescendingly) when Abigail won her hand.

"Don't worry," said Grave, casting a sideways glance to Thomas. "I've had my eye on her all evening."

"Have you?" said Thomas. His jaw tightened as he kept his gaze on the waif.

One of the men at her side put a hand to the back of her chair and leaned down to speak something in her ear. As he watched this interaction, Thomas could feel the thread of reasonableness and civility and calm pulling taut inside himself until it had reached the limits of its integrity. Abigail turned towards the man—her face inches from his—and burst into laughter. As the tinkle of her laughter washed over him, Thomas could feel that thread pulling even tighter until suddenly it snapped.

He strode over to the card table.

"Thomas," said Abigail when she saw him step up, but her face turned wary as she registered his demeanour.

"Get up!" said Thomas.

As he said it, he felt a gentle hand on his shoulder, and the look of devastation on Abigail's face made him turn to see who it was.

"I haven't seen you here in awhile," said Penny.

She was dressed in another nearly transparent frock, a pale blue this time. It clung to her like the foam of the sea and seemed just as likely to blow away on a stiff breeze. Thomas's heart felt like lead in his chest. He couldn't even see straight as Penny threaded her arm through his and peered down at the card table where Abigail was seated.

"What is it tonight?" asked Penny. "Vingt-et-un? I'll order us a round of gin."

Abigail stood from the card table and reached a slightly tremulous arm out towards Penny.

"Miss Abigail Fernside. Pleased to make your acquaintance."

As Penny took her hand, Abigail looked at Thomas with her large hazel eyes, and he found himself unable to move or speak.

"Penelope Roberts," said the woman on his arm. "I'm guessing we have Thomas here as a mutual friend."

"Mutual, yes," said the waif, though her voice cracked slightly on the last word. "If you'll excuse me, I do believe I have run out of luck."

Abigail shifted past them, and Thomas watched for several heartbeats as she made swiftly for the front door.

Fuck.

By the time, he had followed her out, she was some way down the street.

"Abigail!" he called out as he ran towards her. "Abigail!"

She kept walking, but when he finally caught her by the arm, she spun towards him. He could see from the light of the street lamp that her face was streaked with tears.

Hell.

"Go on then," she said. "Apologise, if that's what you want to do."

"Abigail," said Thomas softly. "It's not what you . . ."

"It's all a game to you, isn't it?" she said. "Life is one big

149

playground, and everyone else is simply there to amuse you . . . or take care of you . . . or pine after you. And you stand at the centre of it all—your jests, your stories, your misery. The rest of us are like minor actors in a play, and we eat it all up as if it's the absolute best role we've ever been given."

She wielded her tiny dagger with pin-point precision, and Thomas could feel the sting as it landed. He couldn't think of a single word to say that would measure up to the woman standing in front of him. His words all sounded so trite in comparison to her insight and the emotion with which she conveyed it. Abigail's chin quivered as she wiped at her eyes with the back of her free hand. Then she yanked her arm from him and carried on down the street.

He couldn't leave her of course. There wasn't a hack in sight, and it was the middle of the night, so he trailed behind her like a long shadow, permitting her the space to feel as if she were not walking with him. He was clearly an idiot, but he knew enough not to press himself on her, and he kept his distance as they walked in the direction of Mayfair. Her slippers shushed quietly along the empty street, and Thomas took the next thirty minutes or so to reflect on the words of the woman walking in front of him. She didn't once look back as they walked in and out of the golden glow shed by the streetlamps placed at distant intervals along the way.

Thomas should have anticipated the attack. It was London after all, but he was distracted by his own thoughts as he walked a good dozen paces behind.

The man with the knife materialised out of the darkness like a spectre taking form. He grabbed Abigail roughly by the arm and waved a blade in front of her face. Thomas cursed himself as he slid quietly into the shadows with his heart beating the rhythm of a war drum in his chest and his skin fairly singing with terror.

Abigail glanced back then, just the once as she shrieked, but not seeing him present, she quickly turned to face her attacker once more. Thomas only hoped she wouldn't do anything foolish in the thought that he had abandoned her to walk home alone.

"Your bag," said the man, wrenching her reticule from her hand. "And I'll have the dress as well. Silk, is it? Let's see what's underneath."

He tossed her reticule to the ground as he pulled her in closer to his blade.

Thomas had side-stepped up in the shadows alongside the building with his heart now firmly relocated to his mouth. He gathered every calculating bone in his body to steady his hand as he stole up behind the man. Reaching forward without a tremor, Thomas took the back of the man's neck in a grip he knew to be both painful and paralysing.

"Drop the knife," he said in a voice he barely recognised as his own.

When he heard the knife clatter to the ground, "Unhand the lady."

Once he could see Abigail had stepped back, he punched the man in his kidney so hard, it knocked him to his knees with a grunt. The terror that had gripped Thomas at the outset was unleashed then in a series of swift and brutal kicks that had the man writhing and curling on the ground like an earthworm laid bare after the rain. Thomas's rage was blinding, his body completely untethered as he struck blow after blow, nearly crippling himself in the process.

There was a moment at the height of his rage when Thomas

saw the man not as he was—a dirty footpad in a tattered coat—but as a French soldier in blue uniform refusing to die.

"Thomas!" said Abigail, tugging at his sleeve. "Thomas, please!"

Her voice brought him back to his senses as she tugged him away from the bloody pulp of a man on the ground. Thomas turned to her then in a complete panic, placing his hands to the side of her head, then patting his way down her body in an effort to see if she had been harmed. He was breathing hard, and he felt half mad with the thought of what might have happened to her.

"Thomas," she whispered. "I haven't been hurt."

She took his hands to still them, for they were both shaking.

"Thomas, can you hear me?"

"Abigail? Oh God, Abigail. I'm so sorry. I'm so sorry for everything."

"It's all right," she said.

"No, it's not."

"Come, let's go home." Abigail stole a look at the man on the ground. "Do you think he's still breathing?"

Thomas crouched down and placed a trembling hand in front of the man's nose and mouth.

"Alive," he said, though he did not particularly care either way.

"Let's go," said Abigail.

With the emotional weight of the evening cast over them like a thick woollen coat, they made their way back to the Fernside house in a dead silence. Without a word, Thomas saw Abigail around the back to the servants' entrance. Once she was safely inside, he sat down on an empty crate by the back wall, leaned his elbows onto his knees, and placed his face in his hands.

Perhaps tremors are catching, thought Abigail as she found she did not have the ability in her hands to remove the pins from her hair.

"I'll do it, Miss." The maid's voice was a basket of concern as she carefully pulled the pins from Abigail's hair.

"I don't want to overstep, Miss," continued Betsy, "but do you think it's wise to continue with these clandestine outings?"

Abigail could barely hear her, and it took a moment for the words to land.

"Wise?" said Abigail distractedly. "No, nothing I've done recently has been wise."

When Betsy finally left, Abigail curled up under the covers. She pulled her knees tightly up to her chest, making herself as small as possible, and then the tears began to fall. The fright with which the evening had ended had compounded the emotional toll of the night. She wept until her chest hurt, and her eyes stung, and her pillow was soaked with all the heartache of a girl who knew that she would never measure up—not to her sister, and certainly not to someone like Penelope Roberts. She knew she shouldn't cry over it. She knew Patience would say that it was his problem—not hers. And yet it hurt her anyway. It pained her in a way that made her feel as if she would never properly recover, as if the scars would torment her for the rest of her life.

In the morning, she found she could not rise from her bed. She felt blank and numb, and when her mother came to see her, all she could do was stare at the ceiling and answer her mother's questions in as few syllables as possible.

"Well, if you're not up and about by this afternoon, I shall call the physician," said her mother. "A good bleeding is what you want."

Then she swept out of the room in a swish of violet skirts to leave Abigail to contemplate Dr. Philipps and his jar of leeches. Abigail knew it for the threat that it was, and she also knew that her mother would follow through. Old Dr. Philipps would arrive and enter her bed chamber, greeting her with a smile through his yellow teeth and holding his jar of precious little blood suckers aloft. A cleansing of the blood would follow, and Abigail would only feel queasier and weaker for it.

By late morning, she was sitting up in bed and contemplating getting dressed. Leeches were rather persuasive in that regard.

"You've a letter, Miss," said Betsy, stepping into the room. "And a small parcel."

She held up the items as a kind of offering, and Abigail beckoned her into the room. Having deposited the tiny package and the letter in her mistress's lap, Betsy stood back and waited.

"You'll want to open them, Miss."

Abigail gave her maid a penetrating look.

"Yes, Betsy, I will."

They then stared each other down until Betsy finally gave a quick curtsy and reluctantly left the room. Abigail proceeded to open the letter first.

Dear Abigail,

I cannot undo what has been done, but I hope to be able to atone for it. I hold you in the highest regard and cannot bear to have been the cause of any distress.

Thank you for the care and consideration you have shown me which has been significantly more than I merit. You are no minor actor in a play. If anything, you have garnered the leading role, and I always find myself waiting with bated breath for you to deliver your next line.

Yours,

Thomas

Abigail lowered the letter and stared across the room, through the window, and out over the rooftops of Mayfair.

It doesn't make me feel better. It doesn't, she told herself as a tear tumbled down her cheek.

She then fumbled with the tiny package wrapped in brown paper. It was tied with a small bit of white ribbon edged in gold thread, and she was struck with a pang of familiarity as she undid the ribbon and lifted it in front of her before placing it down on the bed. Inside the brown paper package was a small white box, and inside that was a tiny dessicated rose which might have once been either pink or peach in colour.

Abigail didn't know what to make of it. She sat in her bed contemplating the thing for several minutes before deciding that the meaning of it all was beyond her ken. She placed the ribbon with the rose in its open box on her dressing table and locked the letter away in a drawer. She then mechanically set about her ablutions and rang for Betsy to help her dress.

She spent the rest of the day lost in her music. Having been away for so long, she was somewhat rusty when it came to the harp, but there was a satisfaction in refamiliarising herself with the liquid feel of the instrument, and by the end of the day, she felt rested and a little bit restored. She had even begun a new composition which so engrossed her mind that she had forgotten to change for or even attend dinner.

"Ah, my little enigma is back in the land of the living," said her mother from the music room door. "The leeches have done their job."

She walked into the room and put her hand to Abigail's golden harp.

"It wasn't easy raising two girls all by myself," she said. "Dr. Philipps saw us through some difficult times."

Abigail gave her mother a smile despite the fact that her memories of Dr. Philipps were not particularly fond ones. When she and Harriet were growing up, her mother had always eschewed talking for threats. Talking was hard. Threats often yielded immediate results . . . or at least the appearance of results.

"The Winters will be arriving in London soon," said her mother. "Apparently, they have cousins visiting. Not cousins of the viscount, mind you. These will be Pembertons."

"Yes," said Abigail. "I know. But it's a bit early, isn't it? Patience hasn't written to say."

"My information is sound. I have a network of informants, didn't you know?" Her mother gave Abigail an enigmatic smile.

"There's nothing more enigmatic than the look on your face right now," said Abigail. "I thought you said enigmatism was to be avoided."

"'Enigmatism' is not a word, dear. And I didn't say it was to be avoided. I said gentlemen don't appreciate it. There's a difference." She looked around the room dramatically. "I don't see any gentlemen about."

Abigail had to laugh. It was so rare that she had an opportunity to do so with her mother that she took it when it was given.

The next day passed in similar fashion—staying at home and immersing herself in her music—and so did the next and the one after that as well. She poured all her emotions out through her fingers, attacking the ivory and ebony keys with a passion that seemed to have a will of its own.

Abigail saw no need to respond to Thomas's letter. As lovely as it was on the surface, it floated on an ocean made out of a transparent blue sea-foam dress. Abigail tried to put the stunningly beautiful Penelope Roberts from her mind but found that she could not quite do so. The woman appeared often in front of her, hanging from Thomas's arm with an air of familiarity that set Abigail's heart pounding in her chest. She knew that he had been with this woman—kissed her, touched her, removed her transparent dress. Of course, she had technically known this about him from the start . . . but it had been an abstract concept, one that hovered at a distance rather than one which slapped her across the face like a wet rag.

Abigail sat at her dressing table as Betsy did up her hair.

"Shall I decorate your coiffure with a flower?" she asked. "There's a bouquet in the drawing room that wouldn't miss a sprig of baby's breath or a tiny rose."

"No thank you. It's fine as it is," said Abigail, glancing up at her maid in the mirror.

A fortnight had passed, and Abigail found that time had

slowly hemmed up the frayed edges of her emotions into something resembling normality. She was ready to go out and take part in the world. Her family had been invited to an early ball for those members of the beau monde who had found their way to London before the proper start of the Season. Patience would be there. And her relatives as well. Patience had many lovely and positive things to say about her cousin Samuel. Abigail squeezed her eyes shut to remember the name of his sister.

Arabella.

Samuel and Arabella Pemberton, she reminded herself. She would be meeting them for the first time that evening.

"Oh Abigail!" said Patience upon seeing her friend amidst the crush of the ball. "You look so . . . sophisticated."

Abigail glanced down at the dress she had chosen—it was white, but it was not at all like her other white dresses. She had chosen it for the flattering cut and the feel of the silk against her skin.

"Come with me. I must introduce you to the cousins."

Patience took her arm possessively and led her through the crowd. On the way, Abigail caught sight of a mop of brown hair over a rather serious face. It was Thomas standing alone at the edge of the room. He was wearing his red officer's jacket, and Abigail had to still an urge to wave at him as Patience pulled her along.

Cousin Arabella was like an autumn whirlwind, and spinning about her were several colourful leaves in the shape of young ladies all twittering and laughing and delicately shouldering their way in through the crush to be introduced to the brightest, most fashionable young lady ever to make her debut.

"Popular, isn't she?" said Patience from outside her cousin's circle of new friends.

"Has she been to London before?" asked Abigail.

"Never," said Patience. "She's only seventeen."

Abigail caught a few snippets of conversation like sparks issuing forth from a crackling flame.

"The lace is French . . . height of fashion . . . we should all arrange ourselves in a row according to the hue of each dress, like a rainbow. Then the gentlemen can can survey us with some sense of order in mind."

The young ladies surrounding Arabella giggled. They liked the idea.

"Blue to one end. Pink to the other." Arabella was now issuing orders.

Abigail shook her head. She had never seen someone hold an entire audience of ladies so thoroughly rapt with such empty, silly words. It had always been such an effort for her to make new friends, and she had always wondered what the secret might be.

Inanity, she thought to herself. *And a pail full of confidence.*

In the end, Patience and Abigail had to give up on Arabella for the time being—she was so thoroughly surrounded and so completely occupied in entertaining her flock.

"We'll seek her out later," said Patience, "once the rainbow has dissipated."

Abigail didn't see how that was going to happen. She imagined Arabella trailed a rainbow behind her at all times, like the tail of a comet.

Cousin Samuel was easier to access since he was standing alone by a large arrangement of red roses. He was a giant of a man, though perhaps not much older than Abigail herself.

He had short blonde hair and friendly, earnest brown eyes set into a rather pleasant face. When he spoke, his voice was such a deep baritone, Abigail found that his words vibrated through her body like the lowest note on a base cello. If there was a man in the world who could melt you by tossing out a casual sentence, it was this man.

"Charmed to make your acquaintance," he rumbled as he took her hand and bowed over it.

Abigail gave Patience a wide-eyed look. Patience had to press her lips together to keep from laughing before excusing herself to go and hunt down a glass of champagne.

"I've heard so much about you, Mr. Pemberton," said Abigail.

"All good, I hope." He relinquished her hand.

"Of course. Will you be in London long?"

"Only for the Season," said Samuel. "It's Arabella's coming out."

He looked suddenly anxious and darted his eyes about the ballroom.

"There she is," he said with some visible relief at having found her. "She tends to slip away when I'm distracted. Makes friends very easily as she is quite the conversationalist. Not a talent of mine, I'm afraid."

His words rolled through Abigail's body like distant thunder. It was actually quite a nice feeling.

"Oh I think you're doing quite well," she said.

A flicker of red caught the corner of her eye and tugged at her face until she turned her head.

"Do you know the officer?" asked Mr. Pemberton, following her line of sight.

Thomas was walking towards a group of gentlemen who

160

greeted him with big smiles and something of a cheer as he reached them.

"I . . . ah . . . yes. He's an acquaintance." Abigail forced herself to turn back to the massive man at her side.

The strings started up a country dance, and Abigail thought the music entirely too merry for her current mood.

"Would you care to dance?" asked Mr. Pemberton, leaning down and offering her his arm with a rather lovely smile. "I'll not step on your feet," he added quite seriously when she hesitated.

"Oh," said Abigail. "It's more likely I'll step on yours."

He laughed then. It was sweet and genuine and plain. There was not an ounce of guile about the man, and Abigail felt suddenly quite taken with the simplicity of it all. She accepted the enormous arm he had offered, and they walked out to join the dancers in the centre of the room. Abigail took her place in the circle holding Mr. Pemberton's hand on one side and another gentleman's on the other. Music being the wondrous thing that it is, it was not long before Abigail's mood matched the lively tune. She stepped in time with the group of dancers, into the centre of the circle and out again, and then Mr. Pemberton was swinging her about before she was passed on to the next gentleman in the circle. She found herself smiling and laughing, and it was only when the song ended that she looked up to see Thomas in the corner of the room watching her. She quickly looked away, but some time later when the dancers had dispersed, she chanced another look in his direction. He was still watching her from across the room. He pressed a hand to his thigh as their eyes met, and Abigail had to fight to control the sudden swell of concern that rose up in her breast.

161

She would not walk over. She would not speak with him. She most certainly would not.

Eleven

The Earth Stops Spinning

The night of his and Abigail's meeting at The Black Dagger—the same night he had beaten a knife-wielding thief into a bloody pulp on the street—Thomas made his way home pulling the heavy cartload of insight he had been gifted.

"It's all a game to you, isn't it? Life is one big playground, and everyone else is simply there to amuse you . . . or take care of you . . . or pine after you. And you stand at the centre of it all—your jests, your stories, your misery. The rest of us are like minor actors in a play, and we eat it all up as if it's the absolute best role we've ever been given."

Her words dogged him all the way back to his bachelor apartments. He was a grown man for heaven's sake, an officer in His Majesty's army . . . but he lived his life as if he were revelling in some recent freedom granted . . . as if he were a youth in his first year at university.

As Thomas stepped up to his front door, he reached down into his pocket for his keys and was nearly knocked over by a memory that came to him like a bright blink of lightning in the dark. Abigail in her peach silk dress was pressed up against his front in the very spot where he was now standing, reaching her hand down into his trouser pocket as his arm came around to pull her in closer. She was being all business-like with him, her voice a scold, and it had amused him no end. There was a chuckle in his heart as he gazed down at her before finally letting her go to unlock the door.

God, she was lovely.

Thomas entered his apartments, lit a lamp, and looked around. The place was no more than a few rooms. The furniture was functional if not particularly fashionable, and the walls were completely bare. He could afford more, but he had never bothered much about his accommodations. It wasn't as if he did any entertaining at home. Not unless it was in the bed chamber.

As he pulled at his cravat, he walked towards his bed, dropping down onto it with all the weight of the evening. He threw himself onto his back, and it was only then that the remaining memory of that past night with Abigail came back to him.

She had struggled to help him to the bed, and tangled as they were, they had fallen together on top of the blankets. Thomas winced at the memory. That she would go to such effort for an inebriated man with wandering hands who had once told her that he would resent her and make her cry if they became emotionally entangled . . .

Well, he certainly *had* made her cry.

Thomas reached down to pull at the laces of his boots before kicking them off one by one.

She had done this for him. She had removed his boots.

Don't leave me.

Fuck. Had he said that?

As he undid the buttons of his jacket, he felt her small fingers doing the same. He could see her straddling him on the bed in that insanely sensual peach dress, yanking at his sleeves somewhat impatiently. He had gazed up at her with the warmest and most ardent swell of emotion before giving in to an impulse to reach up and pull her body flat on top of his.

Thomas!

She had been rather annoyed as she rolled from him and onto her side.

And then?

Thomas sat up and shrugged his jacket from his shoulders before lying down once more. In his memory, Abigail lay beside him . . . They were holding each other . . . and then . . .

As the remainder of that night washed over Thomas in a sudden deluge, his heart seized in his chest.

Holy hell.

To say they had talked was an understatement of magnanimous proportions. He hadn't talked to her so much as cut open an artery and bled all over her. She had held him weeping like a miserable child against her breast. Time stretched out into the night. There had been bouts of it—the fucking confessions and the weeping—and she had stayed for it all, holding him to her. He could feel her tears wet his hair and slide down his cheek to mingle with his own.

The unbelievable shame of it practically broke him, but he

refused to allow the memory to slide away. He knew there was something else. Somewhere in the quiet spaces between the sobs of grief, he could hear her speaking softly as she stroked his head, his shoulder.

"You're hurting," she murmured, "because you are a good man. You feel responsible, and responsibility is a frightening thing . . . but we can only do our best. There's nothing more that can be given."

He could feel her cool fingers trace their way up and down the side of his neck in a soothing stroke.

"I know you," she said, "and I know with perfect certainty that you did your very best. No one could have done more . . . It's over now . . . and you're alive . . . and there is now only the question of what to do next. Life blooms in front of you like a rose, Thomas."

He remembered how he had tightened his grip on her then, holding onto her in a way he had never held onto anything in his life.

"Don't worry," she said softly, "I won't leave. You can sleep now."

As he rested his head against her, she began to hum a soft folk melody that was both familiar and comforting. Slowly, liltingly, she added words to the tune:

"No sheep on the mountain nor boat on the lake,
No coin in my coffer to keep me awake,
Nor corn in my garner, nor fruit on my tree,
Yet the maid of Llanwellyn smiles sweetly on me."

Thomas couldn't help but whisper the last line of the verse as the memory trickled over him. Lulled by the soothing sound of her voice, he had fallen asleep in her arms. And she had stayed the whole night. He had not truly appreciated that fact until now. She would have been ruined if she'd been found out, but she had remained with him simply because he needed her.

And then tonight . . . the look on her face when she had seen Penny take his arm. It nearly killed Thomas to relive the moment, but he did it again and again as he lay there in his bed, scoring her pain across his heart with the edge of a dull blade.

Eventually, he rose from the bed and slid open a drawer in his bedside table. He reached in and removed a small white box. Lifting the lid, he looked down at the dry rose and the piece of white ribbon he had kept there since the Season last. He had known from the very start that she was special, and he had turned away in fear—fear that he would not measure up, fear that he could not shoulder the burden of that kind of responsibility if it was granted to him.

God, he had been such a child. And now, after everything that had happened . . . would she ever be able to forgive him?

In the morning, he spent three hours writing a note to Abigail that consisted of only a few sentences. With it, he packaged up the dry rose and the ribbon and sent them off. She should know that she meant something to him, that she had always meant something to him, even if she could not now bear to look at his face.

There had been no response from Abigail, and he had expected none. But now, here she was flushed and beautiful after her country dance with that lumbering great Pemberton man. She was wearing a white silk dress that clung to her like gossamer, and she looked absolutely radiant. Thomas watched her all night with a forlorn sense of loss and was not in the least bit surprised that Samuel Pemberton kept to her side like a fucking limpet to a rock. He did not take an inappropriate second dance with her, but they shared a drink and much conversation, and she made him laugh his stupid barking laugh. Just the once, Thomas saw the man touch Abigail on the bare portion of her arm above her long white glove. The young man was smitten. Of course he was.

"And how are you feeling tonight, Lieutenant Colonel Walpole?" It was Lady Leveson-Gower, all decked out in pearls and pink coral, her snow-white hair shimmering under the chandeliers.

"Oh . . . ah . . . well, thank you," said Thomas, tearing his eyes from stupid Samuel and lovely Abigail.

"They make a fine couple, don't they?" said the lady.

She was as shrewd as a snake.

"That Samuel Pemberton has a heart of gold," she continued. "Sweet young man. And that voice." She pressed a hand to her heart and rolled her eyes up to the ceiling.

"You dance a fine dance, my lady," said Thomas. "I wonder if you can speak plainly."

She cocked her dainty head at him and laughed.

"You've always been a favourite of mine, Lieutenant Colonel. I've been watching you closely."

"Have you now?"

"Mm," said the lady. "Last Season, especially."

"I see . . ." said Thomas warily.

"It's a strange thing to have two people cry ill to leave an evening of poetry and music before it has barely begun." She leaned her shoulder into his. "But don't worry. While I like to speculate, I always keep my speculations to myself."

"Except for now." Thomas stiffened as he spoke the words.

Lady Leveson-Gower grinned at him. She was clearly

having fun at his expense.

"Oh yes, there are always exceptions to the rule," she said, taking his arm. "Look, your quarry has disappeared. Let us take a turn about the room together."

Thomas found himself trapped for the next half an hour.

"Abigail Fernside reminds me of a Miss Jane Savage," said Lady Leveson-Gower as they strolled casually around the perimeter of the ballroom.

"And who is she?" asked Thomas.

"If you were a lady who played the pianoforte, you would have several of her books of composition. You would even know some of her pieces by heart. Her father was a composer as well—a friend of Handel's if I'm not mistaken."

Lady Leveson-Gower broke off their conversation to nod at a group of gentlemen before continuing.

"Miss Savage was the first woman to compose an anthem for the Church of England. It is called *Hymn for Christmas Day*, and I was fortunate enough to see it performed by the Asylum for Female Orphans in London. Perhaps this will give away my terribly advanced age, but this would have been about thirty years ago now." She caught Thomas's eye and gave him a little wistful smile. "So much talent for one so young," she said, shaking her head.

"Where is she now?" asked Thomas.

"I haven't the faintest," replied Lady Leveson-Gower, "though I do believe she still lives."

"Did she not continue to compose?"

"No. She married." The words needed no further explanation, and Thomas asked for none.

They continued to tour the room as Lady Leveson-Gower spoke about her late husband. Something about how his death tore a hole in her soul that would never be mended—to be honest, Thomas wasn't really listening. He was too busy casting his eyes about the room searching for Abigail. She was nowhere in sight, and neither was the Pemberton oaf.

"It's a bit stuffy, don't you think?" said Lady Leveson-Gower, interrupting Thomas's thoughts. "Let's take some air on the balcony."

Thomas had a brief image of himself pressing Lady Leveson-Gower forward onto the balcony and then retreating quickly to close the glass doors and lock her out. He would give her a little impish wave and a wink to keep her sweet and then turn on his heel to find Abigail.

Obviously, he could do no such thing. Instead, he stepped out onto the dark balcony with the lady on his arm. As they moved in silence to the railing in order to look out over the garden lit with torches, he felt the older lady clutch tightly at his arm and try to pull him back. Confused, Thomas looked at her face—it was alarmed—and then turned to look behind him. There, at the far end of the balcony, tucked into a dark corner, was Abigail in the large arms of the oaf. She was looking up into his face. A hesitation. And then the man bowed his head and kissed her quite soundly on the mouth as his hands slid down the silky length of her dress to rest lightly at the top of her buttocks.

The earth stopped spinning.

Thomas could feel the pricking of tears behind his eyes. He struggled to take a breath, and when he could not, his eyes went wide, and Lady Leveson-Gower pulled him swiftly back into the light-filled ballroom.

"For heaven's sake," she whispered. "Breathe!"

He was doubled over with his hands on his thighs.

Christ, he couldn't breathe!

Lady Leveson-Gower cast an assessing eye about the room to see if his little episode was being witnessed.

"Stand up, Lieutenant Colonel. Now. Or a fuss will be made, and it will draw a great deal of attention to us here by the balcony."

Abigail, thought Thomas. *If she was found to have been alone in the dark with the oaf, her reputation wouldn't survive it.*

He struggled for a breath, taking it in with a low straining wheeze as Lady Leveson-Gower placed a delicate hand to his back. With that first breath accomplished, Thomas righted himself and drew in another. The ballroom was spinning like an amorphous ball of glitter. He felt tingly all over, and he hoped to God he wouldn't collapse as the lady steadied him with a firm hand. With Lady Leveson-Gower's attention directed his way and his faculties compromised from lack of air, neither of them noticed the two ladies glide up along the wall and slip out onto the balcony behind them.

Abigail was having a rather pleasant time with Samuel Pemberton after their country dance. The man was so warm and genuine, and he seemed to be rather taken with her which was something of a surprise. They chatted and laughed, and Abigail found he was quite funny when he managed to get the words out. He took his time to respond to her as his big brown eyes held hers with a sincerity that was rather attractive. The effect was both charming and refreshing. Abigail felt completely at ease and was able to relax into the evening in the way one might slide down into a particularly soft and comfortable chair.

Mr. Pemberton's deep voice was soothing, and Abigail found herself watching his mouth as he spoke. His lips were full and sensual, his jaw square. She wondered what it might be like to kiss him. Thomas had turned her world upside down with a few words in a darkened hall and a feverish kiss in an alley . . . but maybe that was only because of Abigail's own inexperience. Maybe someone easier . . . someone like Samuel . . . maybe kissing him would be just as intoxicating, provoke just as many feelings. How would she ever know?

"I could use some air," said Abigail to Samuel. "It's rather hot in here, don't you think?"

She had never manoeuvred a man into a kiss before, but she imagined this was how it was done. As far as bravery went, this hardly even ranked compared with venturing into a gaming hell in the middle of the night and haggling over the price of drunken man.

"Of course." Mr. Pemberton offered her his arm. "Let's take our conversation outside."

He dutifully escorted her out onto the balcony under the stars, and as he did so, Abigail idly contemplated whether if she threw a stick, he might fetch it.

"That's much better," said Abigail as she took a few steps to the balcony railing and slid along to the far corner.

She turned to Mr. Pemberton with a smile and saw him dart a glance down to her bosom. The night air was cool, and in the light cast by the torches down in the garden, the shape of her hardening nipples was visible through the thin silk of her dress.

"Are you cold?" asked Mr. Pemberton, reaching a hand to the bare skin of her upper arm and squeezing gently.

He had touched her there earlier in the evening. It had been inappropriate then, and it was inappropriate now, but he appeared to make the gesture without thinking. Abigail smiled to herself. He really was artless. She liked it. She stepped in towards him and saw the black flare in his eyes.

"Yes . . . but your hand is warm."

She spoke the words, but it didn't feel as if it was her speaking at all.

His large hands came to rest on her ribcage. As he slipped them down the length of her torso to her buttocks, his head bowed over hers, and he kissed her.

Oh.

It wasn't unpleasant so much as it wasn't anything at all—just lips touching lips. He was warm, and his mouth was soft, and that was as much as she could say about the experience. She did feel a little tingle between her legs, but it wasn't particularly urgent, and she was certainly not inclined to explore it any further with him. She had thrown the stick, and he had fetched it. That was about the sum of it.

The kiss was rather brief as far as kisses went, and he lifted his face from hers with a quizzical expression.

"I don't think . . ." said Abigail.

"We don't suit, do we?" he said. "Despite how lovely you are."

"Despite how lovely *you* are," said Abigail with a rueful smile.

Hearing a gasp, Abigail turned her head to see two middle-aged ladies standing stock still on the balcony watching them. Mr. Pemberton's hands were still resting below her hips, and the enormity of the situation came slamming down over her like a wave.

Oh God.

By the time she reemerged from the balcony beside Mr. Pemberton, Abigail could feel all the blood draining from her head. As she took a few hesitant steps into the ballroom, the shifting colours of the room were obscured by large black splotches. As the entire world turned dark, she felt her legs give way, and she crumpled into a pair of rather strong arms.

When she regained consciousness, she was lying down on a settee, her head propped up with a cushion. Her mother was leaning over her as was Patience. One of the ladies she had seen on the balcony was standing just behind her mother, and Samuel Pemberton was standing beside Patience looking rather like a guilty dog who regretted very much his impulsive stealing of the ham hock from off the counter.

I'm the ham hock, thought Abigail.

As she sat up, she briefly caught a flash of red at the far end of the room. There and gone. Her heart fluttered momentarily as if ruffled by a breeze.

"I'd like the room, please!" said her mother rather forcefully to the people gathered.

As everyone made to file out, she said, "Obviously not you!" and grabbed Samuel Pemberton by the coattail.

Samuel threw a rather worried glance Patience's way, but she simply patted him on the shoulder and took her leave. When the room was emptied, Abigail's mother heaved her bosom up to take a large breath . . . and then she let them have it.

"Taking small liberties with a lady you fancy is one thing," she said to Samuel, "but at a ball?! On the balcony?! Are you plain stupid, or are you simply out of your mind?"

Samuel opened his mouth, but she continued.

"And you," she said turning to Abigail. "What in heaven's

name has become of my little girl? It will have been carried in whispers across the ballroom by now. Tomorrow, across London. You know these people are bored, Abigail. You can't give them anything to latch onto."

"Sorry, Mother," said Abigail.

She found herself looking anywhere but into her mother's eyes. She made a studious effort to avoid Samuel's gaze as well.

"I'm afraid 'sorry' won't do," said her mother. "This is a question of reputation. You will have to marry to put a line under the whole affair."

"Marry?" said Abigail. "I don't need my reputation if it means ruining my life . . . not to mention Mr. Pemberton's."

Her mother threw her hands up in the air with exasperation.

"This may come as a shock, Abigail, but the world does not revolve around your person. This is a question of family. Your sister Harriet . . ."

Abigail could only make out bits and pieces of what followed. How was this about her sister Harriet? Slowly, she adjusted her mental faculties to comprehend the words her mother was speaking.

"Harriet's husband is a member of Parliament. He relies on votes, my dear. He relies on the reputation of our combined families. How would it be if he and Harriet found themselves cut from polite society on account of Harriet's wanton little sister?"

Wanton.

"Mr. Anderson and I cannot survive in a social vacuum either. And you will have no prospects whatsoever, my dear. None."

Abigail looked to Mr. Pemberton whose face had gone grey.

"I will announce the betrothal tomorrow," said her mother. "It will appear as if the kiss were in anticipation of the engagement. We will set a date. You clearly have some affection for one another. Everything will be well."

Mr. Pemberton's mouth opened and closed like a goldfish.

"Don't worry." Abigail's mother patted him on the arm. "She comes with a tidy inheritance. I'm sure you will find a way to be happy."

Mr. Pemberton spared a look at Abigail. He forced a smile.

"It's possible we could suit," he said. "I will, of course, do the honourable thing."

How romantic, thought Abigail.

When Mr. Pemberton finally left, her mother surprised Abigail by tossing her a grin and a wink.

"I'm sure it will all work out for the best," she said. "You've snared yourself quite the slab of roast beef. Such kind eyes. And so strong. Unfortunately, he's not the brightest button in the box, and it's a shame about his reflexes, but you can't have everything."

"Reflexes?" said Abigail.

"It was Lieutenant Colonel Walpole who caught you when you swooned—practically flew to your side. A soldier, I imagine, is always on alert. To his credit, Mr. Pemberton was very apologetic for having neglected to notice your collapse. That will also serve you well, my dear. You want to have a husband on the back foot if you can—apologising if possible."

Abigail was barely listening. Thomas had caught her. The flash of red had been him. He had been with her in this very room, only leaving once she had regained consciousness. She glimpsed a memory of his face when she had been attacked on the street. The blind fury with which he had kicked that man

176

into a bloody mess. The panic as he patted her body down afterwards looking for injuries, making sure she was sound.

Oh God—the rumours that must be circulating the ballroom right now . . . What must he think of her?

"I can't marry Samuel Pemberton," said Abigail quietly to herself.

"You can," said her mother, "and you will."

Twelve

The Perfect Family

Thomas sat in the parlour of his bachelor apartments wearing only his shirtsleeves and contemplating the decanter of whisky on the table beside him. When he had arrived home from the ball, he had thrown his red officer's jacket to the floor and ripped the cravat from his neck. The clothing had felt like it was strangling him.

Seeing Abigail in the arms of the Pemberton oaf had knocked the wind clean out of his body. He had never felt anything like it—an anguish and agony beyond all reason and sense. It was the kind of anguish that twisted his soul like a wet towel, wringing every drop of comfort and joy that had ever been gathered up. He was now quite empty except for the pain which was a rather exquisite thing all told—like the gleaming blade of a knife slicing its way slowly through living flesh.

He was reminded of the look on Abigail's face when Penny

had threaded her arm through his at The Black Dagger.

She had been hurt just like this. God!

He threw his face up to the ceiling. Being the unbelievable coward that he was, he had hurt her on more than one occasion. Thomas put his hand to the decanter and left it there as he stared into the space in front of him.

He couldn't believe he had been too busy struggling for breath to protect Abigail from the raging gossips that qualified as members of the ton. He would flagellate himself over that for a good long time. The repercussions for a woman stepping out of line would be severe. There is nothing quite as cold as a social shunning. He imagined her mother would put things to rights soon enough. A wedding engagement. He had seen it done before.

Thomas found his hand returning from the decanter to his chest and clutching frantically at his heart.

She must at least like the man if she kissed him.

Thomas knew he was in no position to judge. He had kissed plenty of women and at least a couple of men who were bare acquaintances at the time. It was just a bit of fun . . . The problem was that he knew Abigail didn't do things like that, not because of any notion he had of her innocence or purity but simply because she was so thoughtful and serious. It wasn't just a bit of fun to her . . . which suggested to him that Mr. Samuel Pemberton must be *special* to her.

Oh God, he wasn't entirely sure he could endure even the thought of it.

In the end, he decided that he didn't deserve to have his agony drowned out in gulps of golden liquor. He went to bed cold fucking sober and lay there all night with one hand clawing into his chest as if he might be able to get a grip on the pain and tear it free of his body.

Eventually, in the small hours of the morning, sleep took him, and he dreamed.

Abigail's mother was standing beside him among his battalion on the field at Waterloo. She was wearing a bright yellow dress and a bonnet and was holding a rather fancy rifle upright. His men had formed the square, muskets ready, nerves strung taught. The French cavalry was thundering toward them.

"HOLD!" he shouted.

Hooves smacked the ground. Musket smoke hung in the air like a fog.

"Rather a lot of trouble, don't you think?" said Mrs. Anderson, leaning her rifle against her leg and adjusting the ribbons on her bonnet.

"HOLD!"

"I SAID, RATHER A LOT OF TROUBLE, DON'T YOU THINK?"

Thomas turned towards her as the cavalry advanced.

What the hell was she playing at, distracting him?

"Excuse me?" he said.

"You've gone to all this bother," she continued, "but you haven't managed to protect her."

Thomas put up a finger to stall the woman for a moment as he turned back to the advancing French. He lifted his musket.

"AIM!"

A thousand muskets were settled against a thousand shoulders. Thomas could see out of the corner of his eye that Mrs. Anderson had also lifted her fancy rifle to take aim. The war horses were two heartbeats from the thirty yard mark.

"FIRE!"

A cacophony of sound tore through him.

And then nothing. Complete silence. The battlefield was empty except for him and Mrs. Anderson whose pearl-smattered yellow skirts were not even dusty. He looked down at his own ensemble which was streaked with mud and blood.

"You'll want to soak that jacket in cold water," said Mrs. Anderson, "before you do a proper laundry."

"What are you talking about?"

"If you don't soak it, the stain will set."

"No," said Thomas. "What do you mean when you say I haven't managed to protect her?"

"Look." She lifted a hand to point behind him.

A cold dread suddenly gripped Thomas about the throat. He didn't want to look, so he kept his eyes on Mrs. Anderson.

"LOOK!" she said once more.

Forcing himself, he turned to look. There, in the middle of the field was the waif sitting on a wooden chair. She was wearing a white dress, and a crimson bloom of blood was spreading across one thigh as she gazed down at it.

She'd been shot.

"Now *there's* a stain that won't be coming out," said Mrs. Anderson.

Thomas woke with a cry on his lips and his heart banging against his ribs.

Patience slipped her arm through Abigail's and pulled her in close as they set off through Hyde Park. It was not the fashionable hour—that would have garnered Abigail a few too many stares. Instead, Patience had suggested they meet in the morning to discuss . . .

"Muffins," said Patience in an exasperated tone as they crunched their way down the gravel path. "I didn't think Samuel had it in him to seduce a young innocent. I can't help but feel this is all my fault for playing matchmaker. Oh, Abigail!"

Abigail gave her friend a sideways glance.

"He didn't seduce me," she said. "I object to the term 'innocent', and it is by no means your fault."

"What happened?" asked Patience.

Abigail hesitated for several long silent paces.

"I sort of manoeuvred him into an experimental kiss," said Abigail miserably.

Patience hissed in a breath.

"I'll not judge you," she said. "I can't say I've never manoeuvred a man into an experimental kiss . . . but the man in question did end up marrying me . . ." She cast her friend a look. "It wasn't that sort of kiss, was it?"

Abigail shook her head.

"Mother has agreed to hold off on the engagement announcement for the week, but she's right about what will happen if it doesn't proceed. She's already had two invitations rescinded and absolutely no callers for three days. Harriet's husband Evan had a meeting with a patron cancelled, and even the Ladies' Society are giving Harriet more space than they normally would. What is wrong with the world, Patience?"

"I'll tell you what's wrong with the world," said Patience angrily. "It's rigged to keep us in our place. God forbid a woman express a physical urge or an aspiration beyond stitching a sampler. Anyone she touches would be tainted by the sin. The very moral fabric of society would be torn asunder. Total chaos would ensue!"

She then added several colourful oaths to punctuate the sentiment and glared at an elderly gentleman who threw her a rather horrified expression.

Regardless of the fact that they had not settled on any particular solution to her predicament, her friend's outrage was enough to make Abigail feel marginally better.

"You and your mother and Mr. Anderson are still very much invited to the masquerade my sister-in-law is hosting," said Patience. "I think it would be good to be seen there, despite being masked. Our family will always lend yours its support."

"Thank you, Patience. I'm not feeling up for a party, but you're probably right. I'll let Mother know we're still welcome."

Over the next several days, Abigail was surprised to find Samuel Pemberton calling on her repeatedly at home. The first time he called, he arrived with a fistful of pink freesias, and Abigail's mother gushed over them as if they were for her.

"Oh, Mr. Pemberton," she said, taking the flowers from him and clutching them to her breast, "they are absolutely lovely. How very thoughtful of you."

"My sister Arabella helped me pick them out."

The simple words were like a roll of thunder across the room, and Abigail thought her mother might actually swoon. After a flustered moment, the older lady finally looked at her daughter then back at Samuel Pemberton. She lifted the freesias in front of her.

"I'll just go and find a maid to put these in water."

Of course, she could have rung for a maid, but she wanted to give the two "lovebirds," as she was taken to calling them, some time alone. As she departed the room, she left the door appropriately ajar. Abigail made sure she could hear her mother's footsteps disappearing down the hall before she turned to Mr. Pemberton and spoke.

"What are you doing here?"

Having said it, she immediately realised how ungrateful it sounded.

"I mean . . . why? The flowers . . . You certainly don't have to . . ."

Abigail winced internally. Her powers of verbal cohesion had somehow managed to flee. Mr. Pemberton regarded her with his soft brown eyes.

"I'm here to court the woman who is to be my wife." The words vibrated through her entire body.

Well, when he put it like that . . .

He took a step towards her on his large muscled legs.

"Though I get the feeling that your mother imagines herself to be the object of my courtship."

This caused Abigail to hide a smile of agreement as she looked up at him from under her lashes. A few moments passed before she found she could not hold the smile back any longer, and a short sharp laugh burst from her lips. Mr. Pemberton's sensual mouth responded in kind.

"Abigail." He took her hand. "May I call you Abigail?"

She nodded as she looked down at her hand which seemed suddenly very small in his large one.

"You should call me Samuel," he said. "I should very much like to start again. I am so sorry for my behaviour the night of the ball. To say I would do the honourable thing after your mother yelled at me as if I were a child in need of a scold—it wasn't particularly romantic."

"But it was kind," said Abigail. "Kinder than I perhaps

184

deserve."

"I don't know you very well," said Samuel, "but I have the feeling that you likely deserve quite a bit more than you think. I know our kiss wasn't exactly . . . earth-shattering, but it was just one kiss. Maybe, given a bit of time together, we will be able to find a . . . warmer embrace."

He lifted her hand to his lips which were quite as warm as that warmer embrace he had just mentioned.

The next day, he showed up in a phaeton pulled by two black hunters and insisted on taking her for a ride through Hyde Park.

"I'll not be racing anyone," he said when she hesitated to mount the contraption. "I rented it for the day. At home in the countryside, we have great swathes of open space, and it's quite a liberating feeling to fly along behind the horses with the wind against your face."

At home, thought Abigail. His home would be her home, and she knew absolutely nothing about it.

As she allowed him to hand her up to the high seat of the phaeton, she said, "How have your parents taken it? This surprise engagement?"

He gave a subtle shake of his head, then climbed up and settled himself beside her.

"Did Patience not tell you? My parents passed away several years ago. It's just me and Arabella which, to be honest, has been rather a tax on my nerves. She's quite unpredictable. Though, I shouldn't say that: she's actually very predictable in her unpredictability."

He flashed a wide smile at Abigail which warmed her in a way she could not have anticipated.

"I'm sorry to hear about your parents," she said.

185

"It was a fever," replied Samuel as he took up the reins, and the horses pulled them away from the pavement. He did not elaborate, and Abigail could understand why.

"My father died in his sleep when I was eight years old," she said. "The physician said that a blood vessel had ruptured in his head."

"Life is a fragile thing," said Samuel as he manoeuvred the vehicle around a tight corner causing Abigail to slide against his thigh.

She glanced up to the side of his face as he paid all his attention to the road ahead. The man was handsome and thoughtful and kind, and he was trying to make the best of the situation in which he found himself—honourable and dutiful. She certainly could have done much worse with an experimental kiss. When they came out of the turn, Abigail remained where she was—seated with her thigh flush up against his, feeling the tense and quiver of his muscles as he kept a tight rein on the horses and angled for the park.

After a thoroughly delightful time at the park, Mr. Pemberton brought her home. Jumping down from the contraption, he came around to her side and reached his hands up to her waist.

"It's a long way down," he said with a smile.

"Oh."

She placed her hands to his shoulders, and he lifted her down with strong arms. Abigail's feet settled on the pavement as she looked up into his eyes. His hands were still on her waist.

"As you know, Arabella and I are staying with the Pembertons, and the dowager Lady Pemberton has requested that I extend an invitation for you to come to tea."

"Patience's mother," said Abigail.

She wasn't sure why she said it. Perhaps because the invitation felt strange to her. Going for tea at Patience's brother's house with the Pemberton family but without Patience simply felt all wrong.

"That would be lovely," she said.

His large hands shifted almost reluctantly from her waist.

"They want to make you feel part of the family," said Mr. Pemberton. "And so do I."

Abigail smiled shyly up at him, but she was having trouble focussing on his face. An image of Thomas kicking a man half to death in the street had intruded itself into her mind. Then Thomas's hands holding the sides of her face and the wild look in his eyes as he tried to determine if she had been hurt.

"Abigail?" said Mr. Pemberton.

Tea at the Pemberton house felt as strange without Patience as Abigail had anticipated.

Patience's brother George (or rather, Lord Pemberton) was not present, but all the ladies were—his mother the dowager, his little sister Grace, and his wife Sophie as well, not to mention Arabella. Samuel Pemberton was the lone man at the gathering.

"Abigail!" cried Grace when she saw her sister's friend enter the yellow drawing room.

The girl stood from her seat as a little brown pug jumped down from her lap and made a dash for Abigail's feet.

"Mind your slippers," said the dowager Lady Pemberton as

she stood. "Potato considers them edible."

"Potato! Come!" commanded Grace, but the dog paid her no mind as it sniffed at Abigail's shoes and then scampered around her several times.

Abigail crouched down to allow the dear little dog to sniff at her hand before giving her a pat on the head. Unfortunately, this only seemed to excite Potato even further, and Grace had to come over to wrestle her away.

"She loves the love," said Grace as she retreated back to her seat with the dog clutched to her chest.

"And who wouldn't?" said Sophie, laughing and coming to take Abigail's hand in order to lead her over to a seat.

George's wife, the baroness, always looked to Abigail like a princess stepped out of a fairytale with her midnight black hair and large amber brown eyes.

"Thank you for the invitation," said Abigail, glancing around at everyone. It all felt just a little overwhelming.

"Abigail," said Samuel, "this is my sister Arabella. I don't believe you've been introduced."

"How do you do?" said Arabella. "I've always wanted a sister."

The word 'sister' struck Abigail in the solar plexus with unexpected force, and she found she couldn't respond.

Arabella was wearing a pale green dress which was cut to the height of fashion, though perhaps a smidge too daring for a girl of seventeen, and her wheat-gold hair was done up as if it had been swept into place by a paintbrush.

"Let me pour the tea," said the dowager, placing a cup in front of Abigail.

Despite Abigail's initial hesitancy, the afternoon rolled by on a wave of friendly conversation and laughter as Potato made surreptitious attempts to steal the biscuits from the tea table. At one point, Arabella even shooed her brother from his seat beside Abigail so that she could have "a proper conversation" with her new sister-to-be. This proper conversation mainly involved her opinions on what Abigail might wear for her wedding day.

"I wouldn't go with white," said Arabella, biting into a shortbread. She lifted the biscuit in front of her to look at it with some appreciation. "These are quite good, aren't they?"

"It's Cook's special recipe," said Sophie.

Arabella turned back to Abigail.

"As I was saying, white is rather . . . tedious, don't you think?"

"Tedious?" echoed Abigail.

"I've read that in India, many ladies wear red on their wedding day," said Arabella. "Red is blood and passion and life. Wearing white simply feels as if you want none of that."

"Don't listen to her," laughed Samuel, "or she will be dressing you for the foreseeable future."

Abigail glanced over to him with a smile. He was seated on a chair which was much too small for him holding Potato in his lap. The dog had one of Samuel's big hands between her teeth, and he was tugging it back and forth with some amusement as the dog let out a low growl. Grace and Sophie were on the settee buried deep into the middle of what seemed like a very important conversation, and the dowager was surveying the scene with some satisfaction as she sipped at her tea.

I'm marrying into the perfect family, thought Abigail. *So why is it I can't stop thinking about Thomas? When will it stop hurting?*

189

"You look lost," said Christopher Grave as Thomas wandered into The Black Dagger.

Thomas was momentarily distracted from his quiet contemplation. He looked around. It was late, and the place was buzzing—dice rattling, women laughing, drinks clinking under the golden light of the lamps.

"Are you looking for your wee lass?" asked Grave.

"She's not mine," said Thomas. It was hard to keep the misery from his tone.

Grave placed an arm around his shoulder and shook his head.

"What you need is a distraction, Walpole. Have you ever thought of selling your commission? My brother Aaron is in need of a business partner—someone with connections who can charm the coins out of a purse. Aaron is a completely upstanding businessman, poker-up-the-arse sort of bloke."

Thomas simply stared at the man.

"Not interested in talking business?" asked Grave. "Too sad? There, there." Thomas was momentarily warmed by the man's purposefully condescending words. "Perhaps what you want right now is a quick fix, something to pick you up. The more money you spend, the better you'll likely feel."

Thomas looked at the man through narrowed eyes.

"No?" said Grave. "A bottle of whisky then. It's worked for you before. I imagine she'll show up to rescue you only moments after you've drained the bottle. And if you're not still standing, we can always roll you out to the hack. A lady loves a drunk—that's what they say, isn't it? I'm sure that little adage has been sewn onto a number of cushions which are no doubt decorating the chairs and settees of several drawing rooms across town."

Grave pulled him in close to his side then, as if to confide a secret.

"Your last option, and I'm afraid this one is your best, is to funnel all your pent-up frustration and desire and hurt into ploughing the first available woman who crosses your path. Penny over there seems quite sweet on you, and I've a back room the two of you could use for a modest sum."

Thomas shrugged the man off his shoulder angrily.

"You're a right fuckwit, Grave."

Christopher Grave blessed him then with one of the most charming smiles in all of Creation before allowing it to fall away like a slide of rock from the side of a mountain.

"Fuckwit I may be, but I'll not have a good man and a celebrated officer in His Majesty's army come into my establishment in order to destroy himself. Walpole, whatever your problem is, work it out. I'll not serve you another drink or allow you to spend another shilling in here until you look good and sorted."

"How do you know I'm not 'good and sorted' right now?" asked Thomas.

Grave fixed him with a stony look that brooked no opposition.

"Sort it out," said Grave sternly before taking Thomas by the arm and escorting him out onto the pavement.

But how is that even possible? thought Thomas. *She hates me.*

As he wandered home through the pale yellow haze of the street lamps, all the details of the world around him seemed suddenly quite alien to him—as if his boots hitting the cobblestones made no sense at all, as if his body were a foreign thing with which he had been burdened for some unknown reason. He looked up, but the smog of the city coupled with the glow of the street lamps hid all the stars from view, and he wondered whether if he couldn't see them, they existed at all. The only thing that seemed in any way real to him just then was the image of Abigail Fernside seated on a wooden chair with a stain of blood spreading across her leg. When he finally arrived back at his empty rooms, he threw himself down on the bed, and falling asleep, he dreamed of someone else's bride.

Thirteen

The Songbird and the Soldier

"I don't understand," said Mary Robins as she took a seat opposite Thomas in her small parlour. "William's at work. Why are you here?"

She was wearing a simple blue cotton dress, her smooth blonde hair was pinned up, and her sharp eyes settled on him warily.

"I need some womanly advice," said Thomas as he sat down, "from someone who dislikes me."

Mary's pale cheeks flushed pink.

"I don't dislike you."

"But you're not thrilled to have William in my company."

Mary started to fuss with the arrangement of her skirts and kept her eyes averted from his.

"Mary."

"Yes?"

"I don't have time for etiquette," said Thomas. "This is

important."

Mary suddenly looked up and fixed him with a gaze that stung him as much as if she had struck him across the face.

What had William said about her? Beautiful, clever, antagonistic?

"All right," she said slowly, "let's say I dislike you. Now, why would that be?"

Thomas found he couldn't help himself.

"You can't stand my charm?" he suggested impishly. "I'm too handsome, too clever, too witty?"

"I like all of those things about you," said Mary quietly. "It's the flippancy I find offensive. I don't want William walking down that path with you . . . seeking out one distraction after another in an effort to drown out what is difficult and worthwhile and important."

"I've done difficult things," said Thomas.

"I'm not saying you haven't. But you do know what I'm trying to say, don't you?"

"I need to grow up," said Thomas.

Mary leaned back in her chair.

"You can still be handsome and charming and clever and witty. And kind. You are also very kind."

Her words touched him in a way he hadn't expected. He shifted forwards in his seat.

"There's a lady. A special lady. I fear she dislikes me even more than you claim not to."

"Ah." Mary's eyes opened wide in understanding. "You'll not want to go gifting her a shawl . . . though I don't mean to sound ungrateful. It's just . . . it won't fix anything."

"No," said Thomas. "I had already feared that wouldn't work."

"You need to show her that you can be serious, that you can do the difficult thing," said Mary. "Be an adult."

A baby started to cry somewhere in the house, and Mary rose to her feet.

"She'll want a feeding."

"Of course," said Thomas. "Sorry to barge in on you like this."

Mary offered him a pinched smile—he was fairly certain she still didn't like him. However, he left the house feeling significantly lighter than when he had gone in. The fall day was crisp and bright, and a cool breeze stroked his face as he stepped down the street contemplating Mary's advice.

Do the difficult thing.

He knew exactly what that was, and it caused him to reach a hand to his chest and clutch distractedly at his heart.

She may never forgive him.

The image of Abigail tilting her face up towards Samuel Pemberton's struck Thomas once more with the force of a canon ball. He steadied himself to remain standing under the impact. It was a lot like being on a battlefield, he thought, but it wasn't a fight, so there was no option of winning.

He would do the difficult thing, but he would not be able to do it with an audience, so visiting Abigail at her home was out of the question. That mother of hers would be all over him like a rash, and he could not see how he could ask for a private moment alone. It would be completely inappropriate.

She must be invited to George and Sophie's masquerade ball, he thought. *I'll find her there.*

Abigail wasn't sure if she could do it—dress up in the playful spirit of a masquerade, dance, make conversation. She entered her mother's dressing room to find her mother seated at the vanity as her maid arranged her hair for the evening. She was going as the Queen of Hearts.

"Is it really necessary for me to come tonight?" asked Abigail.

She had bathed, and she was now wrapped in a white dressing gown with her wet hair splayed about her shoulders and moisture slowly seeping into the fabric at her back.

"You can't not go," said her mother.

"Perhaps, I'm unwell," said Abigail. "Perhaps I need a little bit of time to myself. These past few days have been a whirlwind of socialising."

"With your future husband and his family," replied her mother. "It's not 'socialising' when it's with your husband."

Abigail was briefly horrified by the realisation that her time with Samuel, though nice, was something of an effort. It *was* socialising. Would it be that way for the rest of her life?

"Sit by the fire and dry your hair," said her mother. "Then I want you to put on your costume and your best smile. It will be a fine party—a night to remember. And you don't want Samuel thinking that you've gone off him. The man is a Godsend. Could you imagine what might have happened if it had been someone else?"

Someone else.

What might have happened if it had been Thomas? Would he have done the honourable thing and then resented her for the rest of his life? Would that have pained her more?

She knew one thing for certain: however it might have turned out, it would never have felt as if she were socialising

196

with Thomas. Talking to him—even yelling at him—was never an effort. Time with him, no matter how bruising, was always like time at the beach. It felt as natural and inevitable as the tides. With Thomas, she always felt more like herself, or at least more like the person she wanted to be—someone brave, someone willing to allow her passions to propel her. He never failed to provoke her in some way, whether it was to arousal or laughter, contemplation or anger. With him, every moment was lifted up like the clear chime of a bell.

"BETSY!" called her mother.

Abigail knew that the argument was over if her mother was yelling for the maid instead of ringing for her. They could hear Betsy's footsteps running along the hall before she peered into the dressing room somewhat out of breath.

"Make sure Abigail dries her hair," said her mother. "Then put her in costume, and set her by the front door."

"Yes, my lady." Betsy dipped a quick curtsy before glancing over to her mistress.

Abigail heaved a sigh.

Thomas was usually one for revelry and whimsy, but he did not truly have the heart for a masquerade at this particular point in his life, and he could not spare the mental resources to think up a costume. So he simply wore his officer's uniform as he always did to such events, topping it off with a black demi-mask that framed his eyes and made him look quite dangerous. There was something about a disguise that gave you courage, and Thomas was glad of any extra boost in that regard.

As he entered the ballroom and surveyed the scene, his heart sank. Everyone was either in full costume or sporting masks. It was going to take some time to find Abigail.

The atmosphere was anticipatory, alive with excitement, and Thomas knew exactly why. The masks gave their wearers permission to do things they might otherwise not do, and he knew something about what people might otherwise not do because he had done it all. He even knew where they would be doing it later on in the evening—the darkened rooms, the hidden corners, the empty carriages waiting outside.

"Walpole," said a man's voice. "You're not exactly playing along are you? It's meant to be a masquerade, and you've come dressed as yourself."

It was Patience's brother George—Lord Pemberton. He was dressed all in grey and sported a demi-mask that was painted with rain clouds. His grey eyes shone through the mask as if he were looking down from on high. Despite everything, Thomas couldn't help but flash George his most charming smile. Patience's brother was altogether disturbingly handsome, quietly serious, and tightly wound which was a combination that tended to provoke Thomas into a teasing kind of behaviour. It was a knee-jerk reaction. He would have done it in his sleep.

"And what are you supposed to be, Pemberton?" asked Thomas.

"Isn't it obvious? My wife has dressed me as a storm."

"So you've come dressed as yourself as well then," said Thomas.

He was not prepared to hear George laugh. The sound was infectious, and it made Thomas want to find Abigail right away to tell her about it.

198

"And where is that gorgeous wife of yours?" said Thomas. "I should like to ask her for a waltz." He was momentarily gratified to catch a brief flare of irritation in the baron's grey eyes. "She will have no doubt organised a games room," continued Thomas. "If my memory serves me, the two of us make quite the pair for Whist. I imagine she's dressed as Lady Luck herself."

He watched with some amusement as George visibly unclenched his jaw and tried to smile.

"Don't push it, Walpole. You know you're always welcome in this house."

"Lady Luck wouldn't have it any other way, would she?" said Thomas with a wink.

George Pemberton made a fist with his right hand, and for one childishly celebratory moment, Thomas thought he might have actually done it—he might have actually provoked George Pemberton into punching him.

The moment, however, was short-lived. George unclenched his fist and leaned his face close in beside Thomas's own. For a storm, he smelled altogether too good—like a pile of cut wood warmed in the summer sun.

"Some might say that we're always in costume," said George into his ear. "I imagine you spend a good deal of time hiding behind yours."

He then stood back and took Thomas by the shoulders.

"Have a wonderful evening," he said, and then the storm turned and disappeared into the crowd.

The baron was bloody observant. It made Thomas feel naked and vulnerable and . . . ashamed of himself—George Pemberton certainly knew how to land an upper-cut without throwing a fist. The difficulty and importance of the evening came rushing back to surround Thomas as the playful moment slid away.

He scanned the ballroom once more.

Where was she?

He spied the hulking Samuel Pemberton speaking with whom he imagined was Lady Leveson-Gower—her snow-brilliant coiffure was a giveaway, and her costume suggested the title Ice Queen. Finally, his eyes alighted on the songbird. Abigail was standing alone in a corner wearing a blue-and-black feathered dress and a cobalt blue demi-mask that dropped down along her nose to a point. Her sharp little beak.

Thomas gathered up his courage and made his way towards her. She spied him well before he was near, but she didn't look away, only continued to watch him as he approached. Her little pink mouth was set, lips pinched tightly together.

The small orchestra had started up a quadrille, and dancers were finding their places on the floor.

"Miss Fernside," he said. "May I have this dance?"

She stared at him for an extended length of time.

"No." The word appeared to cost her.

"Miss Fernside," he started again.

Oh God, he couldn't do it here. Not in the ballroom with all these people eddying about them.

He could feel the tears start to well, and he tried to press the tide of emotion back down.

"May I have a word with you . . . alone?" he asked.

She appeared to contemplate this behind her beautiful hazel eyes, more green this evening than brown.

"Where?"

"Down the main staircase. There's a door on the right with

an acorn embossed into the panelling. A reception room. If you make your way there first, I will follow at a reasonable distance."

She said nothing, but she turned and made her way from the ballroom.

Time to be an adult, to do the difficult thing.

Thomas found her waiting for him in the reception room. A fire burned in the fireplace giving off a golden glow of light to complement the few candles burning in sconces on the walls. A small table, a few chairs, a rug, a bird. Thomas took stock of the room where his life would for all intents and purposes end.

"I just wanted to say," said Thomas. "That is, I wanted to extend . . ."

She waited with the same tense air she had held herself in the ballroom.

"I imagine your mother will be announcing your engagement to Mr. Pemberton in due course, and I just wanted to say that I wish you all the happiness in the world. You deserve . . . Abigail, you deserve the very best."

There. He had said it. He had done the grown-up thing. He hadn't maligned the oaf or questioned her choices or taken her by the shoulders and shaken the sense back into her. He was being fucking respectful, and he was destroying himself in the process.

"I know you don't think much of me right now," he said. "I have been cowardly and shameful and hurtful, and I can only hope that you can find it in your heart to forgive me. As a friend," he added. "In the future, you must know that I will always be there if you need anything at all. No questions asked. And I will behave as a perfect gentleman."

He took a step back as if to allow her room to think, room to forgive him. Her forgiveness was all he could expect. It would help him sleep at night.

What he did not understand was why Abigail was clenching her little hands into fists at her side not unlike George Pemberton. She then opened her mouth and let out an exasperated sound that he only hoped was not audible from outside the room. Before he could blink twice, the songbird had thrown herself furiously forward and toppled him to his back on the rug. She pummelled his chest with her tiny fists as the visible portion of her face flushed a lovely shade of pink.

Well, thought Thomas, *this is certainly another surprise.*

Fourteen

A Dance with a Stranger

Abigail looked absolutely furious. Blind with rage. A woman possessed. Lying on the rug beneath her, Thomas allowed the songbird to batter him with her little fists until she was good and tired. Then he took both her wrists firmly in his hands and tried to still her.

"Miss Fernside, I'm trying to be a gentleman here, but it is rather difficult when you are sat atop me."

She twisted and struggled in his grip. Sounds forced their way from her lips but no actual words. Finally, Thomas allowed her right hand to break free of his grip, and she proceeded to slap him quite soundly across the face. As he closed his eyes to receive another blow, she leaned down over him and pressed her lips to his in a kiss so violent and so angry it made his whole body come alive. His arms came around her as he attempted to soften the kiss, but she wouldn't allow it. Instead, she shifted her face to bite down on his ear in such a way that he thought she might have actually drawn blood. One of her hands fisted in his hair and pulled his head sideways. Her other hand ripped at his cravat to expose his neck.

Oh God, thought Thomas. *She's going to kill me. With her teeth!*

His erection didn't seem to mind.

Before she could bite down on him like the little vampire she was, he flipped her to the rug as she writhed and struggled angrily beneath him.

"Abigail," he said. "Abigail, you need to calm yourself."

She was looking at him through her blue feathered mask like a wild bird he had wrestled down from a tree. She didn't speak, but she stilled herself and reaching a hand down, began pulling up her skirt between them.

Holy hell.

They stared at each other through their masks for several seconds as she inched her skirt higher and higher. Thomas even shifted himself slightly to allow her to pull it all the way up to her waist. She was bare beneath him as their ribs expanded in tandem with the labour of their breaths. His heart was pounding so hard, he thought it might actually escape from his chest.

Fuck it, thought Thomas.

He didn't have the strength to resist her, and he certainly knew how to calm a raging female.

"Is this what you're looking for?" he said softly as he placed his hand to the curls between her legs.

She nodded. Still no words.

He used his entire hand, fingers flat together, to stroke down firmly over her mound until he slipped over the softer folds between her legs. Their eyes were locked. She only blinked once. And then he pulled his hand back up through those softer folds forcing them apart, opening her to him. Her mouth parted slightly, but she didn't shift her eyes from his. Down again with his hand. This time harder. And up—she let out a small gasp. Down again. This time, she spread her legs further apart as he pulled the flat of his hand with a steady pressure up over her sensitive bud.

"Ah!"

She tipped her head back, and he took the opportunity to kiss her neck, then lick up the length of her throat until he reached her mouth. He hovered his lips over hers as he rhythmically stroked his hand down and up, down and up between her legs. On each up-sweep, she lost a little more control, her breath came in small bursts into his mouth. She reached her lips towards his, but he kept his mouth just out of reach. He wanted her desperate—desperate as he himself felt.

She tried to clutch him to her, pull him closer, but again he held himself away, rubbing her firmly between her legs, taking a little more from her on each stroke. She seemed to calm beneath him for a time, then slowly tense again. He could feel her release coming in the quiver of her thighs. He could see it in the arch of her back as she tried her hardest to hold it from him. She finally gave in on a cry that he muffled with his mouth.

He kissed her then, as frantically as any man might kiss a woman who was about to slip from his grasp, and she responded. God, she responded. Her hands came up to tangle in his hair in a frenzied grappling as she plundered his mouth. It was an unforgiving kind of kiss—carnal and insistent. Thomas had never known anything quite like it.

As they kissed, he allowed her to shove him over onto the rug so that he was lying on his back. She threw a leg over his lap to straddle him, and kneeling up, she pressed herself, soft and bare, over his trouser-covered erection.

Good God.

Thomas closed his eyes to steady himself, but as he did, he could feel her tugging at the buttons of his falls. His eyes flew open, and he reached for her hands.

"Abigail."

Staring fiercely down at him through her feathered mask, she tugged her hands roughly from his, and putting them to the low neckline of her dress, slowly pulled it down to expose one small perfect breast. Thomas propped himself up on his hands until he was seated with his face to her chest.

"Abigail," he said again, but as he said it, one hand was sliding under her dress to stroke the back of her thigh, teasing its way up to find her hot and wet. He slipped his fingers along the petals of her flower, caressing her in soft tantalising sweeps that made her pant.

She pressed her breast roughly to his lips as she held him in place with her hands fisted in his hair. As he manoeuvred his tongue around her nipple and began to suck, he pressed two fingers gently up between her legs.

"Aah!"

She lifted herself slightly before pressing her sensitive flesh down along the protrusion of his cloth-covered erection. With his fingers inside her and her breast in his mouth, she continued to rock against him in a wild frenetic rhythm that he realised would soon unravel his own control. Little mewling sounds issued from her lips as she rode him, and when he placed the gentle pressure of his thumb near the entrance of her bottom, she came so hard that she collapsed on top of him, knocking him to his back. His fingers were still inside her as her chest expanded into his, breathing heavy. As he tried to remove his fingers, she whimpered and pressed herself down to take them back inside her, sliding slowly along his erection as she did so. The small gesture undid him. He wrapped his free arm around her, gripping her to him as he thrust up against her with a few short sharp movements until he was trembling. He rocked against her one last time, and his vision was obscured by a multitude of white sparks as he spilled his seed, warm and wet, into his trousers.

It was only when they heard voices outside the room that they managed to pull themselves apart. Breathing hard, Thomas quickly pulled down Abigail's skirt as she yanked up her own bodice. He took her arm to lift her to standing, but her legs gave way, and he had to wrap an arm around her to hold her up.

"All right?" he asked.

She nodded.

"We may not have much time before someone comes in," he said. "Hide behind the curtain so that no one sees you when I open the door. Wait for at least five minutes before venturing out after me."

His instructions seemed rather business-like given what had just occurred between them. She looked down at his trousers where a wet stain was spreading.

Hell.

He cast his eyes about the room before they landed on an arrangement of pamphlets laid out on a side table. Grabbing one to hold in front of his trousers, he opened his mouth to say something to her, but before he could speak, she said, "Go!"

The word was sharp and clipped.

"Abigail," he said softly.

"Go!" she urged once more.

It was not the kind of word he expected after what they had just done, and it made him feel confused and adrift. Clearly, she was still upset with him.

Abigail gestured to him, as if to wave him out of the room before she silently stepped behind the curtain. And then he was at the door, turning the knob, heading back out into the world in his red infantry jacket with the scent of her on his fingers and the taste of her in his mouth. Thomas felt as if he were dreaming—as if nothing was real and yet everything was significant.

Abigail's breath shuddered through her as she stood behind the curtain.

What had come over her?

Anger wasn't a sufficient word to describe it. She had been practically frothing at the mouth with frustration over him.

When he had asked to speak to her privately, she had thought . . . Oh, she was such a simple, hopeful girl . . . She had thought he would try to dissuade her from her imminent betrothal to Samuel Pemberton. She had imagined he might express some affection for her beyond friendship, beyond his inclination to slip a hand up her dress in a darkened hallway. His staid and polite and distant little speech added insult to all the injury he had caused her.

She would never have imagined that her anger could turn so amorous, that the only thing she wanted in this world was for him to touch her, to want her, to love her. Because she loved him. She knew that for a certainty now. The taste of him was liquid joy, the touch of his body a wonder. And when he shared himself with her as he had done that one night in her arms, she felt as if his words and his tears had stitched her soul to his. This was no passing fancy—it was an actual madness, a sickness from which she would never recover.

Behind the curtain, she removed her mask to wipe the tears from her eyes.

After she had managed to steady her breath and dry her tears (they kept coming, so it was not at all an easy task), she slipped gingerly from the reception room and made for the stairs. Reentering the ballroom was like stepping back out onto a stage—an entire cast of characters laughing and dancing and talking with the soft strains of violins in the background. This is what her life would be like married to Samuel Pemberton. It would be absolutely lovely, a beautiful masquerade. Abigail wondered how tired one would become if one was never able to remove the costume one was wearing, never able to truly live as oneself.

As the violins died out and silence began to settle around them, the sound of metal striking crystal rang out over the crowd.

Ding, ding, ding!

Everyone turned towards it. It was Lord Pemberton dressed all in storm grey, standing in front of the orchestra.

"If I might have your attention," he said. "I've been asked to convey a joyful piece of news. It is with great pleasure that I announce the betrothal of my cousin Mr. Samuel Pemberton to Miss Abigail Fernside." He raised his glass. "Congratulations to the wonderful couple!"

A murmur broke out among the crowd, and then some smattered clapping slowly turned into a ballroom full of applause. Samuel stepped up beside Abigail and placed a hand to her shoulder.

"I think your mother couldn't wait," he said.

"No," said Abigail miserably, "she never can."

The orchestra started up a waltz as they stood gazing out into the ballroom. Samuel and Abigail hadn't yet turned to look at each other.

"May I have this dance?" Samuel offered her his very large hand. When she hesitated, he said, "I do believe it's what is expected of us."

"Well then, we mustn't disappoint." She placed her hand in his.

As they stepped out onto the dance floor, she couldn't help but scan the room for Thomas, but he was nowhere to be found.

Samuel placed a warm hand to her waist, and she slid hers to his shoulder. As they stepped in time to the music, she couldn't help remembering the first time she had danced with Thomas. It had been a waltz just like this one, and she had stepped on his feet and stumbled. He had, of course, caught her up in his strong arms. She hadn't even known him then, but it had made her feel so safe. She had imagined a proper gentleman—an experienced man, a serious soldier—would have been put out by her clumsiness, but he had only laughed good naturedly. He had paused the dance to readjust their stance as the rest of the couples swirled around them.

"Follow my lead," Thomas had said, "and we'll count. One, two, three, one, two three . . ."

When they had established a rhythm, he had actually looked

into her eyes.

"Green," he said, "flecked with amber and brown. The colours of a forest."

"Excuse me?"

"Your eyes, Miss Fernside. A man could find shelter there in that forest."

She must have flushed crimson.

"Oh, come now," he said. "This can't be the first time a gentleman has commented upon your eyes."

It had taken her some time to form the words to respond.

"It is. So you'll forgive me if I'm suspicious of your motivations."

"Nothing suspicious," said the captain, laughing. "Flirting is one of my reflexes."

"Is it now?"

She felt him tighten his grip on her waist.

"Is it your first Season?" he asked.

"How did you guess?"

"Because you look as fresh and as pure as the driven snow."

Another blush.

"And you are clearly in need of some dancing lessons," he added, dropping his forehead down towards hers in a rather intimate gesture. "I do believe I could be of service in that regard."

"I'm afraid my mother is unlikely to hire a reflexively flirtatious officer as a dance instructor," said Abigail.

Thomas threw his head back and laughed.

"Touché. You're certainly sharper than a pile of driven snow."

The compliment pleased her, and she tried her best not to show it.

"All right," said the captain, his face gone serious. "No formal lessons then. But I should be quite humbly obliged if you would save me a dance at the next engagement. Not a stupid country dance, mind you, or a quadrille. Only a waltz will do. An informal dance lesson of sorts."

He gave her a boyish grin, but there was something behind it she couldn't quite put her finger on. As if he was holding his breath at the same time. She looked down at her dance card which was tied to her wrist with a white ribbon edged in gold. It's not as if it was anywhere near full or ever would be. She glanced back up into his handsome face.

"All right," she whispered. "I could do with the instruction."

"There we go," said the captain who seemed more than pleased. He proceeded to swing her around in a celebratory gesture that was completely out of step with the other dancers.

When the dance ended, she returned to Patience who was standing by the wall looking rather distracted.

"How do you know Captain Walpole?" asked Abigail.

"Oh, I don't," said Patience, looking across the room.

"Then . . . How? . . . Only, you just introduced us, and . . ."

Patience turned back to her friend, her face transforming with a worried-looking smile.

"Well, if you must know," said Patience, "earlier in the evening, I spent a bit of time yelling at a friend of his—it turns out that man is the Viscount Winter."

Abigail placed a shocked hand to her mouth.

"Don't say anything," said Patience. "I'm well aware of my own skills for self-sabotage. Anyway, a few minutes later, the captain approached us—fairly impertinent, if you ask me. I think he found my display amusing. Well! So I pretended to know him and offered you up as a ballroom sacrifice. Though

I daresay, it looks like the two of you hit it off quite well. He looked thoroughly enchanted to have you in his arms. And judging by the shade of pink that is spreading across your face right now, I do believe you may have been somewhat enchanted as well."

"He was kind," said Abigail.

Patience gave her an incredulous look. "I saw him quite literally sweep you off your feet."

As Abigail slid across the dance floor with Samuel Pemberton, her heart ached with the unfairness of it all.

"I can't bear to be the cause of your tears," said Samuel in his deep purr.

She had almost forgotten she was dancing with him, so lost had she been in the past.

"You're not." She forced a smile.

"Your eyes are sparkling. I think that I am."

Abigail took in a deep lungful of air. She had been forgetting to breathe.

"Abigail, I promise you, I will do my best. The situation isn't . . . ideal, but I will do my utmost to make you happy."

Why did he have to be so bloody honourable?

She half wished she could hate him so that she didn't have to hate herself so much.

"I'm sorry," she said. "It's all my fault. It was a foolish thing to do."

"I don't recall trying to fend off your advances," said Samuel, ducking his head down to hers. "We should try again."

"A kiss?" Abigail asked.

"More if you like. It may soothe your sorrow. You may even change your mind about how terrible this all is. We'll be married soon anyway." He paused, clearly thinking, trying to formulate his next sentence. "Abigail, I have the greatest respect for you, and I will devote myself to being your husband."

Looking into his big earnest eyes, she didn't doubt it. He would never work her up into a frustrated fury or weep onto her chest or have a trail of beautiful women in transparent dresses following him wherever he went. She had caught him young—without a past, without any experience, without any wounds to sully his perfect intentions.

"Thank you," she said.

And she did mean it. She *was* grateful. It could have been so much worse.

Thomas's boots hit the pavement in a strategic retreat. He knew what hateful congress was, but he had never before provoked it. Women usually bloody loved him!

Why couldn't Abigail just accept his respectful sentiments? Then he could go home and rest in the knowledge that he had left things between them on a positive note. He couldn't sleep if she hated him, and he was fairly certain that despite her . . . indulgences . . . with him tonight, she still detested him and the way that he was.

The way that he was—God, she didn't even know the half of it.

Thomas charged home where he changed his trousers before setting out into the night once more. He had removed his mask, but he was still wearing his red officer's jacket when he used the brass knocker to pound at William's door in the dead of night. He heard the baby start to cry. The voice of a child called out. Then a long pause. Thomas banged on the door once more until he heard a galumphing down steps, and finally, the door creaked open to reveal William, bleary-eyed and bare-chested.

"Thomas! What the hell are you doing here? You woke up the children."

Thomas pushed his way in.

"Where's Mary?"

"Calming the baby," said William impatiently.

They both lifted their eyes to the top of the staircase to watch as Mary made her way down in bare feet. She was wearing a green dressing gown over her nightdress, and the baby was cradled in her arms.

"Go back to bed," whispered William. "It's just Thomas."

"No," said Thomas, "I need her."

William gave him a hard look. "That's my wife."

"I need her *advice*," corrected Thomas. "I'm completely sober," he added, as if that might sweeten the pot.

"It's all right, William," said Mary. "Here, come into the parlour."

Once she had settled herself in a rocking chair with the baby, she said, "So what's the matter?"

Thomas couldn't sit. He was pacing to and fro.

"I did the difficult thing. I did the grown-up thing . . ."

"And?" asked Mary.

Thomas stopped pacing and fixed her with a look.

"She attacked me, Mary. She bloody well attacked me! She knocked me to the ground and battered me with her fists, pulled at my hair. She bit me!"

Mary and William exchanged an amused look.

"What exactly did you say to her?" asked Mary.

215

"I told you. I said the difficult thing. I congratulated her on her engagement and wished her well . . . as a friend. It practically killed me to say it."

"I see." Mary glanced down at the baby. "William, I think you need to knock some sense into your friend here since his lady clearly wasn't successful."

William was only too happy to oblige. He stepped up to Thomas and gave him a quick cuff up the side of the head.

"Ow! What's that for?"

"Thomas," said Mary, "Think. Why was she so angry? What might she have been expecting you to say instead? What is the *more* difficult thing?"

"What's more difficult than letting her go?" asked Thomas.

His mind whirred past the answer again and again as if it wasn't even an option. William and Mary stared him down.

"She despises me," said Thomas. "With good reason."

Neither William nor Mary said a word. They simply waited as Thomas's mind flailed and spun and tumbled past the answer again and again and again. In the end, it was almost as if he tripped over it accidentally, such was his own surprise to see it lying in his path.

"Oh fuck."

"I think he's got it now," said Mary, rising to her feet.

As she left the room, William wrapped a hand around the back of Thomas's neck and looked him in the eye.

"Don't you ever wake up my wife in the middle of the night again. She's tired enough as it is."

"Sorry," said Thomas. "I've been told I have a bad habit of making everything about me."

"Your lady told you this?"

Thomas nodded.

"I like her," said William. "I like her a lot."

Fifteen

They're Only Ribbons

"What a fabulous night," said Abigail's mother as they handed their coats to the footman. "Wasn't it, Horace?"

"Oh, ah, yes, thoroughly enjoyable," said Mr. Anderson. "Thoroughly." He looked at Abigail. "It's possible I said so earlier, but that is an absolutely marvellous costume, Abigail. Marvellous. You look like a New World songbird—perhaps a black-throated blue warbler or a honey creeper. Though the honey creeper has red legs, so you'd want to be wearing red stockings."

He laughed, and then realising that he should not be speaking of his stepdaughter's stockings, quickly straightened his face.

"Yes, well," said Abigail's mother. "The deed has been done. You're now officially betrothed. The ton will have to swallow its whispers."

As Mr. Anderson made his way up the main flight of stairs, Abigail's mother leaned in towards her.

"And it looks like your big slab of roast beef isn't too put out by the arrangement. He's been courting you for the last several days as if you had a choice in the matter." She laughed. "All's well that end's well."

Abigail had pulled off her mask in the carriage and was fiddling with it in her hands. She hadn't heard a word her mother had said. She was still thinking about the fact that she wasn't wearing red stockings . . . She wasn't wearing any stockings at all. She had exposed herself to a masked soldier, pressed herself down over his fingers, and ridden him as if the four horsemen of the apocalypse were bearing down on them. It had been so frantic and urgent, almost a fearful thing—like a raging fire licking its way up her body, burning its way into her very soul.

Now, she felt charred—the stinging pain of it did not want to recede. She was chafed and sore between her legs, and her face and lips were raw from the brush of Thomas's emerging stubble.

"Goodnight, Mother," said Abigail before putting a hand to the bannister and pulling herself up the stairs.

She cried herself to sleep that night, and when she dreamed, she was still crying in her bed, but Samuel was holding her in his massive arms. He stroked her hair down the length of her back in several long soothing sweeps and murmured softly into the side of her head about the wonderful life they would have together.

"Love will come," he murmured. "It's bound to come if we try our best."

He wiped the tears from her face as she hiccuped with

another sob.

A sound drew her gaze to the window within her dream. She pulled herself from the man in her bed, stepped to the window, and lifting it open, peered out into the night. Thomas was standing down in the street looking guilty. He had thrown a handful of pebbles at her window like a young boy might to get a girl's attention.

"I have twenty pounds in my pocket," he called up. "Do you want to try our luck at The Black Dagger?"

"Who is it?" said Samuel from behind her.

She ignored him.

"Will Penny be there?" asked Abigail.

She had a picture of the woman in her mind—all rounded breasts and curving hips.

Thomas shrugged.

"Maybe."

"Will she touch you?" asked Abigail as her chest tightened to restrict her next breath.

"She will if I ask her nicely," said Thomas with a boyish grin. "You can touch me too."

He winked up at her. The gesture was so casually dismissive in such an obliviously friendly way that Abigail felt it like a knife to the heart.

"Jump!" said Thomas, holding out his arms to her. "Don't forget you can fly!"

Abigail looked down at her body which was covered in blue-and-black feathers. She lifted one wing and then the other in confusion.

"Come back to bed," rumbled Samuel from behind her.

She turned her head to see her husband-to-be waiting for her on the bed without a stitch of clothing on him. His hard muscled body rested in contrast to the tender look in his eyes.

"I'll make it better," he said softly. "I promise."

Abigail woke with a choked sensation in her throat, her eyes puffy and sore from all the crying she had done the night before. She rolled over onto her back.

Had her . . . altercation with Thomas actually meant anything to him? He seemed to share himself around without a second thought.

Nothing serious, he would say. *Just a bit of fun. Just a bit of comfort.*

As far as Abigail was concerned, what had happened between them was neither fun nor comforting. If anything, it had been raw and desperate and painfully fleeting.

Was this how it was between him and his other women?

Abigail resigned herself to the knowledge that she was now one of many. She likely didn't even rank in comparison to the others—women like Penny, women like the vicar's beautiful wife. Both of them with bosoms and hips and full pouting lips that made Abigail feel as if she were simply a novel and amusing little distraction for him between his more serious . . . conquests? Was that the word she should use? Thomas didn't appear to conquer anyone. He was like a brightly coloured fishing lure bobbing on the surface of a lake, and it seemed to be none of his business if anyone was enticed close enough to be skewered through the cheek with a rather sharp hook.

Abigail heaved a sigh.

It wasn't an hour past breakfast when Samuel came calling. As he was ushered into the drawing room by a footman, Abigail's mother sprang to her feet and rushed over to take both his hands in hers.

"Oh, Mr. Pemberton, what a lovely surprise."

"You must call me Samuel," he purred.

Abigail's mother cast her a wide-eyed look.

"Sa-mu-el," she said, enunciating each and every syllable. "Do take a seat."

As he walked over to the settee, Abigail couldn't help but follow the lines of his thighs. The image of his naked body in her bed was still fresh in her mind. When he took his seat, his light grey breeches were pulled taut over his groin, and Abigail found she had to actually tear her eyes up to his face. When she did, he was already watching her, so he had definitely seen where her gaze had been caught.

Abigail felt her face heat which made everything so much worse.

"I was wondering if I might escort you outside for a walk in the park," said Samuel. His eyes didn't waver from hers.

"Of course. Of course," said her mother. "I can send Betsy along to make things proper."

"So?" asked Samuel with his eyes still fixed on Abigail's likely crimson complexion.

"So what?" said Abigail's mother.

"I'm asking Abigail if she'd like to come out for a promenade."

"She would love to," said her mother.

Abigail tried to wilfully cool her hot face.

"I would," she said.

They stepped out into the street and walked several blocks in silence with Betsy trailing a few paces behind.

"How are you feeling?" asked Samuel.

They turned a corner to see Hyde Park's wrought-iron gates which were swung open to reveal the verdant green lawn and sparkling green waters of the Serpentine.

"How do you mean?" asked Abigail.

"You seemed rather sad last night," said Samuel. "I imagine you feel trapped, and I would like to set your mind at ease."

"Why?" Abigail stopped suddenly and turned to him. "Why are you being so bloody nice?"

"Bloody?" said Samuel with an appreciative smile. "She's beautiful and talented, and she swears like a sailor."

Abigail had to fight back her own smile.

"I thought it might put you off me."

"Well, you thought wrong," said Samuel. "It only makes you more interesting."

He took her arm and led her into the park.

"I don't think it's so surprising that a man should want to be nice to his bride-to-be. I should like to lay out some options," he added.

"Options?"

"So that you don't feel . . . anxious."

"Oh."

"For one thing, I was thinking that we should not feel obliged to consummate our marriage on the wedding night. I mean, I would not be averse to such a thing. You are absolutely lovely as you know, but I shouldn't want you to feel pressed and then later resentful."

He placed his hand gently to hers where it rested on his arm. As he continued to speak, he rubbed his thumb across the back of her hand.

"I should want you to come to my bed willingly," he said, "which I don't doubt will happen in time as we grow closer. You can take all the time you need."

Abigail looked down to his large hand resting over hers. The soft stroke of his thumb was not unpleasant.

"In addition, moving out to my country home right away should be optional as well. We could stay in London for as long as you wish—a transition period, if you will."

"You would stay here . . . for me?" asked Abigail.

Her voice was very quiet. She was feeling altogether undeserving of his solicitousness.

"Abigail," he rumbled, his tone entirely earnest, "you should know that I will do absolutely anything for my wife and the future mother of my children."

Children!

That woke her up.

"Jump!" she imagined Thomas saying, arms outstretched.

Abigail sat at her dressing table in a pale pink blush of a dress as Arabella Pemberton stood behind her. Her new sister-in-law-to-be had somehow wriggled her way into the house, charmed her mother ("That is exactly how a young lady should comport herself"), and managed to dismiss Betsy so that they were now the only two people in the room.

Arabella was dressed for the evening in deep blue satin which matched her eyes. Her wheat-gold hair was pulled up in a series of swoops and swirls which boggled the mind. She reached down beside Abigail and picked up a hairbrush.

"This pink dress you're wearing is exactly the sort that would benefit from a good spritzing," she said.

"Excuse me?"

"Wetting your dress is all the fashion right now," said Arabella as if she were an older matron explaining a rather simple point of etiquette. "It's one way of emphasising your more feminine qualities. It's also a way of thumbing your nose at the morality brigade."

Arabella tugged the brush through Abigail's hair.

"Are you wearing a chemise?" she asked.

"Of course," said Abigail.

"I would take it off. A damp dress simply doesn't have the same effect if you're wearing layers."

Abigail pondered this, and as she did, she remembered Thomas's furious face when he had seen her in that peach silk at the modiste's.

Would he be there tonight?

Wearing a dress with the specific intention of provoking a man was not something she had ever done before. She hadn't thought she was that sort of woman. Then again, she hadn't thought she was the sort of woman to attack a man with her fists before exposing herself to him in the hopes of receiving his rough yet intimate attentions.

"The rumours were certainly hushed by your engagement announcement," said Arabella as she tugged at Abigail's hair with the brush. "I can't say I'm sorry you were caught in the act though. You're quite a fine catch for Samuel. He tends to have a gaggle of ridiculous women swarming around him, and in all honesty," she continued, leaning her head down beside Abigail's, "I was worried he may be led astray be someone older—you know, a lascivious widow in want of a pet."

Abigail looked up at Arabella in the mirror. The girl was truly something else, and it made her smile.

"The trouble with Samuel is that he doesn't know how to say no. But I do believe he likes you very much. He speaks quite highly of you."

Abigail opened her mouth to say something nice about

Samuel Pemberton since it seemed the appropriate thing to do at this point in the conversation, but Arabella ploughed on without a pause.

"Myself, I plan on kissing at least seven men before I marry, but I've learned from your mistake—no balconies at balls." She fixed Abigail with a mischievous look in the mirror. "I plan on getting away with it. To that end, I'm compiling a list of kissing locations that are more likely to go undetected."

"Oh, really?" said Abigail. "What have you come up with so far?"

"The back of a hack," said Arabella without hesitation, "is number one. He hops out in one location. I hop out in another. The perfect crime. Coming in a close second would be a linen cupboard. If you're found out, it will likely be a maid, and one could easily pay her off."

Abigail laughed. The girl really had thought this through.

Seeing that her audience was appreciating the exposition, Arabella continued.

"If we happen to be staying in the same house for an extended house party or some such, then the kitchen at night is a perfect location. The servants will be asleep, and no one who isn't a servant will be likely to venture in."

"Hah!" laughed Abigail. "Tell me, do you have a dark alley on your list?"

Arabella's eyes twinkled.

"Seems a bit grubby," she said. "But I like it." Then thinking, "How would I even manoeuvre us there when I have a maid following me about?"

"Ask her to hang back, so you can converse privately with the gentleman as you walk. Then march off ahead, and lose her in the busy shuffle of the street."

"Something tells me you've done this before," said Arabella with a dazzling smile. "I knew I would like you!"

The girl leaned forward and wrapped her arms around Abigail from behind. The gesture touched Abigail in an odd painful way. It was a moment between sisters, and the fact that she had never had anything similar with Harriet dug into her like a thorn. Abigail lifted her hands to hold Arabella's arms against her chest in a burst of protectiveness.

"Arabella," she said, "I know we're having fun with this list, but it is rather a dangerous thing to go kissing men willy-nilly. It could ruin your life."

Arabella looked up at her in the mirror.

"If I marry a man I've never even kissed," she said quite seriously, "my life may be ruined anyway."

There was nothing Abigail could say to that. She had uncharitably imagined the girl to be rather silly all told— frivolous, puerile, empty-headed. Arabella wasn't any of those things. Attempting to direct a situation in which you were expected to give up all but the most reactive type of agency demonstrated not only courage but intelligence.

Arabella loosed her embrace and reached down to Abigail's dressing table. She picked up the white ribbon that was sitting in its box with the dried rose.

"Is this one of the ribbons from your first Season?" she asked.

"Excuse me?" said Abigail.

"I already have several," said Arabella. "Why do the hostesses of these events insist on marking us out as being in our first Season? White ribbons to tie our dance cards to our wrists so that the gentlemen can know that we're the purest of the lot." Arabella grimaced in disgust. "I take my own ribbon now.

Can you guess what colour it is?

"Red!" declared Arabella with a grin. "Not that it dissuades the gentlemen. It seems red is as good as white as far as they're concerned." She giggled.

Abigail said nothing. She took the white ribbon edged in gold from Arabella's fingers. It was the ribbon that had tied her dance card to her wrist at the Crampton Ball in her first Season. It was the ribbon she had been wearing when Thomas had asked her to dance for the first time. If it wasn't, it bore a remarkable resemblance.

Abigail pulled the little white box towards her across the dressing table. Lifting the dry rose from its box, she turned it this way and that, sieving her memories like water through her fingers until she finally trapped the appropriate recollection like a gem in her hand. When it was fresh, the rose had been a pale blush pink. Betsy had taken it from an arrangement in the hallway and pinned it in her hair. She had been wearing it the second time she danced with Thomas which had been on a Wednesday at Almack's. He had made straight for her when she entered the hall, a pencil in his hand.

"Miss Fernside, I do believe we have a dancing lesson scheduled."

Blushing furiously, she had allowed him to lift her wrist in his hand as her dance card dangled from its white ribbon.

"Hold it there." He released her to take up the card and write his name upon it. Glancing up into her face with a mind-melting smile, he said, "The first waltz is mine."

She was frozen and couldn't respond. The attention from such an incredibly handsome and kind gentleman was altogether overwhelming, and she had the sudden urge to hide.

"I won't bite, Miss Fernside. Unless, of course, you want me to."

He punctuated this outrageous statement with a boyish wink which, looking back now, Abigail felt was altogether unfair of him. Her heart had leapt from her own chest and into his hand, and he had strolled away from her taking it with him, tossing it casually up into the air and catching it again like a boy with a ball.

. . . And yet he had kept the ribbon (it must have fallen from her wrist) and the rose as well (perhaps it had not been pinned securely). The man was a jumble of contradictions. They had danced together at least five times that Season, but by the end, he had clearly been avoiding her. She had imagined he had tired of the novelty since she was neither as beautiful nor as witty or worldly as the other women he seemed to find enticing.

What was it he'd said at Avery House? Waifs are off-limits?

"Abigail," said Arabella. "Abigail." She waved her hand in front of Abigail's face.

"I think," said Abigail quietly, "I think I shall bring my own ribbon tonight."

She lifted her left wrist and handed Arabella the white ribbon. The girl was positively scandalised with delight.

"Ooh! What sort of commentary are we making with this particular fashion choice? It's almost too clever. I'm thinking you're making a statement about purity and value: you may be a wanton in their eyes, but your soul is unblemished. You with your white ribbon, and me with my red—we're going to provoke quite a murmur. The kind of murmur that makes people think," said Arabella gleefully.

Good Lord, thought Abigail. *They're only ribbons.*

Sixteen

The More Difficult Thing

I f Thomas had any hope of doing 'the *more* difficult thing',
it was going to have to be in stages so as to give Abigail a
chance to think before she made any decision about how
her life would proceed. She wouldn't be married for another
few weeks yet. He still had time. It was important for her
and the oaf to be seen about town, so he was fairly certain
Mrs. Anderson would insist they both attend Almack's on
Wednesday.

Boots polished and coat brushed, he climbed up the stairs
to the assembly hall feeling as if he had a belt secured tightly
around his chest. He paused at the top of the stairs and took
a breath before turning his charm against the gorgon at the
gate. Lady Jersey, one of the six patronesses of the hall, stood
armed with her own charismatic smile as he approached.

"Lieutenant Colonel Walpole, how lovely to see you."

She eyed him up and down, and he only hoped he hadn't

tied his cravat with last Season's knot or worn the wrong type of boots. It had been over a decade since she had turned Lord Nelson away for wearing trousers instead of breeches, but the incident was still fresh in everyone's mind.

"You are looking as ravishing as ever." Thomas took her hand and bowed over it. "I imagine your dance card is already full."

"Not at all," said Lady Jersey on a titter. "Not at all, Lieutenant Colonel."

"May I?" He pulled a pencil from his jacket and proceeded to write his name on the card dangling from her wrist. "A shame all your waltzes have been taken," he said and was gratified to see her flush a soft shade of pink. That blush was his ticket inside.

When Thomas stepped into the hall, he spotted Abigail at once. She was standing with Arabella Pemberton among the throng.

What the hell was she wearing? How had she even made it past the gorgon in that dress?

As he stepped closer, his heart throbbing up into his ears, he couldn't quite take his eyes from her breasts. She was wearing a pale pink gown that clung to her as if it were damp. Her nipples looked as if they might pierce through the thin material at any moment. The dress clung to her hips, her sweet little belly. God, he couldn't even imagine what she looked like from behind.

As he came closer, he realised that, yes, the dress was indeed wet. Arabella Pemberton was talking excitedly into Abigail's ear, practically bouncing on the toes of her slippered feet. Out of the corner of his eye, he saw the oaf approaching through the crowd, and Thomas had the insane urge to punch the man across the jaw before throwing Abigail over his shoulder and carrying her off.

Arriving in front of her, he had to tear his eyes up the length of her body to her face which was . . . Did she look satisfied? Expectant?

"Miss Fernside, Miss Pemberton," he said, well aware that he had only a minute or so before the oaf would be on them.

"Lieutenant Colonel Walpole," said Abigail, "how nice to see you again."

He gave her a strained smile as the oaf closed in.

"Forgive my impertinence, but Lady Leveson-Gower has been asking after you. May I take you to her?"

He held his breath. She had kissed him a few days ago, but it had been more furious than affectionate.

"Of course," said Abigail, taking his arm. "Arabella, tell Samuel I'll be back soon for our dance."

As he led her away at a clip, he had the unfortunate impulse to speak his mind.

"What the hell are you wearing?" he whispered.

"It's the fashion," said Abigail calmly.

"I know it's the bloody fashion. Why are *you* wearing it?"

"I thought Samuel would like it," said Abigail as he tugged her around a large arrangement of cream and pink roses out of sight of the crowd. "And do you know what? He did. He liked it very much. In fact, I think he's going to try for another kiss tonight. Maybe more."

"You love him?" asked Thomas with some exasperation.

"I'm marrying him." Abigail kept her hazel eyes on his.

She was challenging him. Somehow, he approved. Thomas knew he was here to do things carefully. In stages. Step-by-step. Give her space to think. Instead, his instincts took over, and he pushed her gently up against the wall beside the roses, holding her in place with the length of his body.

"Do you know what I did when I left you in that reception room the other night?" he asked.

He could feel her ribs expand as she took a breath beneath him and let it shudder out through her lips.

Fuck. Her lips.

"I licked each and every one of my fingers until I had consumed every last drop of you," he said.

Her black pupils expanded into the forest of her eyes. After a few silent moments laden with the weight of unspoken words, she wriggled free of him and held up her left wrist.

"Are you going to ask me to dance?"

He looked down at her dance card, and that was when he noticed it. She was wearing the white ribbon he had sent her—the one he had secretly teased from her wrist after their first dance together. The gesture settled over him like a light snowfall—cool and fresh and bright. She was actually offering him an invitation, a small piece of hope.

Silently . . . reverently . . . he pulled the pencil from his pocket and attempted to write his name beside the second waltz of the night, the only waltz of hers that was free. His right hand held the pencil, but the tremor in his left hand had returned, and the dance card shook in his grip. Abigail put her hand over his to hold it steady. When he had finished writing his name, he glanced up into her eyes.

"Abigail, there is something I need to tell you."

"You can tell me while we dance."

"And after," said Thomas, "I want you to think very carefully about what I have said."

"I will." She looked up at him from under her lashes before

darting a quick look out past the arrangement of roses. "I had better get back."

As she made to slip past him, Thomas placed a hand to her upper arm, and she turned her face back to his.

"Don't kiss him again, Abigail. Not yet."

"All right. But I won't kiss you either. I'm engaged now."

The other two waltzes of the evening were taken by Abigail's husband-to-be, and Thomas tortured himself by watching the two of them dance. The oaf was handsome as all hell—he had to give him that. And he was certainly solicitous as far as Abigail was concerned.

"Time's running out," said a familiar deep voice—an irritating voice. Richard had sidled up beside him.

"Why aren't you dancing with your wife?" asked Thomas.

"She's sweet-talking the Earl of Pembroke for me. I need him onside for a vote coming up in the House." Richard nodded in Abigail and Samuel's direction. "Lady Leveson-Gower says they make a lovely couple. She also says you quite literally couldn't breathe when you witnessed the rumoured kiss. She's quite concerned that a terrible mistake has been made . . . on your part."

Thomas refused to look at his friend.

"I'm working on it," he said. "It's complicated."

As Thomas continued to watch Abigail dance, his conversation with Lady Leveson-Gower about a female composer named Jane Savage came back to him.

"Did she not continue to compose?"

"No. She married."

He hadn't thought anything of the exchange at the time, but he realised now that it had been a cautionary tale. Lady Leveson-Gower was both shrewd and farsighted.

"Do you love her?" Richard's words pierced through Thomas's thoughts.

"Jesus, Richard. What do you want me to say?"

"The truth. It's quite simple."

"It's not simple."

Thomas was having a hard time keeping his voice down, and a few heads turned their way. He grabbed the sleeve of Richard's jacket.

"Let me do this my way," he said. "She needs time to understand . . . I can't just . . . There are some important things she needs to know first."

"Ah," said Richard with some sense of comprehension.

He patted Thomas's hand where it rested on his sleeve. The gesture was as warm as it was reassuring, and Thomas had to fight to keep the tears at bay.

As the evening wore on, Thomas found it more and more difficult to refuse the glasses of champagne that were being offered around. Instead of drinking, however, he kept his eyes on Abigail who was proving remarkably popular in her new look—both with the ladies and with the gentlemen. After an age had passed, it was finally his turn to lead her out onto the dance floor.

"How is it Mr. Pemberton has not reserved *all* of your waltzes?" he asked as they arranged themselves in the familiar position—his hand to her perfect waist, her hand resting on his shoulder.

"Mother has trapped him," said Abigail with a quick smile. "She fancies him quite the slab of roast beef. Her words, not mine."

Despite the fraught nature of the evening, Thomas had to laugh. Abigail had that effect on him.

"Slab of roast beef. I haven't heard that one before." He turned his head to catch a glimpse of Mrs. Anderson dancing with the large and rather swoon-worthy Samuel Pemberton. "She's not wrong," he added.

Abigail lifted her eyebrows.

"That's quite the concession," she said as they glided over the floorboards.

"I can see why you kissed him," said Thomas.

All trace of humour vanished from Abigail's face as she registered his words.

"No, you can't," she whispered.

They continued to dance, and Thomas thought that perhaps she would not elaborate, but eventually, she spoke again.

"You can't possibly remember what it's like to have absolutely no experience, no foundation of knowledge, nothing with which to compare anything else."

Her words shocked him. It hadn't occurred to him to think about her choices in this way. He had simply assumed that she had some serious affection for the man.

"And how . . . ?"

God, could he ask it?

"How did the kiss compare?"

Apparently, he could.

They stepped their way through several bars of music before she answered. Her eyes never left his.

"It was the difference between drinking water and drinking champagne. No flavour, no bubbles, and no rising sense of intoxication."

"Ah." Thomas tightened his grip around her waist.

They stepped and turned in time with the music for several more beats before Abigail asked her question.

236

"And how do I compare?"

"To what?" Thomas didn't understand.

"Kissing-wise," said Abigail.

There was a note of anxiety in her tone that Thomas felt was completely unwarranted. But it was not as if he wanted to answer the question.

"I think we're putting the cart before the horse here," he said.

"What's the horse then?" asked Abigail.

"My past," said Thomas, "my present . . . who I am. Listen to me, Abigail. Do you remember when I spoke about my brother Alexander?"

"The one you terrorised with worms down his pants?"

"I didn't tell you everything," said Thomas.

She shifted her hand in his to grip him just a fraction tighter.

"The fact of the matter is that Alexander was—is—the Walpoles' real son."

Abigail stared at him with incomprehension.

"My last name is Walpole," he said, "but I'm not related to the Walpoles by blood. They took me in as an infant when my parents both passed away. My father was Mr. Walpole's land steward, and the two of them were by all accounts good friends."

It was the kind of personal history one didn't speak aloud, and he had never spoken it aloud before. For some reason, it felt good to do so, and he wondered at that fact: *why would bringing something shameful out in the open feel like such a relief?*

"The Walpoles did not have any children of their own at the time, and they raised me for the first few years quite as they would a child of their own blood. I was showered with attention and what I thought at the time was love. They even gave me their name, and I believed them to be my true parents. No one told me otherwise, although I daresay several of the servants must have known. Things changed, however, when Alexander was born."

"He was favoured," said Abigail.

"He was their son, and I was not," said Thomas. "I've been in disguise, you see. With the name Walpole, everyone assumes I'm related to the first prime minister in some way. It's the only reason I'm permitted entrance to places like Almack's."

"You didn't have to tell me . . ." started Abigail.

"No," said Thomas. "Given your family's position in society . . . Abigail, you're related to an earl for heaven's sake. You need to know that I'm no gentleman. Just the son of a steward who did not live long enough to give me his name. I have no inheritance, no land, and only an officer's income. You've seen where and how I live. I mean, I can afford better, but it still wouldn't be . . . That is, I have nothing of significance to offer you."

"Nothing of significance," repeated Abigail slowly.

The dance had come to an end, and Thomas found he could not relinquish his hold on her. As the remaining dancers stepped away, the two of them remained standing there, hands held tight as if they were about to start up again.

"There's something else," said Thomas eventually.

"What is it?" asked Abigail.

"Think upon what I've said for a few days, and then we'll speak again."

As Abigail released his hand and stepped away, Thomas felt himself thrown backwards into the past, tossed unwillingly like a rag doll into the midst of a scene he wished he could forget. In his mind, he was a young lad of sixteen once more, and his parents—the Walpoles—were staring at him in disappointment and horror. His brother Alexander was only eleven, slinking from the room with a smirk on his face.

"This is what we get for taking you in?!" yelled his father.

Alexander had seen him fumbling in the back shed with the gardener's son and had gleefully reported the incident to their parents, but Thomas didn't understand what his father was saying. What did he mean by "taking you in"?

"He shouldn't be in this house," said his mother quietly. "Alexander cannot think that we are tolerant of such things."

"Do you understand," said his father, lowering his voice to a near whisper, "that if it were anyone else who found you out, you would be reported to the nearest constable? Do you *want* to swing from the gallows? Do you have no sense of family? Do not think that you would be hanged alone—our name would hang with you."

"Why, Thomas?" asked his mother in her most beseeching tone. "Why? When we've given you everything!"

Since Alexander's birth, Thomas's parents had receded from his life, becoming more and more distant to him until one day, he had been reading a book of Greek myths and decided that they were, in fact, no longer truly parents. Instead, they were more like Greek gods sat up on a mountain somewhere, occasionally looking down on him with indifference.

Well, thought Thomas, *at least they're not indifferent today.*

His mother was in tears, and his father's face was red with fury. If it had been over some concern for him, it might have been love, but their only concern was for Alexander and for themselves.

That was the day he found out he wasn't theirs, that he was only a steward's son. That was also the day they sent him

239

from their home. They would pay for his schooling and set him up with a commission when he came of age, but he was not to set foot in their house ever again. While he had known in his heart that they didn't love him, it was still a bitter pill to swallow for a boy of sixteen as he set out into the world alone.

"The lieutenant colonel cuts rather a dashing figure," said Arabella when Abigail returned from her dance.

"What? Oh, yes," said Abigail distractedly.

"Is he the one you kissed in an alley?" asked Arabella in such a surreptitious tone that it took Abigail a few moments to register the remark.

When she did, her eyes flew wide open, and she grabbed the girl by the arm.

"That's a yes then," said Arabella excitedly. "Don't worry, I won't tell. We're kissing sisters."

"That's not a thing," said Abigail.

"All right, it's not a thing," agreed Arabella, "but the fact remains that I will keep your confidence. Samuel certainly doesn't need to hear about all the men you kissed before him."

All the men?

Abigail suddenly felt rather guilty in the light of Arabella's kept confidence. She tried to shake it off, but the feeling clung to her like a wet dress.

Which is completely unfair, she thought. *How many women has Samuel kissed? Or Thomas? Do they feel guilty?*

As Abigail took up her third and final waltz with Samuel, she couldn't help notice the difference between the way he and Thomas held her. Where Samuel's grip was warm and light (he was a perfect gentleman), Thomas held her with a strength and steadiness that suggested he was ready to catch her at the first stumble. Thomas's eyes actually followed her hand when she placed it in his as if the simple gesture were a thing to behold. Where Samuel looked down upon her in a friendly, considerate manner, Thomas held her gaze with an intensity and directness that made the entire room fall away.

"What are you thinking about?" asked Samuel as he spun her carefully about the room.

"Oh . . . Me? . . . I was just thinking about how different people can be," said Abigail.

"In what way?"

"With each other," she responded truthfully.

"Ah."

Despite the fact that they proceeded to dance in silence for some time, Abigail could practically hear the gears whirring inside Samuel's head. He didn't speak again for the remainder of the waltz.

The next morning after breakfast, Abigail found her mother embroidering in the drawing room with her sewing basket resting on the small table at her side.

"Mother," said Abigail, taking a hesitant seat opposite. "I'm wondering . . . that is . . . is it entirely necessary for me to marry Samuel Pemberton . . . socially speaking?"

"Of course it is," said her mother without looking up from her needlework. "And why wouldn't you want to? The man's a beefy angel."

241

This was technically true.

"It's just . . . well . . . I may have kissed him, but I don't actually love him."

"Well, then, you shouldn't have been caught kissing him, now should you? If you want to behave a certain way, you should at least do the rest of us the courtesy of not making a big show of it. Or is it the show that appeals to you, my dear? You do seem to love an audience."

Abigail was momentarily stung by her mother's words, but a sudden realisation stepped in to replace the pain. The words themselves betrayed the speaker. "Show"? "Audience"? They were strange words to use. Was her mother envious of her musical talents? Was this the reason for her barbed compliments, her lack of encouragement?

Abigail's mother squinted at her sampler as she pressed the needle through the cloth once more.

"It's possible I'm in need of a pair of spectacles," she said. Then looking up, "Abigail, do you think I'm getting old?"

Abigail felt the question as some sort of trap.

"I wear spectacles on occasion," said Abigail diplomatically, "and I'm only twenty-one."

"Too true," said her mother, smiling. "Too true."

She then placed her sampler in the basket beside her and shifted herself forward in her seat as she landed a pair of assessing eyes on her daughter.

"Abigail, I can't imagine what you are thinking, but stop thinking it right now. You will marry Samuel Pemberton. You will put these whispers to bed. And you will do it with a smile on your face. Do you hear me?"

Abigail didn't respond for several seconds, but she couldn't let the matter drop. It was too important.

"Would our social predicament . . ." began Abigail. "Could it be solved if I simply married *someone*, rather than Samuel Pemberton in particular?"

Her mother's eyebrows lifted.

"My dear," she said. "Who did you have in mind? One of the footmen? Mr. Banfield may have been interested after your musical performance at Lady Leveson-Gower's, but you did not exactly endear yourself to him that evening. And then you raced off to . . ."

She shook her head with disappointment, and Abigail was reminded of the way her mother had sniffed at her the following morning. She knew Abigail had been with a man.

"Your behaviour has not been ladylike," continued her mother. "Seriously, Abigail. Do you not have a thought for the rest of us? It's too late now. The die has been cast. You will be forgiven all your sins once you are seen to be firmly under the thumb of a respectable man. And that respectable man is Samuel Pemberton."

Abigail could feel her face heat. She wanted to flee the room, but she stood her ground.

"Do you think Lieutenant Colonel Walpole is a respectable man?" she asked, knowing full well that in asking the question, she was admitting not only to a dalliance with the soldier but also to her affection for him.

Her mother narrowed her eyes.

"Has he proposed?"

"Not as such," said Abigail quietly. She was feeling less sure of herself by the second. "He says there are a few things he would like to talk about."

Her mother huffed.

"Listen to me, Abigail. There's not a man alive who will

purchase a chicken when eggs are raining down on his head."

What?

"This is serious, my dear. Do not scupper your engagement with Samuel Pemberton. It will bring ruination down on you and your sister's family, not to mention me and Mr. Anderson. It's possible you have some fairytale dreams of being rescued by a soldier in a bright red jacket with a bayonet hanging from his belt, but men will treat you as they see you, and I'm afraid that based on your recent behaviour, they are likely to see you in a very poor light . . . Samuel Pemberton notwithstanding of course. That man's heart has somehow remained unstained by your antics."

Abigail realised in that moment that the support she was looking for would not be forthcoming. Why had she thought it might be? It was time to take a decision for herself.

Dear Thomas,

I know you said I must think carefully for a few days, but I don't need a few days. Your origins do not concern me. Earls and stewards and kings and paupers are all food for worms in the end. We are all equal in that regard.

You may have realised by now that I am no pauper. I have a tidy sum put by—a modest inheritance from my father. I do not mean to dangle this as an enticement. All I mean to say is that wealth and station are not the things I need from you.

When you say that you have nothing of significance to offer me, I disagree. I'm certain you can find something in your pockets that will tempt me. Try again.

Yours,

Abigail

Thomas read the letter at least fifteen times while Abigail's footman waited.

"Give me a moment," said Thomas to the footman.

He penned a quick note.

Dear Abigail,

I'd rather not tempt you with the contents of my pockets before you come to know me better. It wouldn't be fair. If we are to talk, it needs to be somewhere completely private with no possibility of eavesdroppers—I'm not saying your mother is an eavesdropper, but then again . . .

Let me know of a location that would suit you.

Yours,

Thomas

He sent off the note with the footman, and within an hour she was outside his door.

Alone.

Thomas looked down at her slight figure standing on the doorstep in a pale green muslin day dress. She tugged at the ribbons of her bonnet and lifted it from her head. Thomas peered past her, looking up and down the street.

"I took a hack," she said, pushing past him and stepping inside. "So? What is it I need to know?"

"Abigail."

His hands were sweaty, and he could feel the blood draining from his face.

"Abigail, I didn't expect you to show up like this."

"There's nowhere else to talk that wouldn't risk eavesdroppers," said Abigail. "Thomas, are you all right?"

"I think I just need to sit down."

Taking his arm, she led him to the parlour where they took seats opposite each other among the sparse furniture and the even sparser walls.

"The last time I was here, I held you in my arms as you wept," said Abigail softly as she looked down to the bonnet on her lap.

That brought the blood rushing back into Thomas's face. Why would she mention that now? He was ashamed enough of his behaviour as it was.

"You don't need to be drunk to tell me how you feel." She lifted her gaze from her lap to his eyes. "I will always keep it in confidence."

"Abigail."

"Yes."

"Abigail," he said again.

Good Lord, he was feeling quite dizzy. Thomas leaned his elbows to his knees and placed his palms together as if in prayer. He leaned his body forward in his seat so that he was looking at the ground. Breathing was becoming difficult.

"What is it?" asked Abigail, a sharp note of concern at the edge of each word.

"Abigail." He glanced up briefly to her then down to the floor once more. "I should very much like to ask you for your hand in marriage . . ."

Fuck. This was not the way to propose.

". . . but I'm not perfect," he said.

"No, you're not."

"I'm a coward," said Thomas, eyes still lowered.

"I wouldn't go that far," said Abigail gently.

"And I'm a rake . . ."

"Hmm." She wasn't disagreeing.

". . . I do not distinguish between men and women in that regard," said Thomas.

Lifting his eyes, he found hers to be exactly as he had feared they would be—startled and confused and grappling towards an alternate meaning behind his words that would be more appropriate and moral and natural.

Seventeen

A Talisman

A bigail tried to swallow but managed to choke on her own saliva which resulted in a fit of coughing that had Thomas rise from his chair in order to rub her gently on the back.

She knew that men sometimes . . . Well, she knew that they were sometimes tried and hanged for . . . She took a deep breath.

"Please don't say anything now," said Thomas. "I couldn't bear it if you did. Go home, think about it, and if in a few days, you still want to see the contents of my pockets . . . then you can send me a note. Otherwise, I wish you all the best, Abigail. I really do." His voice cracked when he spoke her name.

"Thomas." She stood from her chair.

"No, don't," he said quickly. "Not now."

His eyes were awash in unspilt tears as he took her by the elbow and led her to the door.

Out on the street, holding her bonnet by its ribbons, Abigail did not even consider waving down a hack. She looked back towards the black door that stood between her and the soldier who had laid himself bare in front of her. Then she turned and started slowly down the street. She walked for at least half an hour pondering Thomas's words.

If there had ever been a moment in her life when she felt naive and unworldly, then it was this one. Casting her mind back through all her time with Thomas, she tried to pick out the relevant clues. The way he had insisted Richard carry him over the threshold and the manner in which he had welcomed James's kiss on his mouth when he had arrived home—those moments stood out for her. She had often seen him teasing Patience's brother George, and now she wondered if it had been more of a flirtation. Thomas's open affection for his male friends was something of an anomaly among men in general and English men in particular.

And he had agreed with her mother's assessment of Samuel Pemberton as a slab of roast beef. This made her smile now again but for different reasons. Her smile twisted away as she wondered how he might . . . The thought gripped itself around her heart and wouldn't let go. She stopped and turned around in the street.

The brass knocker was cold in her hand as she lifted it, and it was some time before Thomas opened the door. His eyes were sunken and bloodshot.

"Don't," he said. "Not now. I couldn't bear it. Wait a few days."

"I only have a question," said Abigail shyly.

Thomas didn't say a word. Neither did he invite her in.

"Will I . . . ? That is, given that you . . . Will I be . . . enough?"

"Pardon?" said Thomas as confusion spread over his face.

She looked down to see his left hand trembling at his side.

"I know I can hardly compare with women like Penny and . . . and the vicar's wife," said Abigail. "That's for starters, but . . . will you not miss . . . ? That is, I feel I can't really compete with . . . with the likes of George Pemberton, if you see what I'm trying to say."

Thomas darted a glance up and then down the pavement before he spoke, and when he did his voice was a whisper.

"Are you saying you are worried I will want others?"

Abigail nodded.

For a moment, Thomas simply stared at her through his red-rimmed eyes. Then he stepped back to allow her in. She hesitantly stepped over the threshold.

"Did my confession not offend you?" he asked, incredulity lacing his voice.

This time it was Abigail's turn to stare.

"There is nothing about you that offends me."

"You seemed quite offended when you attacked me the other night."

"That was different," said Abigail.

A long pause as Thomas waited for her to continue.

"All right, fine. There *are* some things about you that offend me . . . like the fact that you aren't mine. You seem to belong to everybody—and now it appears you belong to twice as many people as I had previously thought."

It was a brave thing to say, and Abigail was momentarily proud of herself for saying it. Thomas remained silent, simply watching her, and she couldn't for the life of her work out what was going on behind his eyes.

"Say something!" said Abigail.

"Do you want to see what's in my pocket?"

Abigail gave him a look. "I'm not in the mood to play that pocket game again."

"No game," said Thomas as he reached into the breast pocket of his jacket.

He pulled forth a ribbon that at some point in time might have been white. It was so dirty, it looked like it had been lying in the street for a week. Abigail took it from his hand and examined it.

"Is this one of mine?"

"I was a bit of a ribbon thief last Season."

"Is this blood?" Abigail slid the ribbon through her fingers. It was stained in several places.

"I kept it with me as a sort of talisman when I was . . . abroad," he said.

"Why?"

"I told you once that in order to do what is necessary in battle, you need to believe that you are protecting something or rather *someone* who is worth the forfeit of your soul."

As the meaning of Thomas's words settled over her, Abigail wiped at a tear which was threatening to spill itself down her cheek. She couldn't quite believe what he was saying, and for a moment, she thought that he must mean something else, that she was crying for no reason.

"You're not in competition with anyone, Abigail. There's no comparison. There never was." He pressed his trembling hand to his leg and dropped his eyes to the floor. "I only hope I can be . . . the way I've lived my life . . . it doesn't exactly scream 'responsible husband material.'"

"Thomas."

Abigail's heart was aching with every pulse. Slowly, he lifted his gaze to hers.

"But I promise I will try my best, Abigail. Being with you . . . it makes me a better person, and I want to continue to be that better person."

She wiped furiously at both eyes, then summoned every shred of her own willpower to shove the ribbon back at him. He tried to reach for her arm, but she pulled it away.

"I have to go," she said.

Thomas stood at the open door holding the dirty ribbon in his hand as he watched Abigail practically fly down the street. She had managed to hail a hack before turning the corner, and after watching her green dress disappear into the carriage, he returned indoors.

What had just happened? Would she marry him?

He was still in shock over the fact that her only complaint was that she would not be able to compete with the likes of George Pemberton.

That did suggest she would marry him, didn't it?

It felt as if a breeze were riffling at the frayed edges of his heart, but Thomas refused to give in to the sensation. Instead, he set about splashing his face, combing his hair, and straightening his clothes. When she had left him after his confession, he had cried alone in his bed until his eyes were burning and he was choking on his own sobs. It felt as if he had lived an entire lifetime of despair in the hour that she had been gone. Then to hear her knock at the door! It had taken some time to gather himself into something remotely presentable.

A Talisman

There is nothing about you that offends me.

Abigail Fernside had surprised him one last time, and now he didn't know what to do with himself. So he simply sat down in a chair and stared out the window. He saw her, cheeks flushed pink, as she hesitantly descended Richard's staircase to greet him upon his arrival home. Knees together, head bowed down towards her shoes as she sat on a chair in the drawing room trying her best not to be noticed. Eyes bright, voice strong and ironic as she serenaded Patience and the dowager with her inane little tune. Her peach silk dress drifting over her breasts, holding her hips in place with a whisper of silk as she brought the entire world crashing down with her music. Soothing whispers as her tears fell into his hair, holding him close. Turning on him in the street, yelling at him and his self-centred manner. The frustrated rage with which she had thrown herself at him at the masquerade . . . and the exquisite taste of her mouth and her . . .

Thomas sat in that chair for an eternity and for no time at all, living inside his memories of her, trying his best not to think about what would or would not come next.

A sharp rapping sounded at the door, and his heart missed a beat. Thomas put his hands to the arms of the chair and attempted to stand, but he couldn't quite feel his legs, and it took him a rather long time to gain a solid footing. Another knock. When he finally opened the door, she was standing in front of him in her green muslin frock, her bonnet hanging from her hand by its ribbons.

"I'm no longer engaged to Samuel Pemberton," she said, "and I should very much like to kiss you."

A tear streaked down Thomas's face—he was paralysed with emotion. With a look of concern lacing her features, Abigail stepped inside. Reaching up, she wiped the tear from his face. Tenderly, she kissed the place on his cheek where the tear had been and then gently pressed her lips to his. Thomas found he couldn't respond—it was all too much. Abigail quietly took him by the hand and led him to his bed chamber. Throwing her bonnet to a chair, she sat him down on the bed and leaning into him, removed his jacket from his shoulders. Slowly, she undid his cravat which allowed his shirt to fall open at the front. Then she stood up and turned her back to him.

"I can't reach the laces," she said. "Could you?"

"Abigail," he whispered.

She turned her head to the side and spoke to him over her shoulder.

"You'll want your wife naked, I imagine, for the initial inspection."

Inspection?

The corners of Thomas's mouth curled up in a hesitant smile. He lifted his hands to the laces of her bodice, and when he had loosened them, she turned to him with one hand to her chest to hold up her dress. Slowly she lowered the bodice down to bare her sweet creamy breasts before allowing the dress to fall into a green puddle on the floor at her feet.

Stepping out of it, she stood naked between his knees as he sat at the edge of the bed.

Christ.

Thomas was used to taking charge of situations such as these, but this time his heart was rattling in his chest as his hands slid up her hips to her waist, then higher to hold one breast in each hand as he looked up into her hazel eyes.

"Too small?" she asked somewhat shyly.

"Pardon?"

"As far as the inspection goes, do you find my breasts to be too small?"

She was actually concerned.

Thomas slipped his hands behind her and pulled her to him. He planted a warm kiss on her belly.

"Never," he said, looking up into her face once more. "My wife is perfect."

He slid his hands down to her bottom and squeezed gently.

"And her arse rivals all others. Turn around."

She giggled as she obeyed him, and taking her hips firmly in his hands, Thomas pressed a kiss to each of her plump cheeks. Then he slipped the fingers of one hand between her legs as he wrapped his other arm around her waist to hold her in place.

"Ah!"

He kept up a rhythm between her legs, his fingers pressing and sweeping over her as she made tiny gasping sounds that drove him up into a heightened state of arousal. Not being able to resist, he kissed and bit at her bottom which sent her into a deep moan. Before she could find her release, he pulled her down to sit sideways across his lap.

To have her seated naked on his thighs seemed an altogether extravagant thing. He slid a hand up her back as she stroked the hair from his temples. He leaned in and pressed his face against her breast, closed his eyes, and inhaled the sweet scent of her.

"God, Abigail, it's almost too much . . . I need to taste you." He tumbled her to the bed.

Crawling up on top of her naked body, he bowed his head down to sip at her lips gently before plunging his tongue inside her mouth to take as much as he could. She was clutching at his shoulders, then his hair as she pulled him in hard for the fiercest kiss he had ever known. Eventually, he managed to tear himself away in order to kneel up and pull his shirt over his head. He was gratified to see her eyes dilate at the sight of his bare torso, and when she reached a hand up to trace the lines of his scars, he was momentarily undone by the tender gesture. She watched without blinking as he unbuttoned the fall of his trousers, and when his erection sprang free, a small sound of surprise fled her lips.

It was her first time, he reminded himself. He needed to be careful.

"Was that not what you were expecting?" he asked playfully.

She pressed herself up to seated and reached a tentative hand out to explore his member.

"Patience's drawings don't quite do it justice," she said with a small smile as her thumb circled the head of his shaft. "It's rather more alarming than I had anticipated."

"Patience's drawings?"

Abigail looked up at him with some embarrassment, so he was surprised by what she did next.

"One of her drawings shows a woman . . ." She shifted herself forward and leaned her face down to his member, "teasing a man with her tongue like so."

Thomas sucked in a breath as she licked him quite roughly from base to tip before experimentally taking him in her mouth.

"Well thank heaven for Patience," said Thomas with a laugh.

Abigail pulled her mouth from his erection with a slight popping sound and smiled up at him.

"Tell me how to do it properly."

"Not right now. I need to taste you again. All part of the

inspection," he added. "Lie down."

As she did so, he removed his trousers, and when he crawled on top of her, he could feel his erection sliding up against her pelvis. He gave her a quick hungry kiss on the lips that left her panting for more.

"Two perfect pink lips that have already been wrapped around my cock." He smiled. "They pass the inspection."

She groaned as he nuzzled his face into the side of her neck, licking and sucking at her until she was wriggling beneath him. He couldn't quite bring himself to pull away from her this time, so he spoke into her skin.

"One soft silky neck, vulnerable and exposed."

She giggled, and the vibration travelled through him, warming the hidden corners of his heart. Slipping himself down her body, he squeezed and lifted her breasts before taking one nipple gently between his teeth as he worked the other with his fingers.

"Aah!"

He replaced teeth with tongue, and then his entire mouth was over her breast, sucking at it hungrily as she grabbed him by the hair and bucked up against his face with a moan. His erection was paining him now, his entire body strung taut with the effort to maintain control.

"Bloody hell, Abigail—your nipples are going to make me spend before we've even started."

Her breath was coming hard, but she managed to respond.

"So they pass the inspection then?"

He laughed before sliding lower, dipping his tongue into her navel, and then lower still, stroking his fingers through the curls between her legs.

"Are you going to . . . ?"

"All part of the inspection," said Thomas, dropping his head between her thighs.

His fingers spread her open to him—gently, gently, until her bud of pleasure was completely exposed. It was swollen and glistening, and Thomas had to take a breath to steady himself. Slowly, he pressed a thumb up over it. Her response was immediate and rather violent—a quick thrash and a cry.

"Oh God!"

"Tell me if you want me to stop," said Thomas, glancing up her body to her face.

Several breaths, and then, "No, don't stop."

He bowed his head to the task, and as he held her parted with his fingers, he reached out his tongue and gave her a soft little lick upwards.

She groaned and clawed her fingers into the sheets.

The taste of her was doing a number on his restraint. He licked her again and again, drinking her up as she writhed and whimpered on the bed. It wasn't enough—he moved his tongue lower and pressed it inside her where she was sweet and dewy as his fingers stroked up and over her bud of pleasure. His erection was pressing down into the sheets, and he couldn't help thrusting along the bed as he swirled his tongue inside her.

Finally, as he felt her quivering and on the edge of losing control, he lifted his face and taking both her thighs in his hands, spread her wide.

"Abigail," he whispered.

"Yes. Please, Thomas. I want you inside me." She pulled him down on top of her.

She was wet and ready, and he slowly slipped himself in partway, pausing to give her time to get used to the feeling.

She gazed into his eyes expectantly, and he leaned down for another soft tumble of kisses.

"More," she gasped as her legs wrapped around his waist.

Thomas pressed himself all the way in until their bodies were flush against each other. She made a muffled sound in her throat as she clutched him to her. He lifted his head to take her in, to look into her green and gold and brown eyes. They were joined now, and it felt a sacred thing.

God, he had never . . .

This was not how it usually . . .

"Abigail, you are . . . I promise . . . I will care for and protect you for as long as I draw breath."

"And I will care for and protect *you* for as long as *I* draw breath. It's not only a soldier's prerogative."

He dipped his head for a gentle kiss, and when he lifted his face from hers, she pulled him back down for another. This one harder and more greedy.

"How does this feel?" he asked as he rocked himself back.

"Oh." She closed her eyes as he rocked forward once more. "Oh, yes . . . nice. You don't have to quite so careful," she added, lifting her hips to take him in deeper.

As she responded by clawing into his back and meeting each of his thrusts with uplifted hips, he gradually surrendered to his body's urge to take her in the most frantic, desperate way possible. In the end, they were sweaty and practically grappling with each other. Tumbling sideways onto the bed, she kept one leg up and over his as he pounded himself into her, revelling in the appreciative and rather animalistic sounds that were issuing from her sweet little mouth. When he sensed she was right at the precipice, he slipped a hand between them and allowed it to move over her little bud with the rhythm of each thrust. Soon she was screaming incoherently into his neck as a paroxysm rocked through her body.

Thomas was quick to pull himself from inside her, and sliding his erection up against her thigh in a few swift strokes, he spilled his seed onto her leg with a heavy groan.

"Christ, Abigail. I might not survive our marriage if it's going to be like this every time."

Her face was flushed, and she appeared to be struggling to form words.

"Thomas," she said quietly as she pulled him into an embrace. "Thomas."

Her tiny hand stroked up his bare back, and he slipped down her body to rest the side of his face against her heart, to listen to the sound of her life blood moving through her.

"I can feel your heart beating against my belly," she said. "Just like that night when I held you here in this bed."

"I'm so sorry about my behaviour that night." Thomas felt a fresh wave of mortification at the memory.

"Don't be," she said. "We were loosely bound until then. The way you shared yourself with me . . . each tear was like a stitch sewing our souls together. I knew when I left in the morning that it could never be undone. No matter our paths in life, I would feel your soul tugging at mine."

Abigail stroked his hair, and he inhaled the scent of her skin, all the while wondering what he could possibly have done in this life to deserve such a partner. As Thomas luxuriated beneath Abigail's caress, an unwanted thought intruded on the blissful moment: they would have to tell Mrs. Anderson that her daughter would not be marrying Samuel Pemberton.

Eighteen

A Wolf in the Dark

~⚬⚬⚬~

A bigail stepped down the street holding Thomas's arm with one hand and dangling her bonnet from the other. Trusting that he would guide her safely, she closed her eyes for several seconds as he led her along. The sun was warm on her face, and it felt a decadent thing to be happy under a blue sky.

When she had fled from Thomas's apartments earlier, she had made her way directly to George Pemberton's house where Samuel and Arabella were being hosted for the Season. It had been a thoroughly awkward affair. Ushered into the drawing room where the entire household was convened, Abigail had felt the eyes of all six people turn towards her. Patience's brother George, his mother the dowager Lady Pemberton, and his wife Sophie were looking at her expectantly. Not to mention little Grace who appeared only too thrilled to be a witness to whatever was going to happen next. Samuel and Arabella were seated with the family taking tea when she entered. The gentlemen stood first when she stepped into the room followed by the ladies with a clinking of cups being settled in saucers and a rustling of skirts.

"Abigail!" said Grace, her blonde ringlets wobbling slightly with the excitement in her voice.

Abigail forced a smile, but the anxiety must have shown on her face. Grace swivelled her head towards Samuel and then back.

"I apologise for interrupting your tea," said Abigail.

"Nonsense, my dear," said the dowager Lady Pemberton. "You're more than welcome to join us. You will, after all, soon be a member of the family, so there's no need to stand on ceremony."

Oh God.

She wanted to fold in on herself.

"Would it be possible . . . ? That is, I should like to have a private word with Samuel."

All eyes turned to the massive young man rubbing a hand over his short-cropped blonde hair.

"Let's give them the room," said George, reaching a hand out towards his sister Grace. She quickly grabbed a biscuit from the tea tray before allowing her brother to lead her away.

Abigail couldn't bear to look at Arabella as she filed by with the rest of the family, but the girl put a soft hand to Abigail's arm and gave it a comforting squeeze. The gesture provoked a rather alarming swell of emotion, and Abigail struggled to contain the tears that threatened to spill.

When they were finally alone, Samuel spoke first.

"We're different," he said, "around different people. That was something you mentioned last night, and I agree. *You're*

262

different around that officer—Lieutenant Colonel Walpole. I saw you dancing with him."

"Samuel . . ." began Abigail.

"You don't need to apologise," said Samuel, "for being in love. Has he proposed?"

Abigail thought of the dirty ribbon Thomas kept in a pocket that rested against his heart. She nodded, and Samuel gave her a soft smile.

"It would have been better than tolerable," said Samuel, "being married to you. I imagine it might even have been wonderful."

Abigail wiped a tear from her eye.

"It's been a privilege to come to know you," she said, "and I can never thank you enough for all that you have done and were willing to do for me. Not many men would have been as honourable."

"I didn't feel very honourable when I was looking at you in that wet pink dress last night," said Samuel with a crooked smile. "Marrying you didn't seem like such a chore at that particular moment."

Abigail felt a hot flush spread over her face, and Samuel laughed. The sound of his laughter vibrating up through his chest broke the wire of tension that was pulled taut inside her. Her entire body relaxed, and she let out a hiccup of laughter herself.

"The dress was your sister's idea."

"Ah," laughed Samuel. "It all makes sense now. I really do have to keep an eye on her, don't I?"

The list of kissing locations Arabella was in the process of compiling floated up into Abigail's mind.

"More than one eye, I should think," said Abigail.

"We would have had fun together." Samuel's face had turned serious.

He was probably right, but Abigail knew it would never have been enough.

"You deserve a proper marriage," she said, "one in which you will be cherished above all others."

Samuel stepped forward and taking her hand, lifted it to his lips.

"You deserve the same."

Abigail wondered briefly if she could ask the question that was plaguing her. Would she be overstepping if she did?

"What is it?" asked Samuel, peering down into her face.

"Could I . . . ? I mean, please say 'no' if this seems inappropriate to you . . . but if Arabella ever needs a chaperone or a host when she is in London . . . I would be happy to support her in any way that I can. I know you have family here, and there are plenty of female relatives to do the job . . . but if she ever needs a friend . . ."

Samuel's eyebrows drew together slightly.

"She sort of grows on you, doesn't she?" said Abigail. "She's grown on *me*."

A slow smile lit up his handsome face.

"Like algae in an ornamental pond," he said. "Bloody insistent and thoroughly ungovernable."

Abigail had to laugh.

"I don't think she would like that comparison."

"Too bad," said Samuel with a deep chuckle. "It fits."

Abigail was shaken from her reverie when Thomas tugged

her to the side of the pavement and pushed her up against a brick wall.

"We'll be in your mother's drawing room soon," he said. "I can't imagine she will wait patiently while I lick you from the base of your throat to your mouth, so I'd best do it now."

It was broad daylight. They weren't even hiding. Abigail's lips parted as she tipped her head back for him. His tongue was like warm velvet stroking up along her skin, and then he was plundering her mouth as his arms came around her, completely heedless of the passersby. A man whistled at them from atop a cart, and Thomas pulled himself from her to turn and wave with a smile on his face.

"She's my wife!" he yelled jovially.

The man gave another loud whistle and doffed his cap with a grin. Abigail hid a smile with her hand.

"I'm not your wife *yet*."

"Details, details," said Thomas, pulling her from the wall and continuing down the street.

They found Abigail's mother sewing in the drawing room. Mr. Anderson was also there. It appeared as if he had been leafing through a book of New World birds. They both looked up as Thomas and Abigail stepped into the room.

"What's this?" said Mr. Anderson, standing.

Thomas quickly pulled his hands out of his pockets and straightened his back.

"Mr. Anderson, is it?" he said, stepping forward to shake his hand. "And Mrs. Anderson. We've met before."

"Lieutenant Colonel Walpole." Abigail's mother glanced to her daughter. "Abigail, what have you done?"

Abigail dropped her gaze to the floor.

It was only a moment before she felt Thomas's hand envelop

her own as it lay dangling at her side. She managed to lift her head.

"I should like to ask for your daughter's hand in marriage." Thomas looked at Abigail as he continued to speak. "She is the light that keeps me from the rocks and the tether that guides my soul. It would be my life's great honour to care for her in a way only a husband can."

The way he was looking at her when he said it made that last line sound almost libidinous.

"Well!" said her mother. The word sounded furious and surprised and . . .

"I'm afraid she's spoken for," said Mr. Anderson, taking his seat and picking up his book. "You're rather too late. There's a Mr. Samuel Pemberton who will be marrying the little bird."

"I've . . ." started Abigail in a faltering tone. "We've . . . Samuel and I . . . we have decided against marrying."

"What?!" Abigail's mother fairly shrieked the word. "I knew you were self-centred, Abigail, but this is of another order. The shame of it! What am I to say the next time I see the Pembertons or the Cramptons, or for that matter, anyone in London?"

"You can say that she is happy," said Thomas, squeezing Abigail's hand. "You can say that she is loved." He paused, and when he continued, his voice had taken on an edge of hard menace. "What you will *not* say is that she is self-centred or shameful or in any way less than the perfect creature God has made her."

Abigail's mother quailed ever-so-slightly before setting her mouth into a hard line and looking Thomas in the eye.

"Do you own any property?" she asked.

"No." He looked at Abigail apologetically. "All I have is my officer's salary."

This time, it was Abigail's turn to squeeze Thomas's hand. Her mother fixed her with a look of disappointment, and Abigail stepped in even closer to Thomas.

Her stepfather put his book down once more.

"Are you saying you would prefer this man?" asked Mr. Anderson, looking Thomas up and down. "He only just now removed his hands from his pockets. Samuel Pemberton *never* stands with his hands in his pockets."

This appeared to be rather a sticking point of etiquette for her stepfather.

Thomas turned his eyes on Abigail.

"Pockets or no pockets, Abigail?" asked Thomas, which made her smile despite the tension of the situation.

"I should like to marry him, Mama. I love him."

Her mother huffed out an angry breath.

"Well, do what you will," she said, shaking her head. "It's not as if you've taken anyone else into consideration." She sat down and picked up her sampler as if the whole thing was beneath her. "Speaking of which, if you do go ahead with this, you will have to organise for the banns to be read for the next three weeks. I can't possibly face the reverend with this sort of news. How to explain that your previous banns are to be abandoned? The girl can't make up her mind. Good Lord . . . "

"Banns?" said Thomas. "Three weeks?"

"He's keen," said Mr. Anderson, opening up his book once more, "I'll give him that." Then glancing up, "You'll not be able to procure a special license unless you're a peer. Are you a peer, Lieutenant Colonel Walpole?"

"No," said Thomas thoughtfully, "but I always knew Richard

would be good for something one day."

Mr. Anderson closed his book once more with a small smack.

"All right then," he declared as if he had any say in the matter. "A songbird for the soldier. It does have a nice ring to it. Could be a poem . . . or a novel (not that I'd be caught dead reading one) . . . or—"

"—Yes," interrupted Thomas. He slid a comforting arm around Abigail's waist. "You are quite right, Mr. Anderson. It does have a nice ring to it."

Mr. Anderson smiled with satisfaction as his wife gave all her attention to her embroidery.

Thomas burst through the door of The Horse and Dolphin later that day.

"Best slip a flouncy apron over your head, Willy," he declared, "because you're going to want to make me a pot of tea when you hear what I have to say."

His friend grinned up at him from the bar, broad shoulders and muscled arms set to the delicate task of wiping a glass with a white cloth.

"Go on then," said William.

"I'm getting married!" Thomas threw his arms wide.

"The special lady who doesn't take any nonsense," laughed William. "And her name is . . . ?"

"Miss Abigail Fernside." Thomas pulled up a stool at the bar.

Saying her name was like speaking a prayer, and he was momentarily thrown emotionally off-balance. He glanced up to see if William had noticed, but William's eyes were on the glass in his hand.

"Richard's going to pester the Archbishop to perform the ceremony in a few days. I never realised it took three bloody weeks to read out the banns. How did you and Mary wait that long?"

"We didn't." William gave him a sly wink as he leaned forward over the bar.

"Being out and not having her with me . . . It feels as if I've left my arm at home," said Thomas.

"Hah!" laughed William.

"Have you ever met the Archbishop?" asked Thomas.

"What do you think?" William picked up another glass and gave it a rub with his cloth.

"I imagine he'll be all dressed up in a very pretty frock for the nuptials," said Thomas. "I should like you to come. You and Mary and the children. If the bishop's in a good mood, he may even let Johnny play with his hat."

"Are you serious?"

"About the Archbishop's hat?" asked Thomas.

"About inviting me to the wedding," said William with some irritation.

"Why wouldn't I be?"

"Who else will be there?" William put down the glass on the counter.

"Richard, Patience, the whole Winter family. The Pembertons . . . Abigail's family. Oh, also my many past lovers who will all likely be weeping big crocodile tears into enormous silk handkerchiefs."

"Don't fuck with me, Walpole. Are you joking, or are you serious?"

William's tone had taken on an edge, and Thomas realised that perhaps he had been too flippant with his invitation.

"I'm dead serious," he said, reaching for his friend's arm across the counter. "You and your family are invited to my wedding."

"With the Archbishop and a viscount and a baron and their respective families?" asked William incredulously.

"All my friends will be there," said Thomas. "I'll have an invitation sent over. Mary would like that, wouldn't she?"

William simply stared at him.

"Yes," he said eventually. "She would like that very much."

In Abigail's dream, there was a wolf howling in the dark as she spread her blue wings and flew over the city. Below her, she could see the silver moon like a shilling fallen in the Serpentine. It was full and bright, and she supposed it was the reason the wolf was howling.

Rat-a-tat-tat.

The sound was distracting, but she maintained her aerial course across the city, dipping and climbing as the cool night air ruffled the feathers of her wings.

Rat-a-tat.

She turned mid-flight to see where the sound might be coming from, but with her concentration broken, she began to fall through the sky. As she did, she casually wondered if the wolf were waiting for her down below.

When Abigail opened her eyes with a start, she found herself lying in bed. The familiar room was dark and quiet.

Tap-tap.

She lifted herself onto her elbows. The sound was coming from her window, and it was followed by the unmistakable howl of a wolf. Pulling back the covers, she stepped barefoot from the bed and padded over to the window. It took her some time to draw back the curtains and lift open the window. Thomas was standing on the pavement below waving up at her in the moonlight. With a tip of his head and a few hand gestures, he indicated to meet her around the back.

Abigail lit a lamp and crept down to the servant's entrance where she found Thomas waiting for her.

"I've been howling and tossing stones at your window for a good fifteen minutes."

"I was sleeping," said Abigail.

She couldn't quite believe he was there, and she imagined her smile was perhaps wider than was ladylike.

"Sleep with me," said Thomas.

The tone in his voice was almost pleading. He leaned his shoulder on the doorframe and dropped his head down towards hers.

"Little pig, little pig, let me come in." His lips quirked mischievously.

"So I'm a pig now, am I?" asked Abigail in amusement. "Is this because you're the wolf?"

"The big *bad* wolf." Thomas dropped his gaze down her body before throwing his head back and letting out another howl.

"Shhh! They'll hear you," whispered Abigail as she lifted her lantern and stepped aside to let him in.

She led him up the servants' stairs and then down the hallway towards her bed chamber. As she stepped down the darkened corridor, she threw a glance back towards Thomas and was surprised to see him following her on his hands and knees. The look in his eyes was altogether feral.

"What are you doing?" she whispered.

He growled rather menacingly which was silly and shouldn't have made her heart start to race . . . but it did. Little pigs, she suddenly remembered, generally didn't let wolves into the house. She picked up her pace—it felt like the best sort of game. She heard him growl and scamper after her in pursuit. Abigail wanted to shriek, but she kept as quiet as she could even when he caught her outside her bed chamber. He had her nightdress in his teeth and was pulling her towards him. She turned with her back to the door of her room as he growled deep and low before sniffing and snuffling his way under her dress. He was on his knees, biting and licking at her legs.

Oh God! She could hardly contain the sounds that were struggling up through her throat.

"Erp! Ah!"

She fumbled for the door handle, and they somehow tumbled inside and onto the floor.

"Thomas!" she scolded. "The lamp!"

He paused his pursuit to take the lamp from her and settle it safely on a table. Then he reached across to swing the door gently shut before turning on her once more with a growl. Taking both her legs, he pulled her towards him along the carpet so that her night dress slid up to her thighs. And then he was biting those thighs, sucking and licking at her until he had his face burrowed between her legs.

Good Lord, his mouth was a ravenous thing.

Abigail was swiftly losing all sense of propriety. She spread her legs wider which seemed to please him immensely. He placed a hand to each of her thighs to hold her legs firmly apart, and Abigail thrashed her head from side to side, whimpering as he sucked at her most sensitive place. Before she came apart completely, he lifted his head and slid up her body to ravish her mouth. Tasting herself on his lips hit Abigail with such erotic force that she lost all control, finding her release without any contact whatsoever between her legs. She gripped tightly at his hair as she panted her release into his mouth, and when she was finally calm, he rose up over her on his knees and undid his trousers to allow his member to fall free.

Abigail actually licked her lips.

"If I do anything you don't like," said Thomas. "I need you to tell me."

She nodded.

"Say you will," said Thomas sternly.

"I will." Abigail gazed up into his hungry eyes from her position on the carpet. "Promise."

Her breath was still coming hard as he took her firmly by the hips and flipped her over onto her stomach. She was aching to have him slide inside her, but he made her wait. Pressing her night dress up to her waist, he leaned forward and gently bit her on the bottom.

"Ah!"

Then slipping his body over hers, he nestled his member between her legs as he gripped the back of her neck between his teeth. The effect was altogether animal. He growled once more, teeth holding her in place as he pressed his hard cock firmly up inside her.

Oh dear Lord, she was going to come again.

It only took a few rough thrusts with his teeth pressing into her neck to send her up and over the crest of an enormous wave. Abigail placed the back of her hand to her mouth and bit down to try and muffle her own cry. He continued to thrust inside her, gentler now, and his mouth came down beside her ear. She could hear his laboured breath and wondered that she could have such an effect on such a man.

Gathering some modicum of control, he said, "I'm going to need your little titties out in the open, my love."

Abigail flipped onto her back beneath him and with his help, wriggled her night dress up and over her head.

"Lord, have mercy," whispered Thomas. "You are so incredibly gorgeous it makes me want to weep."

Abigail looked down to her breasts which she still considered to be quite small, a fact he didn't seem to mind in the slightest. She experimentally took one of her own nipples between thumb and forefinger, and as she did so, she could hear him draw in a sharp breath.

Looking up at him, she whispered, "You're wearing too many clothes yourself. I should like to have your titties out in the open too."

Thomas lifted his eyebrows and grinned appreciatively down at her before snuffling his way into the side of her neck and then taking her mouth in a kiss that was so unashamedly carnal Abigail found her legs spreading wide once more, seemingly of their own accord.

Reluctantly, Thomas lifted himself to kneel over her. She watched him shed his clothing as if it were a show. First the cravat was pulled free in one long sweep to allow his shirt to fall open. Abigail sat up and tugged his shirt from his trousers before he pulled it up over his head. His torso was beautiful, achingly so. The scars of battle criss-crossed his chest, and a smattering of dark hair narrowed and drew the eyes down towards his glistening erection that sprang free of his open trousers. She pulled roughly down on his trousers, and he managed to kick himself free.

"Come on," he said. "We're going to need the bed for this."

She rolled over and made to rise, but he was already lifting her naked body up into his arms. A vision of how they must look together settled over Abigail—his muscled arms with tendons strung taut cradling her against his naked chest as he walked to the bed. He sat down on the side of the bed and seated her on his lap. She stroked a lock of hair out of his face.

"Straddle my lap," he said. "Come up onto your knees."

She did as he commanded, feeling the coarse hair of his thighs against her skin. The temptation was to settle over his erection and press herself down, but as she attempted to do so, he held her up with his hands at her ribs.

"Not yet," he said. "I want this to last."

Lifting herself up slightly, her breasts came to his face, and his tongue darted out to taste one nipple as he stroked her other breast. She pressed herself to his mouth and threw back her head. The sensation was needle sharp, and it darted down between her legs. Spread apart as they were over his lap, Abigail felt an agonising emptiness, a need to be filled. Slowly his fingers came around the back of her thigh to stroke tantalisingly between her legs. This only served to heighten the urgency of her want. She reached down to close her fingers around his erection and angle it inside her.

"Wait," he said, pulling his face from her breasts.

He lifted her to the bed and then shifted himself to lie down with his head on her pillow.

"Straddle me again."

As Abigail crawled on top of him, he pulled her higher.

"Not my cock," he said. "I want you to straddle my face. The wolf is still thirsty.""

His voice was hoarse with wanting, and though he tried to smile, she could see that he was a little too far gone for jokes. The ache between Abigail's legs was now a persistent thing, and her body was practically trembling as she knelt over his face and put her hands to the top edge of the headboard.

He grabbed her by the hips and pulled her down onto his mouth. It was so warm, and his tongue was moving in such a way . . . Abigail could hardly control herself as she squirmed on top of him. And then she could feel his fingers (both hands!) creeping their way behind her thighs and probing her wet soft regions like an octopus crawled up from the deep. She was gripping the top of the headboard, her breasts pressed up against the cool wood. With his fingers doing God knows what and his tongue working her bud into a swollen fever, Abigail whimpered uncontrollably as her climax began to take hold. He continued to mercilessly tug at her with his lips until she screamed so loudly, anyone passing by on the street would have heard and glanced up to her window.

Thomas swiftly tumbled her to the bed, pulled her down beside him, and placed a gentle palm between her legs.

"All right?" he asked.

She nodded quietly, chest heaving. As he began to remove his hand, she quickly placed her own over his to hold it in place.

"Just a moment more," she said. "It's soothing."

"I should like nothing more than to soothe you," he smiled.

A knock at the door startled them to seated. Abigail shot from the bed and grabbing a dressing gown from a chair, wrapped it quickly around herself. She tried to quiet her breathing as she placed a hand to the door knob and partially

276

opened the door.

Mr. Anderson stood before her in an open dressing gown over a very long nightshirt with a white nightcap flopping sideways on his head and a candle in his hand. He looked as if he had just stepped out of a children's nursery rhyme.

"There was a strange sound. Your mother thought there might be an intruder and asked me to check on you."

"I think it came from the street," said Abigail, trying to sound groggy.

She pretended to stifle a yawn.

"That's the most likely thing," said Mr. Anderson. "It's what I told your mother, but you know how she is. I'll take a quick tour of the ground floor to set her mind to rest."

"That's so good of you. Thank you."

By the time Abigail had the door entirely shut, Thomas was standing behind her, drawing the dressing gown down from her shoulders, kissing and biting at the side of her neck, then pushing her gently up against the door with his hard naked body.

"You're going to have to be very quiet now, my little bird," he whispered, adjusting his position to slowly press his hot erection up inside her.

He stretched and filled her in the most sensual way, and Abigail instinctively pressed her bottom into his pelvis to take in as much of him as she could.

Oh God.

His arm wrapped around beneath her breasts, and he held her to him. Abigail's nether regions were now so swollen, every sensation was heightened to an exquisite peak of near madness. She thought she might lose her mind. There was no way she would be able to maintain any control over the sounds that she made . . . but she certainly didn't want him to stop. The feel of him inside her was unlike anything else.

Thomas rocked back and gave a hard thrust up into her which blurred her vision and sent all coherent thought into retreat. Abigail revelled in the strength of him as he held her in place. His breath was hot on her ear as he spoke.

"We'd best make this quick, my darling. Wee Willie Winkie will be back with his candle in a trice, no doubt."

"Hah!" Abigail found the laughter simply flew from her lips.

"Shhh!" said Thomas as he pulled back and took another long firm stroke inside her. And then another. "Do you not know the nursery rhyme? If we're not all in bed by ten o'clock, Willie Winkie's going to come and read to us about New World birds until we fall asleep."

Abigail laughed again, but the laughter turned to small rhythmic panting cries as Thomas quickened the pace of his love-making. She could feel him quivering up against her, and the knowledge of his heightened arousal was enough to tip her over the edge and into oblivion. She leaned forward with the side of her face pressed hard up against the door as her mind splintered on a loud moan.

Thomas immediately withdrew from her body with a growl and spent himself in warm pulsing waves over her buttocks. He then quickly crouched to the floor to pick up her dressing gown and used it to wipe her clean. She turned and watched the beautiful lines of his body as he walked to the wash basin to rinse out the corner of the dressing gown. He then hung it over a chair and looked at her.

"Come sleep with me." He stepped to the bed and reached an arm out to her.

She came to him then, naked and flushed. Standing beside

the bed, he wrapped her in a strong embrace and kissed the top of her head.

"Jesus, Abigail. I can't be without you. I know the wedding's not for a few days, but I will come and howl at your window every night until then . . . And if all you want to do is sleep, I'll hold you fast and count my blessings."

Then slipping down her body, he dropped to his knees in front of her with his arms wrapped loosely around her legs. When he looked up into her face, she was startled to see tears in his eyes.

"I love you, Abigail, and it frightens me half to death because you are the greatest responsibility and blessing of my life. Know that you have my heart in its entirety . . . You had my soul from the very first dance."

Abigail had to wipe a tear from her eye. She then reached down and pulled him up by the arm. Smiling through her tears she placed two hands to his chest and shoved him playfully backwards onto the bed before climbing her naked body on top of his.

"My wife likes it a bit rough, I see," said Thomas with a grin.

"She likes it when you bite the back of her neck," said Abigail, sitting herself astride him and placing one hand to his chest.

"Oho!"

A sharp knock froze them in place.

"I think," said Thomas, sitting up and lifting her from him, "that we're going to have to set Willie Winkie straight about a few things."

He stood stark naked from the bed and walked to the door. Abigail clutched the coverlet to her breast as she placed one hand over her mouth in shocked anticipation. Thomas turned the knob and swung the door wide open to see Mr. Anderson in his floppy night cap poised with his hand about to rap once more.

"We know it's past ten o'clock," said Thomas, "and we're all in our beds, so I suggest you get some shut-eye yourself."

Mr. Anderson's mouth opened, but no sound came out as his eyes darted down the length of Thomas's body.

"Sleep well," added Thomas, "and we'll see you for breakfast in the morning."

Mr. Anderson's voice finally came to him.

"Right," he said. "Breakfast."

Giving him a cheery wave, Thomas slowly closed the door. Abigail idly wondered what her mother would say in the morning and was startled to realise that she didn't particularly care.

"You'll stay for breakfast?" she asked with a smile.

"Well, I have to now, or else I risk Willie Winkie calling me a liar."

Abigail laughed as he tumbled her onto her back. After a small grope and a tussle and several long sultry kisses, Abigail settled herself onto her stomach with her lips to her husband's bare shoulder and her arm thrown over his chest. Drifting off to sleep had never felt more luxurious. That night, she dreamed that Thomas was waiting for her in the street outside her window.

"Jump!" he said, reaching his hands out to her. "And don't forget you can fly!"

Nineteen

Floating Away

⚬~⚬

"I thought you said this was going to be at a church with the Archbishop," said William.

It was out of step with proper etiquette, but Thomas had made a point of being at the front door to the Winter residence when the Robins family arrived for the wedding. He knew what it was like to feel out of place, and he wanted them to feel completely welcome.

"Turns out I don't know much about special licenses," said Thomas with a shrug. "Apparently, His Grace the Archbishop won't sully his hands with anything so common as a wedding. He's probably smack dab in the midst of saving souls right now—has the Devil at the point of a sword no doubt."

William laughed, and Mary couldn't help but smile.

"We only have a regular member of the clergy present—Reverend Stanhope," said Thomas, shaking his head while affecting disappointment. Then to little Johnny, "I know I said you could play with the Archbishop's hat, but you'll have to make do with mine instead."

"Yes, Sir," said Johnny quite seriously.

"Where's the baby?" asked Thomas.

"I'll not bring a squealing baby to a wedding at a viscount's house," said Mary, her tone dripping with incredulity. "She's with my sister."

"Come on then." Thomas placed an arm around William and led him and his family to the staircase. "The guests are all milling about in the ballroom. I'll introduce you."

William spared a glance at his wife who was looking at him with an absolutely terrified expression while holding Johnny's hand tightly in hers.

"They won't bite," said Thomas to Mary in his gentlest tone. "They're my friends for a reason."

When he ushered them into the ballroom, Patience and Richard approached immediately for introductions, and Patience managed to set Mary at ease by simply being herself. Taking Mary's hand, she led her away to make even more introductions, and Mary only cast William the one nervous glance backwards as she left them.

"Patience's sister Grace will entertain Johnny," said Richard. "She has a dog named Potato he will no doubt find amusing."

William gave him a grateful smile, and Richard excused himself to go and find Grace.

A swift movement at the edges of the ballroom caught Thomas's eye, and when he looked over, it was to see George—Lord—Pemberton approaching them at a clip.

"Walpole!" said the baron as he stepped up to the two men and clapped Thomas on the back in an uncharacteristic gesture of good humour. "You didn't say you were inviting celebrities. Can I have an introduction?"

"Lord Pemberton," said Thomas, "this is—"

"—Mr. William Robins!" said George, reaching out his hand. "I know, I know. It's an honour to meet you, Sir."

George had William's hand in both of his and didn't appear to want to let go.

"I've been to every single one of your matches," he said. "You're a legend."

"I wouldn't go that far," said William. "I'm retired now."

George shook his head and reluctantly released William's hand.

"Do you ever . . . box just for fun?" asked George, reaching a hand up through his sandy hair and standing it on end. "A friendly match with no stakes?"

William's mouth curled up into a smile.

"Did you have something in mind?"

"How would you like to punch a baron in the face?" asked George with a grin. "I promise, I'm a very good loser."

Thomas left the two of them to work it out as he stepped from the ballroom and into the hall.

Where was Abigail?

As he walked down the hall, Arabella Pemberton and Abigail's sister Harriet appeared from around a corner. Harriet was the picture of feminine perfection—auburn hair and blue-green eyes and a figure so bountiful, it looked as if she might spill out of her dress at any moment. These were simply facts in Thomas's eyes—nothing that stirred even the vaguest urge or attraction within him. He wondered at that: how could one woman have stitched her own soul to his in such a way that he had not a thought for anyone else?

"Lieutenant Colonel Walpole," said Arabella. "You look

quite fine in uniform—as usual."

The girl was always so forward. He liked it.

"She's almost ready," continued Arabella.

"And she looks a dream," said Harriet. "You're a very lucky man."

"I know." Thomas attempted to swallow past the lump in his throat.

As Arabella continued on to the ballroom in order to inform everyone to take their seats, Harriet put a hand to Thomas's sleeve.

"Don't be too bothered about Mother," said Harriet. "She's sulking, but at least she's here. Abigail and I . . . With the mother that we have . . . it's not always been easy."

"I'm aware."

"But I do love my sister," said Harriet. "She is—"

"—extraordinary," said Thomas, darting his gaze down the hall to where she might appear from around the corner. "She is extraordinary."

Harriet's face lit in agreement.

"I'm glad you know it, Lieutenant Colonel Walpole."

"Thomas. Call me Thomas."

Harriet smiled and patted him on the arm before leaving to find her own seat in the ballroom. Standing in the hallway, Thomas tried to stand up a little straighter. He brushed at one sleeve with his hand, then touched his hair as if he might find it in place. At least it wasn't standing completely on end like George Pemberton's. He then walked around the corner with his heart skipping in his chest.

Abigail opened the door to her changing room just as he raised his hand to knock.

"Thomas!"

He was nearly knocked backwards at the sight of her and couldn't properly form any words for a good few seconds. She was wearing a red dress of thin silk that clung to her bosom like a second skin. It was the kind of fabric that liked to find some purchase, so her skirt, rather than flowing outwards, hugged her hips and thighs as it dropped down towards the floor. As far as dresses went, it looked almost weightless.

"Arabella managed to convince me it was the appropriate colour for a wedding."

Thomas stepped up to her and placed a hand to her silky waist, then allowed that hand to slide over her bottom.

"Abigail, what is this?"

"You don't like it," she said.

Thomas swore under his breath and then started to tug at the fabric at her bottom, bunching it up in his hands until he had pulled her dress up as far as her thighs. She leaned into him as he did so, her breath coming faster.

"I bloody well like it," said Thomas. "But I'm going to need to have it off within minutes of the ceremony. Make whatever excuse you like, and I'll meet you here when all is said and done."

"It's our wedding, Thomas." Abigail kissed his jaw. "We can't just disappear."

"I'm afraid it won't take long." Thomas pulled her dress up a little higher and slid his fingers between her legs.

"Ah."

"It's going to be rough, and it's going to be quick," he said hoarsely. "I won't survive waiting the rest of the day."

Abigail's eyes were starting to glaze over as he worked his fingers between her legs, but she managed to respond coherently.

"Well, when you put it like that, how can I complain?"

Abigail tried to compose her face into some version of solemnity as she walked down the aisle, but she just couldn't do it. Her joy was a fluttery thing. It had lifted up the corners of her mouth and wouldn't let them drop. Thomas was not the kind of man who waited patiently for his bride to be brought to him. Instead, he had taken her hand and was escorting her down the aisle himself, his red jacket a pair for her red dress.

All eyes were on them—the Winters and the Pembertons alike, not to mention the Robins family as well as her own. Arabella was there with her brother Samuel who had turned his beefy and angelic self in his chair to watch the couple approach. Abigail wondered what Samuel might be like given more time and more experience. His heart was so soft, and she hoped that no one would ever take advantage of that fact. As she passed by Grace and Johnny, Abigail gave the boy a wink which was received with a bounce in his chair and a wink of his own. He was a bit of a rascal, that one, and she thought that maybe one day she wouldn't particularly mind having a little scamp of her own. This made her glance over and up at Thomas. Any child of his would be a rascal for sure. She giggled, and Thomas gave her his best foreboding frown which only made her giggle more.

Reverend Stanhope was waiting for them at the top of the aisle. His features were sharp, but his face was kind, and he received them with a big smile.

"The soldier and his bride," he whispered. "Matching ensembles as well."

Abigail's entire body was shimmering with the excitement of the moment, and she could barely comprehend the words the reverend spoke as he began the ceremony. It was only because Thomas squeezed her hand and tossed her a rather ravenous glance that she managed to catch the words, ". . . to satisfy men's carnal lusts and appetites, like brute beasts that have no understanding . . ."

If she was going by the look on Thomas's face, she would have understood that to be one of the prescriptions *for* marriage rather than a warning. Shifting his hand in hers, he slid his thumb up to stroke gently over the pulse at her wrist which sent a tingle travelling all the way down to her toes.

By the time they were facing each other, his right hand clasped with hers, Thomas's face was as solemn as she had ever seen it. He kept his gaze fixed with hers for the duration of their vows, and when Reverend Stanhope said the words, "forsaking all other," tears welled in his eyes. He mouthed the words, "I love you," and Abigail had to choke back a joyful sob.

By the time the ring had been placed on her finger and they had been kneeling for quite some time with the reverend still talking . . . and blessing . . . and praying, Thomas lifted his head and caught her eye. The Reverend's head was bowed, his eyes closed as he stood in front of them uttering yet another prayer. Thomas pursed his lips in her direction and kissed the air which made Abigail fight to maintain her serious composure. Then Thomas slowly sidled up to her sideways on his knees so that he could slide a hand over the silk of her dress and around her body, pulling her into his side. The reverend droned on . . . and on. Every time there was an "Amen," Thomas made as if to stand before realising that yet another prayer was upon them and being forced to settle back into his kneeling position. Abigail found this absolutely hilarious, and she was practically trembling with stifled laughter by the time the last "Amen" was uttered.

"Are we done?" asked Thomas.

The reverend beamed down at him, and Abigail smothered a giggle with her hand.

"Yes," he said. "You may stand."

Thomas supported Abigail to standing with him and then proceeded to take her face gently in his hands. She was actually laughing when he kissed her, but her laugh died away as the kiss turned rather hot and ardent. Strong arms came around her as her husband's mouth plundered hers with all the carnal lust of a brute beast.

Someone in the congregation let out a whistle. Abigail imagined it was either Patience or Michael. And then the clapping and laughing began, and it didn't stop even when Thomas finally released her from the embrace. The reverend's face was flushed pink as Thomas took his hand to thank him for the "eloquent and pithy ceremony".

"There's not a blacksmith in Gretna Green who can compare," said Thomas brightly.

Reverend Stanhope didn't appear entirely sure what to make of that statement, but he smiled beatifically and allowed Thomas to shake his hand and wished him and his wife all the very best.

"You mustn't tease the reverend," said Abigail a few minutes later as Thomas pressed her backwards into the dressing room and up against a vanity table.

"What kind of a wedding dress is this?" asked Thomas as he slid a hand slowly up over her ribs to rub a thumb gently back and forth over her nipple through the thin silk.

Oh.

"Thomas," said Abigail, trying to muster some self control. "We can't be gone long. Someone will come looking."

He placed both strong hands to her waist and lifted her up onto the vanity table behind her. Reaching behind her, he tugged at the laces of her bodice. She could feel the dress slacken, and one capped sleeve fell from her shoulder. Thomas stood back to look at her as he tugged her dress gently down to release her breasts.

"Heaven help me, Abigail," he whispered.

He bent to kiss her neck as his hands came up over her breasts. Abigail spread her legs and slowly tugged up her skirt until she was bare to him. His mouth was hot and wet on hers as he slipped his fingers between her legs. It wasn't long before she was groaning into his mouth.

Eventually, she pulled away.

"This all seems rather slow and gentle," she said. "I thought you were going to be quick and rough."

A wolfish smile spread over Thomas's face as he undid his breeches. Abigail reached down and curled her hand around his searingly hot erection as Thomas stepped closer in between her legs.

"Shift forward," he said.

She liked the no-nonsense command, and it made her ache to have him closer. With one hand to the table and another wrapped around behind her, he thrust himself up inside her with one quick hard movement. Her head fell back as a moan escaped her lips.

"Jesus, Abigail," he rasped. "I said this wouldn't take long, and it won't."

Thomas proceeded to rock himself backwards until he was nearly withdrawn before driving heavily into her once more. It was all she could do to remain upright. She was practically drowning in the erotic tension of his arousal as her body instinctively tightened around him and her mouth opened on a pant. Thomas only took three more hard strokes before heaving himself from her body in order to spend his release on her thigh. He quickly wiped her clean with a handkerchief pulled from his pocket, taking especial care of her dress.

"What?" he said when he caught her looking at him.

"Why do you never come inside me?"

He gave her an odd assessing look as he placed his hand to the side of her face.

"You're still so young," he said. "And you have so much talent that you have yet to fully explore. I don't want to burden you with children before you are ready."

The simple sincerity of the statement sparked its way through her, and Abigail found she had thrown herself at him before she could think, toppling him to the carpet. She kissed his face over and over again—his lips, his eyes, his cheeks—as his hands came around her bare waist. He lifted her higher and took one breast in his mouth.

Oh God, they really should be getting back to their guests.

Thomas tumbled her beneath him and slipped his way down her body kissing her belly. She could feel the slide of the silk along her leg as he drew up her skirts before ducking his face between her legs and taking a quick rough lick.

He lifted his head and said, "This won't take long. I promise," before bowing to his task.

"Breakfast champagne!" said Patience, placing a glass into Abigail's hand.

Her friend leaned in towards her, eyes sparkling.

"I did my best to keep your mother and mine from hunting the two of you down."

Abigail felt her face heat.

"No need to thank me," said Patience. "I trust your little interlude was satisfactory?" She was trying to sound serious, but her lips pursed prettily in an effort to hold back a grin.

Abigail stared at her friend, wondering how she should respond before deciding that there was only one appropriate response.

"More than satisfactory," she said quietly, though the words made her face heat even more.

"Hah!" laughed Patience.

"What are we laughing about?" Arabella stepped up in a marigold silk dress and glanced from face to face.

"Nothing you need to worry yourself about for now," said Patience.

"Ah," said Arabella. "Amorous congress."

Patience and Abigail shared a wide-eyed look.

"Is that not the polite term?" asked Arabella, all innocence.

"Yes," said Patience.

"And what pray tell," asked Arabella rather mischievously, "would be an impolite term?"

Abigail and Patience only laughed.

"No, seriously," said Arabella. "My maid is rather tight-fisted with her knowledge of such things, and Samuel certainly won't give me the time of day."

"Come and see me later," said Patience. "We can have a talk."

"Really?" Arabella lifted herself excitedly up onto her toes and then down again.

Abigail felt a rather sturdy and familiar arm come around her waist as Thomas stepped up beside her. The simple presence of him next to her—the muscled weight of him, the smoky scent—made her heart ache. If this was what it was to have him, she couldn't understand how she might have survived without.

"Come on, my darling," he said. "The Winters have managed to secure strawberries in the middle of autumn, and I want to feed you breakfast."

Patience and Arabella shared a delightedly scandalised glance as Abigail offered her glass of champagne to her husband. Ignoring the glass, he lifted his eyes to hers.

"No thank you," he said. "I'm floating away as it is."

Epilogue

"So how has it been?" asked Richard as he stepped down the street with Thomas.

The winter wind whipped at their greatcoats and tossed a few sparse flurries of snow across their path. The day was a grey one, heavy with clouds that threatened to blanket the city in a festive layer of snow.

"Oh, you know," said Thomas. "She buys me pretty things, and I do my best to please her in the bed chamber."

Thomas eyed his friend sideways to see if the joke had landed and was satisfied to watch as a smile spread across the viscount's face.

"Seriously, though," said Richard, casting a studious glance his way.

They walked on for several paces in silence, their boots hitting the pavement with the determined and rhythmic sound of soldiers on the march. It was a comforting feeling to have someone stepping in time with you. It was a kind of kinship to move as one, and Thomas briefly wondered at the nature of brothers-in-arms.

"She loves me," said Thomas. He might have said, "I love

her," but the wonder was in the first statement rather than the latter.

"*Everyone* loves you," laughed Richard.

"Not like this," said Thomas.

Richard regarded him with eyes that seemed to be rimmed with fire, and Thomas felt suddenly singed by the intensity of his gaze.

"Why do you think they do it?" asked Thomas. "Patience and Abigail . . . Why do you think they love us the way that they do?"

Richard shrugged his massive shoulders, and set his mouth into a serious line. Their boots continued to step in unison along the pavement and then came to a standstill at a busy intersection.

"It's possible they're angels sent to keep us from drowning in the deep." Richard stared out across the road. "That, or they're not entirely right in their heads," he added as he turned a smile on his friend.

"It can only be one or the other," mused Thomas. "Sacred beings or demented women . . ."

Darting another glance out into the intersection, Richard took Thomas's arm with a large firm hand and guided him across the street through a gap in the traffic.

"I'm not a child, you know," said Thomas when they had reached the other side. "I can cross the street on my own."

"I do apologise, Lieutenant Colonel. I only thought you might be flattened by a hack while mooning over your fair wife."

Despite his annoyance, Thomas could feel a flare of friendly warmth heat his chest. Richard often had that effect on him.

"Come on then," said Thomas. "They'll be waiting for us."

As they picked up their pace along the pavement, Thomas looked over to the side of Richard's bearded face. Suffering often hardened a person, ossifying them into a rigid slab of stone, but Richard's suffering had changed him in a different way. It had kindled an empathetic fire in his heart for the suffering of others, and Thomas had often warmed himself in that gentle blaze.

"What are you giving Patience for Christmas?" he asked.

Richard gave him a look before he answered.

"Very expensive flowers," he said. "My own arrangements," he added with only a slight hint of embarrassment in his voice. "One a day for the seven days leading up until Christmas."

"And on Christmas?"

"I bought her a pretty pistol."

"Hah!" laughed Thomas. "Daffodils and a gun—I think she's going to like it."

Richard chuckled.

"And what about Mrs. Walpole?"

"I've got nothing so far," said Thomas thoughtfully. "My pockets are empty."

They walked on between the brick buildings that seemed to hold up the pale grey clouds like a roof above them. A stray flurry of snow hit Thomas in the cheek.

They finally arrived outside the Winter residence and took the stairs up to the front door at a jog. A footman opened the door onto the warm house lit with golden candlelight, and the two soldiers stepped in out of the cold. Shrugging out of their greatcoats, removing their gloves, chafing their cold hands together.

"Your cheeks are all rosy," said Richard with a chuckle. "You look as pretty as a maid."

"Are you hearing this, Martin?" said Thomas to the footman who was very careful to keep a straight face. "I'm a lieutenant colonel in His Majesty's army. The viscount has some nerve!"

Richard laughed.

"Leave Martin alone," he said.

"Lord Winter," said Martin, "they're all up in the drawing room decorating the tree."

"Are there biscuits?" asked Thomas.

"Yes, Sir."

Notes played on the pianoforte stepped their way down the staircase like children running on tiny feet. When Thomas looked to the staircase, there was an actual child standing there—Patience's younger sister Grace. Her big blue eyes danced with merriment as she stepped down from the last step.

"Thomas!"

"What are *you* doing here?" said Thomas with mock annoyance. "I thought I told you that uppity children who own dogs named after vegetables have no business decorating trees and eating biscuits."

Grace cocked her head in a way that suggested she had heard this sort of joke before.

"Come on then," said Thomas with a wink. "The usual?"

"Yes, please!" said Grace.

He swiftly ducked down to lift her up and throw her over his shoulder with a delighted shriek before carrying her up the stairs and back into the drawing room. Richard followed on his heels as Grace laughed herself pink in the face. Thomas stopped short at the drawing room entrance to take in the scene.

Abigail was at the pianoforte playing a tune that twinkled

over the room as if the music were made by the blinking of a thousand tiny stars. A fire crackled in the grate as Patience and Michael hung ornaments on the biggest evergreen Thomas had ever seen indoors. In the corner, Richard's mother sat laughing with James who was sipping at a cup of hot chocolate with his rather angelic lips. Thomas wasn't entirely sure how long he had been standing there, but eventually Grace began to kick at him.

"Let me down!"

"Sorry, poppet," he said, allowing her to slide to the ground. His gaze strayed back to Abigail who was still lost in her music, eyes almost shut, completely oblivious to his presence.

What had he done to deserve this? he wondered.

It all seemed rather miraculous . . . like a baby who doesn't cry even though he's got hay sticking into his backside and a donkey shoving a muzzle into his face.

Grace looked from Thomas to the pianoforte and back again.

"Oof," she said. "I imagine you have no idea what to give her for Christmas."

Startled, Thomas swivelled his eyes to the little girl standing beside him.

"You'll want to give her something meaningful," said Grace. "It doesn't have to be expensive."

"You're a bit small to be handing out advice," said Thomas.

"You're a bit big to be so confused about a simple gift," said Grace.

"Who says I'm confused?"

"Your face," replied Grace, putting her hands on her hips. "I've seen this sort of thing before."

"Oh really?"

Grace lifted her chin towards the viscount who had stepped up beside Patience at the tree and placed an arm around her waist.

"Richard, for one," said Grace, "and George too. When I get married, it's going to be to someone who doesn't have to struggle with the romance."

Thomas laughed. "And where do you intend to find this . . . person?"

"I'll know him when I meet him."

The music came to an abrupt halt as they spoke. By the time Thomas had lifted his eyes from Grace, Abigail was on him. His arms came open just in time to catch her as she threw herself into his embrace. He glanced down to Grace with a wink.

"Thank you very much," he said, "but I think I do just fine with the romance."

Grace scrunched up her face in a manner that suggested she disagreed as Abigail pulled back slightly in his embrace.

"I should like to have William and Mary and the children over for a Christmas tea," she said brightly.

"What? At my bachelor apartments?"

"Where else?" she asked in some confusion.

They had yet to set up house properly. Thomas had managed to fit her pianoforte into the parlour of his apartments, but the harp simply took up too much space.

"I can do without it," said Abigail.

Her words had settled over him like the first frost over a garden.

"No," he said firmly. "You can't. You won't."

Thomas had rearranged his bed chamber to allow for a music corner where the harp could live and be played for the time being until they moved into a proper house. For now, he couldn't quite understand how Abigail could be happy living in his sparse accommodations with only one housekeeper and her maid in attendance. She had not complained even once despite the fact that between them, they could afford a staffed and modestly fashionable house in town.

"Seems like a lot of bother right now," she said when he suggested it.

She had been lying naked in his arms, and she snuggled into him, her skin smooth and cool against the rough scars and hair of his chest. He closed his eyes and shook his head in wonder.

Despite her peaceable demeanour—or perhaps because of it—Thomas wanted to give her more. He had never been particularly ambitious when he had only himself to think of, but now he had one eye on the future as Abigail slid a hand down his body.

"I have such fond memories of this room . . . and this bed," she said. "Can't we stay here a little longer?"

"A little longer, but not forever."

He pulled her close as his mind tossed itself across the possibilities that lay before him. Thomas had connections in both high places and low which was a rather extraordinary thing and would likely serve him well if he ever wanted to venture into business. He made a mental note to speak with Christopher Grave about that upstanding brother of his.

Though Thomas knew Abigail was content right now, in his heart he feared that she would eventually feel trapped in her role as his wife. He knew he would make a mess of things on his own—he was just a man after all—so he sought out some help. Abigail's mother would not offer the support that she needed, but Thomas knew from experience that family can be found in friendly places. Lady Leveson-Gower was only too thrilled to be brought into his confidence and set about hunting for an appropriate house.

"She needs space to breathe, Thomas—a home with a music room that is entirely hers. Leave it with me." She patted his arm and smiled. "I knew you would be good for her."

Thomas had one more request that set Lady Leveson-Gower beaming her approval. He knew she was well-acquainted within several of London's social circles, and he thought to leverage that acquaintance on Abigail's behalf. It wasn't long before Lady Leveson-Gower had organised another evening of music designed to gain Abigail the notice of several highly placed composers and patrons of the arts.

Thomas wanted Abigail to flourish as herself, to explore her talents, to fly. At the same time, he knew a selfishness inside himself that desired her solely as his own. He liked it best when she sang only for him, lying in bed as she idly stroked his bare chest. The sound of her music made him ache, and he couldn't bear to think that it did the same for anyone else. The shadow of a beast often raised its ugly head when he saw her out in company, playing for an audience or delighting some undeserved gentleman with her quick wit, and it frightened Thomas to know that he had that within him.

On Christmas day, Thomas took Abigail riding past the outskirts of London and into the countryside. They took just the one horse. Thomas had her seated snugly between his thighs as he manoeuvred the horse down the well-trodden path. His hands were steady on the reins—the tremor in his left hand had faded with time. Occasionally, he would bring one arm around her waist and hitch her in closer to his body—it was a gesture that made her feel entirely cherished. Fields stretched out to either side of them, their boundaries marked by low stone walls, hedgerows, and the occasional stand of barren trees. Brown earth and what remained of the grasses were coated in a white frost. Little white clouds of her breath rose up in front of Abigail before dissipating into the cold, bright air.

"Warm enough?" asked her husband, leaning in against the raised hood of her riding cloak.

She could see his hot breath drift past her temple.

"Yes." She rested her head against him. "Where are we going?"

"To church."

"You said you didn't want to go to church when my mother suggested it." She tried to twist around to see his face.

"Stop squirming," said Thomas. "You'll fall."

Abigail righted herself.

"Here we are." Thomas pulled the reins to the left and guided the horse up a small hill.

An enormous yew tree stood at the top of the hill, evergreen among the icy fields. It was surrounded by a stone wall into which was set an iron gate. Thomas dismounted at the gate and tethered the horse before reaching up to lift Abigail down. She landed in the frosted grass with a crunch.

"But where's the church?" she asked.

"There used to be one here a long time ago. It looks like the stones were used to build a new one elsewhere or perhaps some other type of building entirely."

Thomas opened the gate.

"It doesn't really matter," he said. "The tree is still here and so is the spirit of the church."

"The tree of life," said Abigail, turning to him with a smile.

"And death." Thomas's face was suddenly quite sombre. "It's quite toxic. Horses have been found dead with the leaves still in their mouths—thus the need for a wall."

He seemed suddenly nervous, and she felt the need to give him time, so she turned and walked in through the gate.

"Abigail." He followed her in and took her gloved hand in his. "I wanted to give you something . . ."

She turned to him underneath the green boughs of the tree.

". . . but everything I could think of seemed so trite in comparison to what you have given me."

"Thomas," she said on a whisper. "You're enough."

"I'm not though. That's the thing," said Thomas, pulling her glove finger by finger from her hand.

He removed his own glove and then took her bare hand in his warm one. He pressed her fingers to his lips, and then she took her hand and slid it behind the collar of his coat to hold the back of his head and pull his lips down to hers. The sensation of his mouth on hers, the way he drank her up like a man dying of thirst never failed to weaken her legs. Gently, he pulled his face from hers and took it in his hands, one gloved and one bare.

"I made a lot of vows at our wedding with Reverend Stanhope beaming over us," said Thomas. "But I want to make you a promise here under this tree that with every breath, I will honour and protect you—whatever it is you want to do in this life, I will support you any way that I can. And in my death, I shall never cease to love you. Abigail, my love for you is like a pail spilling over, and I feel altogether clumsy as I try to carry it around with the contents sloshing out everywhere and making quite a mess."

Abigail laughed though her eyes were brimming.

"Thomas." She reached her arms around him.

"Also," said Thomas as she pressed her cheek to his chest, "I have something for you in my pocket."

She lifted her head to look up into his eyes as her heart gave a happy little flutter.

"Which one?"

He lifted his shoulders and let them fall with a mischievous grin.

She patted at his breast pockets.

"Cold," he said. "You're freezing, my lady."

Abigail wanted to go straight for his trousers, but she knew how the game was played, and there was a certain amount of pleasure to be had in stringing it out. Unbuttoning his coat, she reached in to pat at the side pockets of his jacket.

"Warmer."

Abigail kept her eyes on his as she slowly slipped her hand down over his trousers and between his legs.

"My lady!" said Thomas in his most pearl-clutching tone.

"I think I found something," said Abigail as innocently as she could.

Her hand was over his member giving it a gentle squeeze. The cold day did nothing to dissuade the man from rising to the occasion.

"You'll not want to tempt Mr. Wolf out to play just yet."

Reaching up, Thomas shoved her riding hood back to lick at her ear as she continued to massage him between the legs.

"There's still the matter of your gift," he reminded her in a hoarse voice. "I spent all of six shillings on it, so you'll want to make the appropriate grateful noises."

Abigail giggled as she fumbled in his left trouser pocket, pressing her front up against him to reach all the way to the bottom, but there was nothing there. She tried again with the right trouser pocket, and as she slid her hand down, Thomas held her tightly against him, his member now straining against his trousers and pressing hard up into her pelvis.

"Don't distract me," Abigail laughed.

"But you're the one who tempted him out," said Thomas. "He only wants to play."

Her hand closed around something small and square in his pocket as the giggles continued to bubble up from inside her.

"Aha! I have it!" she said, stepping back and pulling it from his trousers.

It was a small blue box wrapped with a white ribbon. She looked up at him as she teased the ribbon free.

"Don't get too excited," he said. "It's only meant to be a token."

Lifting the tiny lid of the box, Abigail peered inside.

"Oh!"

It was the tiniest little bluebird made entirely of glass resting on a cushion of white cotton. Abigail plucked up the bird between two fingers and held it up to the light.

"It's beautiful."

"Like you," he said softly. "Abigail . . . I don't ever want you to feel that just because you are my wife . . . that you can't or shouldn't . . . What I mean to say is that I don't ever want you to feel trapped. I don't ever want to prevent you from flying."

She furrowed her brow as she glanced up at the darling man.

"I never thought that you would. You're the soldier who will guard my flight."

She could see that he liked that idea because he had a particular glint in his eye she knew well. He stepped towards her and placed a hand to her cheek. He was looking for a kiss, and God knew she wanted to give it to him, but she still had a question that was begging for an answer.

"It's exquisite," she said, holding the bird to her heart, "and I will cherish it always, but . . . I don't mean to malign your financial choices . . . It's just . . . six whole shillings?"

His laugh poured over her like warm honey.

"Too much?"

"I should think so," said Abigail.

"Grace Pemberton drives a hard bargain," said Thomas. "The girl has an entire collection of these miniature glass figurines. She said the bluebird was her favourite, and she couldn't possibly part with it for less than a guinea."

"And you haggled her down to six shillings?" Abigail laughed. "I suppose it could have been worse."

Thomas placed his hand over his heart.

"I promise not to make any more frivolous purchases from enterprising children." There was a merry twinkle in his eye. "Now give us a Christmas kiss, Mrs. Walpole."

Thank You!

Thank you for reading *A Songbird for the Soldier.* I've been waiting for Thomas Walpole to arrive at his happily-ever-after since the moment he walked onto the scene as Richard Winter's friend in *A Soldier and his Rules.* He's one of my absolute favourite characters, and I hope you've enjoyed spending time with him as much as I have.

- **Don't miss out on Book 3.5 in *The Pemberton Series*! It's a free subscribers-only steamy novella called *The Bull of Bow Street Meets his Match,* and it can be downloaded when you sign up for my mailing list at oliviaelliottromance.com. This book features Abigail Fernside's sister Harriet as the heroine.**
- Reviews help other readers decide if a book would suit them. I appreciate all reviews, both positive and negative, so please think about leaving a star-rating or, if you have the time, a few thoughts about my book.
- *A Songbird for the Soldier* is the fourth book in *The Pemberton Series*, and I am currently working on the fifth, so stay tuned!

Also by Olivia Elliott

If you haven't read them already, you may enjoy the other books in *The Pemberton Series.*

A Dangerous Man to Trust? (Book 1)

Bridgerton meets *Jane Eyre* in this spicy, slow-burn Regency romance written with humour and wit. A strong yet vulnerable hero who feels he's unworthy of love, a feisty governess who has sworn off marriage, and a world of heartache and longing between them.

A Soldier and his Rules (Book 2)

He is a stern and brooding soldier who is used to giving orders. She is a passionate artist who rarely does as she's told. His haunted past and secret shame stand like a wall between them in this hot and spicy Regency romance.

A Baron's Son is Undone (Book 3)

He is the uptight son of a baron. She is the banished daughter of . . . a pirate? Each guards their own terrible truth that threatens the blossoming intimacy between them in this emotional—and steamy—Regency romance.

The Bull of Bow Street Meets his Match (Book 3.5)

She is a devastating beauty with a sense of social justice. He is a Bow Street runner with blood on his hands. As the first hesitant sparks kindle a blaze of fire, these two must eventually decide if love is worth the risk.

Receive a free copy of this book by joining the author's mailing list at oliviaelliottromance.com.

Printed in Dunstable, United Kingdom

76719499R00180

WHY I
DISAPPEARED

André King

a selection of poems

Why I Disappeared

ISBN: 9798314699669
Imprint: Independently published

cover design by André King

André King

Contents:

Why I Disappeared

———————————

Why I Disappeared

André King

I disappeared once, in ways both big and small. Sometimes we fade without even knowing why, pulled by something deeper than words can reach. This book is the aftermath of that disappearance — the space between what was and what is yet to come.

These poems are fragments of that journey. Moments of stillness, of searching, of learning to be okay with being lost. Maybe you'll find a piece of yourself here, too. Maybe, like me, you'll learn that sometimes disappearing is just the beginning of something new.

With love,
Andreas.

The Chariot

You could have stayed.
Could have let the weight of it all
·pull you under,
let the past wrap its hands around your ankles
and call it fate.

But you didn't.
You stood up,
stepped forward,
moved even when it hurt—
even when the road was nothing
but dust and distance.

Now, look at you.
Unshaken.
Unstoppable.
A better version of
your past self.

André King

i move through days
like *a river to the sea*
always pulling toward you

no distance is too wide
no time too long
i will find my way back

Why I Disappeared

Dear Diary,

If I could have the perfect boyfriend, he'd be all these things and more.

He'd be funny—like, actually funny, not just meme funny. He'd be nice to me and my friends, because if he can't do that, what's the point? His hair would be soft, and his smile would make me forget why I was ever upset. He'd be book smart (because I can't be the only one with brains here), and he'd have good style—like, effortlessly cool, not "mom dressed me" cool.

I hope he has sisters, so he knows how to actually respect women. And maybe just a little bit sassy, because I need someone who can keep up with me. Oh, and TALLER THAN ME. Non-negotiable.

He'd give the best tight hugs, the kind that make me feel safe. We'd cook together, and he'd smell good all the time (good hygiene is a must). He'd have hobbies, things that make him excited, and he wouldn't do drugs. He'd think with logic but still know when to be soft. And he'd tell me I'm handsome—often.

I want a boyfriend who brings me flowers just because, has stuffed animals (because that's adorable), and gives me random little things that remind him of me. He'd like sushi, go thrifting with me, and actually take me on cute dates. Also, he needs to handle spicy food, or I'll have to eat all of it myself.

He'd watch dramas with me, bring me ginger ale when my stomach hurts, and never get annoyed when I randomly start singing. He'd be good with kids and take care of himself too, because self-care is attractive. I think I'd like him to be 1-8 years older than me, but not so much older that it's weird.

He wouldn't be scared of bugs (because one of us has to deal with them), and he'd like my music taste. Maybe he'd have piercings—just a little bit of edge. He'd charge my phone if I fell asleep, check up on me during the day, and send me TikToks that made him think of me.

He'd let me lay on him whenever I wanted, be more introverted than me, and actually have a skincare routine.

I don't know if this guy exists, but if he does... I hope I meet him one day.

André King

I blinked
and you were gone.

Amor vincit omnia

they say love conquers all
so i let it
i let it wreck me
soft and brutal all at once

i let it tear down walls
i spent years building
let it flood every room
until i was drowning in it

but love is not a warrior
it does not fight fair
it does not win without loss

so here i stand
victorious, they say—
but empty-handed
cause indeed, love conquers all.

André King

i set the table for two
then take away the extra plate

old habits linger
like the ghost of your laughter in the walls

i wish you could be here

Why I Disappeared

i trace the outline of forever
but your face is missing from the picture

i wish i could see a future with you
but love alone
cannot clear the fog

i wish i could see a future with you

André King

wildfire

he has the wings of desire
burning bright, never still
too wild for cages
too restless for roots

i loved him like the wind
knowing he could never be caught

recipe for desire

he is laughter in the kitchen
memories growing between bites
of sweetness and spice

the most amazing character—
soft where it matters
bold where it counts
a flame that never flickers

but tonight,
he is something else entirely—
bare beneath the apron
nothing but heat and mischief
a feast for more than just the table

he cooks,
and i burn.

André King

Denial, denial, denial

i keep denying
that it was the last time
that our paths would ever cross again

i tell myself—
we are just a pause,
a comma,
not the end

i walk streets hoping
for a glimpse of you
every stranger that passes
i scan everything around me
in case i find you

Why I Disappeared

The Harsh Reality of Recovery

No one ever tells you how difficult healing is.

"It gets better," they say. Just wait, they say. But before you learn to breathe again, they don't tell you that recovering feels like drowning. They fail to mention that the road to rehabilitation is confusing, draining, and filled with moments when you question whether it's worth it.

I wake up nauseous.

The side effects of my antidepressants sit heavy in my body—exhaustion that won't lift, weight I didn't ask for, a body that doesn't feel like mine.

I used to try to ignore my appetite, but now it feels like a stranger that I'm not sure how to greet. When I look in the mirror, I question whether this is a better or just different version of me.

Some days, I feel like a failure. Like I should be further along, like I should be happier, stronger, more certain. But I'm still lost. Still distant.

I'm still figuring out how to live in a world that never stops because I need a break.

I am still here, though, and that is the harsh truth.

I've survived every night when I didn't think I would. I have faced the thoughts that told me I would never be enough. I have woken up, again and again, even when I didn't want to.

And maybe that is enough for now.

Perhaps recovering isn't about feeling entire again when you wake up one day. Perhaps it's about the little things, like the meals I eat guilt-free, the days I get out of bed even if I don't want to, and the times I allow myself to be happy without wondering if I deserve it.

André King

I've diverged from who I had been. But perhaps that's alright. Perhaps I should fight for this version of me, the one who endured through everything.

So I'll continue. I'll keep trying. Even in the eyes of bitterness. Even when it's challenging. Because when I look back, I'll see that this was constantly me expanding.

To Myself

Why I Disappeared

I am here,
as just a body in the room.
My mind has already left.
I smile,
because that is what they expect
but inside
I am somewhere else entirely.
Alone,
quiet,
peaceful,
I wonder
if anyone feels the same
or if they
are here
in a way
I never will be.

I hate parties

André King

your body knows.
your tired bones,
your heavy chest,
the way you hold your breath.
you don't have to say it out loud.
but you deserve to be heard.

I'm fine

Why I Disappeared

you don't know when it changed
only that it did
and no matter how hard you try
you can't make yourself
care again

André King

i hope you heal

even from the things

you've convinced yourself

don't hurt anymore

Aries sun

fire in his veins
reckless and radiant
he wants everything
all at once

he burns too bright
loves too hard
leaves too fast
and never looks back

he is chaos and passion
a storm with a heartbeat
born to run
but aching to be caught

André King

I might ruin him

the way he ruined me

strings don't last forever

they weren't lying
when they said
once two souls are no longer meant to meet
they simply don't

even in the smallest town
on the busiest street
in the places you swore
you'd run into them again

they become a ghost
as if the universe
quietly erased the path
between you and them

André King

love or ruins

i want to trace his lips
or bite them hard enough to bleed
i want to hold him close
or push him far enough
that he never finds his way back
i want to whisper his name
or never speak it again
i want to love him
or destroy him
until neither of us
can tell the difference

Why I Disappeared

we were as close as January and December
but now
we are as far as them
seasons apart
drifting like forgotten months.

André King

you are the human definition of sunshine

Why I Disappeared

gone, baby, gone—
like a shadow at sunrise,
like a name in wind.

André King

we don't talk anymore
but you still cross my mind
and although
some **people fade**
you never did.

Why I Disappeared

Unseen, unheard, gone

unseen, unheard, gone—
like a shadow slipping through the cracks,
erasing every trace,
leaving behind only questions
and a name no one whispers anymore.
not missing,
just elsewhere.
not forgotten,
just free.
like i was never here at all.

André King

a heartbreak,
a love unraveled,
a name i can't say without tasting regret.
absence louder than presence,
love with nowhere to go.

Why I Disappeared

a triangle of sadness,
a heart undone.
a body breaking.
a loss too heavy to carry.

three sides,
one tempest.
i am drowning in it.

André King

Seeing you take your shirt off,
makes me want you so bad—
like a flame that keeps calling
even when i try to step away,
like a thirst i can't seem to quench.
My only desire is to see
all your clothing on the floor,
and you naked.

Why I Disappeared

its branches reach high,
yet stay grounded, aware.

bonsai

André King

nothing makes sense,
i don't know where i am,
i just want to disappear,
but still, i stay.

fish out of water

The Protection Spell

I seal myself in light,
wrap my ribs in something stronger
than wanting.
No more chasing hands
that never hold me right,
no more reaching for scraps
of affection,
no more begging for love
like it's the air I breathe.
I ask for peace,
for the hunger to settle
and the ache to soften.

André King

Maybe he forgot.

Maybe he changed his mind.

Maybe he was never coming at all.

Why I Disappeared

The Historians

At some point, we all become historians,
keepers of touch, collectors of moments,
tracing the echoes of laughter,
the imprint of a name long gone.

We archive love in folded letters,
store heartaches,
rewrite memories until they feel like truth,
or bury them deep, hoping they fade.

Some histories are whispered at 2 a.m.,
some are left unfinished,
some we tell ourselves differently each time,
but none ever truly disappear.

André King

I whispered it anyway,
just in case he was listening
somewhere in his dreams.

midnight confessions

Why I Disappeared

Winter

Cold air sneaks through the cracks,
curling around my fingers,
settling in my bones.

Your hands used to be warmer than this.

André King

The Writing Retreat

There's something about the isolation—
just me, the notebook, and the mountain air.
The blank pages don't scare me here,
because I know they'll fill,
they always do.

It's just a matter of time.

Why I Disappeared

Caress Me for the Diamond That I Am

Touch me softly, like I'm something rare,
a treasure hidden in plain sight.

Run your hands over the edges,
the sharpness of what you haven't seen yet.

I am not here to be taken for granted,
but to be admired—
flawed and perfect all at once.

Caress me for the diamond that I am,
not just for the sparkle you see,
but for what I carry.

André King

I can't believe I was your first—
the first to touch your skin,
the first to see you so unguarded,
so raw.
the one to carve my name into your memory,
and I wonder if I'll be the one you never forget.

So Sick of Dreaming of You

Every night, you come back—
and I let you,
but I'm tired of playing this game
where you're everything,
but never enough.

André King

We Aren't Really Strangers After All

Maybe we never were.
Maybe our souls recognized each other
before our eyes ever met.

Maybe that's why you felt familiar,
like a memory I had somehow forgotten.

Maybe we were always meant to find each other.

To Write Love on My Thighs

Trace your name where only I can feel it,
soft letters pressed into my skin.
Let your hands spell devotion,
let your lips leave poetry,
let every touch be a love letter
written just for me.
No ink, no paper—
just longing,
just you.

André King

Pull yourself together.

Pull yourself together.

Pull yourself together.

Pull yourself together.

2-2-2: Balance, Alignment, Becoming

The universe whispered in triple twos,
Reminding me that I'm exactly where I need to be.
That patience is power,
and what's meant for me is already in motion.
Everything is unfolding,
even when I can't see it yet.

André King

I Don't Belong to You

I am not yours to claim,
not yours to hold too tight.
You may have touched my skin,
but not my soul.
You may have traced my body,
but never my depths.
I don't belong to you.
I belong to myself—
to my dreams, my freedom,
the love I choose,
not the love that cages me.

Lucky Number 7

Seven steps ahead.
Seven wishes whispered.
Seven signs from the universe,
telling me I'm on the right path.
Seven chances,
Seven changes,
Seven doors
waiting to be opened.

Luck, or destiny?
Maybe both.

André King

Mirage

A perfect illusion,
something so close,
yet just beyond reach.
I chase you through desert skies,
dazzled by your beauty,
your promise of all I've ever wanted.

But you vanish the moment I get close,
slipping through my fingers like sand,
a dream that never quite solidifies,
leaving me thirsty,
longing for more.

A mirage—so real,
and yet, not at all.

I reach for you,
knowing, deep down,
that I will never catch you.
Still, I keep running,
because for a moment,
you felt like everything.

Why I Disappeared

The Illusion of Control

Two years ago (19th of March, 2023), I walked into a man's apartment, thinking I knew exactly what I wanted.
A one-night stand, no strings attached, no expectations. Just a brief moment of passion to fill the emptiness.
But that night, something shifted.
What was supposed to be a temporary escape became a nightmare I didn't see coming.
A man, whose words were sweet when they should have been sharp,
whose hands were gentle when they should have never touched me like that.
I didn't know it then, but I'd walked into what felt like a prison,
and the worst part was, I didn't even know how to leave.

They say men cannot be "sensitive," but they are wrong.

No one talks about how it feels when you ignore the warning signs—
when your intuition whispers, but your heart ignores it.
I walked into that night thinking it would be fine.
And I left feeling broken.

It wasn't just the bruises on my skin.
It was the ones that never showed up.
The ones that still linger when I look in the mirror.
I wonder, sometimes, if we ever fully heal from something like that,
if we can ever reclaim the parts of ourselves we lose in moments of violence,
even if they were just minutes long, hours even.
Does time really heal, or does it just teach us to live with it?

I never told anyone. Not then. Not for a long time.
Because who would believe that the guy I thought was just another name in the long list of "could-have-beens" could turn into something so dangerous?
But I wish I could say I walked away stronger, wiser,
as if the experience somehow gave me a new sense of power.

Instead, I spent months questioning myself, wondering if I did something to deserve it, if I didn't walk away soon enough, or if my silence somehow invited it.

Two years later, I still wonder: Can you love yourself back to the version of you before that night? Can you unlearn the fear, unlearn the shame, unlearn the feeling of being small?

Why I Disappeared

i am happy again

new light fills my chest
morning doesn't feel so dark
i welcome the sun
i think this is joy

André King

am i happy?

happiness looks close
but when i reach out for it
it fades like a dream

Why I Disappeared

La La La(thos)

i saw what i wanted to see
not what was real.

i held onto the good things
as if they could erase the bad.

i called it love
when it was just
a beautifully wrapped warning sign.

André King

Who Was Prey, Really?

he made me look like
a lioness stalking my prey
as if i was the hunter
and he was the helpless thing
caught in my gaze.
as if i was the one who circled,
who waited, who struck first.
but he forgot—
a lioness hunts to survive.
he played the game,
then cried when he lost.

Why I Disappeared

i wiped his tears as he hung from my lips

he called it surrender
i called it a mistake.
his sadness dripped between us,
like salt and silk.
i kissed him like a promise
i never meant to keep,
held him like he was mine,
even when i knew he wasn't.

André King

i can calm them down,
be their safe place,
but when it's me,
i can't find the peace.
if i can be there for my friends
in stressful situations,
why can't i do it for myself?

L.A. is on fire

i crave **liberty**
but it feels like a wild thing
and always just out of reach.

my mind is a battlefield
fighting for freedom
while **anxiety** wraps its hands around
my every breath.

André King

no pills to swallow,
no balance to maintain.

Reminder:
Even a small step forward counts as progress.

André King

The fear to fear

i fear the fear
that keeps me from living,
that keeps me in place,
frozen in the thought
that i might never escape.

Exposure Therapy

i expose myself
to the things
i fear,
the things
i'm sick of,
the people
i can't stand.
i face them
because avoiding
only feeds them,
turns them into
monsters
that live in
the dark corners
of my mind.
each moment of
discomfort
is a step closer
to freedom,
and though
it hurts,
it's the only
way
to take back
control.

André King

what if this is the universe
whispering,
"not this way,
but this way"
in a language, only my soul can understand?

Why I Disappeared

A boy in colours

a child born with colours
too bright for the world around him,
but told to hide,
to dim his light,
to pretend he was someone else.

he learned silence early,
swallowed his truth
to fit into a broken world
that wasn't ready to see him whole.

his heart screamed quietly,
but his lips were stitched shut,
living under the weight
of expectations that never felt like his own.

but even silenced,
his truth still lived inside,
waiting for the day
the world could finally hear him.

André King

are there any silver linings between us?

Why I Disappeared

i wonder if you meant them
but couldn't say them,
or if you never felt them
and simply left them unspoken

i go over the things i did not hear from you

André King

I can't tell if I was sleeping
and dreaming,
or this was really happening.

Why I Disappeared

I'm still in your sheets,
half awake, bare.

You are pressed on me,
the heat burns between us,
your touch keeps me tangled up,
and I am not ready to leave.

André King

I know I'm not perfect,
and I feel like I've failed
by loving in a way I can't control.

I just want to be accepted,
for the love I feel.

my letter to god

Why I Disappeared

Pineapple milk

a burst of sweetness,
a splash of cream,
you make my mouth water
with every drop of
your golden nectar.
very salty,
sweet and sour,
but I can't stop tasting it.

André King

trace me again,
like you did last night,
and remind me
of everything I never want to forget.

Why I Disappeared

sometimes the paths we don't take
are the ones that save us
from the hurt we didn't know
we couldn't handle.

André King

he came as a butterfly

on my birthday,
a butterfly, soft and golden,
landed on my hand,
politely touched my skin,
as if carrying a message
only my heart could hear.
that moment I knew
it was him,
my grandfather,
and
I felt it,
as if he was wishing me a happy birthday,
and showing me that
he never really left.

The Men Who Think They're Gods' Gifts
(But Aren't Even Good in Bed)

I once read that confidence is the sexiest thing a man can wear. But what happens when confidence tips over into full-blown, delusional ego? You end up on a date with a man who treats you like a supporting actor in The Movie of Him, and—if you're unlucky—you might even end up in bed with him.

Spoiler alert: It's never worth it.

Take my most recent misadventure: A dinner date with a man I'll call Ego Man, who spent two hours telling me about how his job was not what he wants to do (honey most people hate their jobs or what they study, I am one of them), his exes (who were all "crazy"), and his gym routine (which, honestly, I could see, but at what cost?).

When I tried to chime in, he'd nod vaguely and then circle right back to his favorite topic—himself.

By the time the check arrived, I was exhausted but intrigued. Could someone this self-obsessed possibly bring that same energy to the bedroom? Could there be a silver lining to all the monologuing? Call it curiosity, call it a lapse in judgment, but I went home with him.

And fuck, I should have known.

There's a particular kind of man who believes his sheer existence is enough to satisfy his partner. Ego Man was one of them.

He undressed like a man revealing a masterpiece, but the performance that followed? Rushed, mechanical, and tragically underwhelming. There was no foreplay (he didn't believe in it, major red flag), no concern for my enjoyment (he assumed it was happening), and no real effort (he was just happy to be there).

Afterwards, as I lay there calculating the amount of sleep I had sacrificed for this, he rolled over, exhaled like an Olympic champion, and said, "Wow, we're so compatible."

Were we? Because I was already planning my escape.

As I left his apartment, still unsatisfied but now extremely self-aware, I wondered: How many of us have been fooled by the false advertising of male ego? The men who think they're Casanovas but haven't mastered the basics? The ones who believe "being there" is the same as showing up?

Confidence is sexy. But self-awareness? Now that is orgasmic.

So here's to fewer egos and better endings (ps. better men).

Why I Disappeared

From left on read, to late-night in bed

There's something thrilling about the unexpected. A plot twist, a chance encounter, a late-night knock on your door that wasn't in the script but somehow ends up being the best scene in the movie.

When I first matched with 80s Time Traveler—a man with rockstar hair, a confident smirk, and an energy that screamed I'd make you a mixtape but in a totally cool, not cringey way—I was intrigued. He wasn't the type to waste time texting. He had a whole date planned before I could even overthink it. It was bold. Refreshing.

And, of course, life had other plans. I had to cancel. And then, life kept happening. Dating apps became an afterthought, and I unknowingly left his message (and number) in the void.

Ten days later, swiping back into the game, I messaged a faceless but intriguing profile on Grindr—only to realize I had walked straight into my own romantic comedy.

Turns out, faceless Grindr guy was 80s Time Traveler. And he was not thrilled. He was abrupt, a little mean, and clearly convinced that I had ghosted him. I almost blocked him on sight, but something kept me there, typing out explanations, smoothing out misunderstandings. And somehow, through the mess, apologies were exchanged, and next thing I knew, he was offering hugs as reparations.

It was past midnight. I was impulsive (as always). I told him to get dressed and come over.

Twenty-five minutes later, there he was, knocking on my door. Holding yellow flowers. Looking even better in person (was drooling inside).

I should have known then—this was about to be a night.

Tea was poured, music played (his playlist was insanely good, the kind that makes you re-evaluate your own taste), and the conversation was effortless.

And the hugs?
He didn't lie—they were everything. Warm, deep, the kind that make you forget how cold the world can be.

We talked for hours, kissed for hours, and, well… I'll let you fill in the blanks. (him being versatile made it even sexier, and oh boy him naked in my bed, wow).

He stayed the night. Left for work in the morning and after that I knew I would see him again.

To my conclusion, this was a date that almost never happened.

So take it as proof that sometimes, even after a rock start, the universe delivers a damn good plot twist (if you are worth it).

The Man Who Never Forgets

He carries every wound,
every missing apology,
forging his past
into walls of stone.

André King

Closure

No final words,
no last goodbye-
just the silence
that spoke louder
than love ever did.

The sleepless nights
were closure.
The unanswered calls,
the hollow stares—
they were closure too.

Neglect wrote the ending,
disrespect sealed the pages.
So close the book,
walk away,
and for once—
choose you.

Crying in the Subway

no one looks too long.
that's the rule.

my tears slip between the sound of the train,
the hum of tired bodies,
the static of an old speaker
announcing a stop i don't care about.

i wipe my face with my sleeve,
pretend i have somewhere to be,
pretend i am not falling apart
between strangers who pretend not to see.

the doors open,
people rush out,
and for a moment,
i almost disappear with them.

André King

all good things must come to an end

he devoured me like a last meal
like hunger had a deadline
like the sunrise was a thief

so i left first

took my name back from his mouth
took my heart back from his hands
watched him sit in the ruins
of what he thought would never break

funny, isn't it?

how men only call it love
when it's slipping away.

Why I Disappeared

Dawn and Desire

The morning after,
waking up at your place,
in your bed,
right next to you.

The sheets smell like you—
a mix of your sweat, your perfume
it made me want to drown in them.

Sunlight spills through your corner window,
striping your back in gold,
casting lines I want to trace with my mouth
for a millionth time.

Your arm drapes over my waist,
heavy, certain—
as if even in sleep,
you're keeping me close.

I should leave
but your breath is warm on my neck,
and my body still remembers
how you said my name last night.

So I stay—
a little longer,
maybe forever.

André King

some lovers are like fire
meant to burn
never meant to last

but god—
didn't we burn so well?

Why I Disappeared

skyfall

he kissed me like gravity didn't exist
like the ground would never find us
like he could keep us suspended
somewhere between the stars and the earth
but all I could see was the sky falling.

André King

there is no funeral for love
that died of neglect.

Why I Disappeared

some men expect tears
as proof they mattered
as if heartbreak is the only way
to measure love

but darling—
i left dry-eyed
and that
is the real tragedy.

no more wasting tears

André King

car sex

he picked me up,
parked the car,
and pulled me onto his lap
like I was the only thing
he wanted.

we squished together
in one of the car seats,
but it felt right,
felt like fire.

he leaned back,
the chair groaning beneath us,
and kept his eyes on mine
as he fucked me—
like he was marking every inch of me.

I couldn't look away.
His gaze locked on mine,
burning through me,
making me feel things
I never knew I needed.

Why I Disappeared

therapy does not hand you answers
it holds up a mirror
and asks you to look
until you finally see yourself
clearly

self-discovery

André King

the fallen angel

i told myself
i would never fall again

but then you said my name
and suddenly
i was losing feathers

one by one
i let my guard slip
let my heart soften

and now i wonder
if i am falling
or if i am finally learning
how to *land*

Why I Disappeared

André King

As I started moving forward, I slowly began to fade,
to disappear.

I never saw him again.

Why I Disappeared

André King

A special chapter called '**Men**'.

We cross paths with countless people, but there are a few that stand out—
men whose presence shifts the air around us, whose energy leaves an imprint.

They come in many forms.
Some bring joy, others bring pain, but all of them teach us
something we never expected to learn.

This chapter is dedicated to the men I've met along the way
or the versions of the man in me.

Why I Disappeared

Part I: The Promiscuous Man

hiding behind pleasure,
he moves through bodies
like seasons change.

he seeks pleasure
in the arms of others,
never realizing
he's still searching for something
he can't touch.

his bed is never empty,
his hands always reaching—
but none of them
ever get close enough
to touch what he's really hiding.

he's good at pretending,
but never at staying.

Part II: The Hollow Man

he's cute in a way
that makes you smile,
funny enough
to make you forget
his lack of depth.

he knows how to charm,
how to make you laugh
but when the jokes fade,
there's nothing left.

his words are sweet
but his actions never match,
a boy with a face
but no heart to hold.

he's a momentary high
that leaves you empty
when it's over.

Part III: The Golden Man

his aura is vibrant,
radiant,
shiny,
like sunlight.
his hair glows with warmth
that lights up everywhere,
and his eyes—
bluer than the ocean,
deep and endless.
there's something about him
that feels like warmth,
like light,
and I cannot help
but be drawn to him.

Part IV: The Miserable Man

he wakes up with a frown
and carries it through the day,
his mind always searching
for something to complain about.

nothing ever feels right,
everything falls short,
and everyone else
is never enough.

he judges,
criticizes,
blames the world
for his unhappiness,
too blind to see
that the problem is inside.

he's trapped in his own misery,
never realizing
that he holds the key
to his own peace.

Part V: The Charming Man

He walks into a room,
and the air shifts.
Eyes follow him,
drawn in by
the ease of his presence,
the way his words
drip like honey—
smooth and intoxicating.
He knows exactly what to say,
exactly when to laugh,
exactly how to make you feel
like you're the only one
he's looking at.

André King

Part VI: The Broken Man

he holds you close
but never lets you in.
his hands are warm,
his heart is locked.
he's been hurt too many times
to believe in forever,
too many promises broken
to trust the sound of yours.
you try to love him
gently, patiently,
but love is a language
he no longer speaks.
so you stand there,
knowing—
some walls don't fall.

Part VII: The Long-Distance Man

he is here,
but never close enough.
his voice travels through the phone,
his love measured in time zones
and missed calls.

you count days instead of moments,
hold his words instead of his hands,
memorize the way he says your name
because you can't taste it on his lips.

you tell yourself distance is temporary,
but so is love
when it lives in the space
between waiting and wanting.

André King

Part VIII: The Violent Man

his hands were not made for softness,
his love laced with fear.
you learn quickly—
his kindness has an expiration date,
and his temper does not ask for permission.

you tell yourself it's not that bad,
until you flinch at shadows,
until his anger lingers in your bones,
until you forget what safety feels like.

Part IX: The Toxic Man

he says he loves you
but only when it's easy.

he pulls you close
then pushes you away,
just to see if you'll stay.

his words are sugar,
his actions are venom.

you tell yourself
he doesn't mean to hurt you,
but that is all he knows.

André King

Part X: The Ego Man

he walks like the sun
was made to shine on him.

every room is his,
every conversation
a stage for his voice.

he loves to be admired,
but never truly seen.

you try to reach him,
but his heart is buried
beneath the weight
of himself.

Part XI: The Sad and Lost Man

he carries his past
like stones in his pockets,
too heavy to move forward,
too familiar to let go.

his eyes hold stories
he never tells,
his smile never quite reaches them.

you try to love him whole,
but he is a map with no destination,
a wanderer with no home,
a man lost inside himself.

André King

Part XII: The Sensitive Man

he feels everything—
the weight of words,
the shift in your tone,
the silence between sentences.

his heart is like
an open window,
letting in light,
but also every storm.

he loves carefully,
gives gently,
hurts deeply.

the world calls him soft,
but you know—
it takes strength
to feel this much
and still stay open.

Why I Disappeared

Part XIII: The Soft and Tender Man

he holds you
like you are something delicate,
not because you are weak,
but because he knows
love is meant to be
handled with care.

his words are warm and sweet,
his touch gentle, like a whisper.
he does not need to be loud
to make you feel safe.

his love is steady,
gentle, constant,
and exactly what a
person needs.

André King

Part XIV: The Hunting Man

he moves through the world
with sharp eyes and steady hands,
always searching,
always wanting,
never satisfied.

his words are bait,
his touch a trap—
soft at first,
until you realize
you were never the one hunting.

he takes what he needs,
leaves before morning,
already chasing
his next prey.

Why I Disappeared

Part XV: The Dying Man

he holds my hands
like they are the last thing keeping him here

his lips tremble against my skin
whispering prayers i do not answer

his eyes beg for forever
but my love was never a god

i watch him fade
his memory slipping from my bones

he dies slow
and i do not mourn

some men think love
is the only thing keeping them alive

but darling—
i was never your oxygen.

André King

I hold no grudge but he does.

Why I Disappeared

André King

Acknowledgments

To *him*,
the one who unknowingly became a part of my disappearance.
Your absence, your presence, and everything in between have shaped these pages more than you'll ever know.
Thank you for the lessons, the silence, and the moments that led me to myself.

To those who stood by me,
even when I was too lost to recognize their presence:
your support has been my anchor.

And to my readers, for taking the time to walk through these words with me.

Why I Disappeared

André King

About the author:

I started writing poetry at 17 after discovering a poetry workshop exercise online.

Inspired by the challenge, I gave it a try—and haven't stopped since.

My work explores themes of love, longing, conflict, and the delicate balance between passion and destruction.

Find more by visiting:

Instagram / TikTok
@andrekingpoetry

Printed in Great Britain
by Amazon

61849614R00070